The Rumrunners
A Prohibition Scrapbook

by C. H. Gervais

Firefly Books

Firefly Books Ltd.
2 Essex Avenue, Unit 5
Thornhill, Ontario L3T 3Y7

Printed in Canada

ISBN 0-929668-08-9

Contents

Dedication — This book is dedicated to all those who survived the Roaring Twenties.

ACKNOWLEDGEMENTS

Acknowledgements for assistance in compiling information go to the following persons or institutions: Frances Curry of the Windsor Star Library and her staff, the Windsor Public Library, the Detroit Public Library, the Public Archives of Canada and the Public Archives of Ontario, the Southwestern Regional Library of the University of Western Ontario, the Windsor Police Department, the United Church of Canada archives; the Ontario Historical Society, the University of Windsor, Larry Kulisek of the University of Windsor History Department, the Hiram Walker Museum, John Marsh of the Amherstburg *Echo*, Elton Plant, Jack Geller, the Sandwich United Church, Paul Vasey, Les Trumble and family, the Vuicic family, the Spracklin family, the University of Windsor Drama Department, the Detroit *Free Press*, the Detroit *News*, Jim Cornett, Jack Kent, Gerald Hallowell, James Reaney, Frank Rasky, David Lawrence Jr., Executive Editor of the Detroit *Free Press*, and, of course, to all the rumrunners and people interviewed in this book and to anyone whose name may have been overlooked here.

Special acknowledgements to Alan Abrams of Detroit who spent several frantic weeks combing through the manuscript for accuracy, and to Lionel Koffler of Firefly Books who helped push the project to completion.

Permissions were given by the following: Walter Goodchild for the priceless photographs of rumrunners on the ice; Bill Johnson for his drawings of the Chappell House and Edgewater Thomas Inn, the Vuicic family for photographs of the Rendezvous Tavern; Peter Frank of Gale Research in Detroit for area maps; Alan Abrams for the Kunsky Theatre news letter photograph; the Detroit *Free Press* for photographs of the Purple Gang and the Jerry Buckley murder; the Windsor Police Department for photograph of the blind pig in Sandwich, Ontario; the Public Archives of Ontario for the photographs of the Elk Lake blind pigs, and the photographs of William E. Raney, and to the Windsor *Star* for the photographs on pages 8, 11, 12, 15, 21, 27, 28, 31, 38, 43, 45, 48, 50, 53, 54, 57, 62, 64, 66, 69, 74, 76, 78, 80, 82, 84, 86, 88, 92, 95, 96, 104, 105, 106, 107, 108, 110, 117, 122, 125, 126, 127, 128, 142, 146; UPI for photographs on pages 90, 137; Allied Artists for picture on page 134.

Permissions to quote passages from articles were given by the following: the Detroit *News*, *Maclean's* Magazine, the Windsor *Star*, the Detroit *Free Press*, *Today* Magazine, the Windsor Separate School Board, the Toronto *Star*, Ron Scott and CBE Radio, Gayle Holman and *Windsor This Month* and the Woodstock *Sentinel-Review*.

Help in preparing photographs was given by Stan Andrews, Walter Jackson, Kyle MacMullin and Rod Rieser. Thanks also goes to Karen Bashucki, who typed the manuscript.

Bibliographical background for the text came from Gerald Hallowell's *Prohibition In Ontario* (Ontario Historical Society), *Nostalgia, Spotlight On The Twenties* by Michael Anglo (Jupiter Books), *Prohibition, The Era of Excess* by Andrew Sinclair (Atlantic Monthly Press Book) and *Playboy's Illustrated History of Organized Crime* by Richard Hammer (Playboy Press).

Biographical Note

C. H. (Marty) Gervais, known as a poet, playwright and journalist, is book editor and religion editor at the Windsor *Star*. He is the author of six books of poetry, one play, one children's book and has edited a collection of essays on a British Columbia writers' movement. Gervais, who has an M.A. in English from the University of Windsor, is 34. He is married and has two children.

6

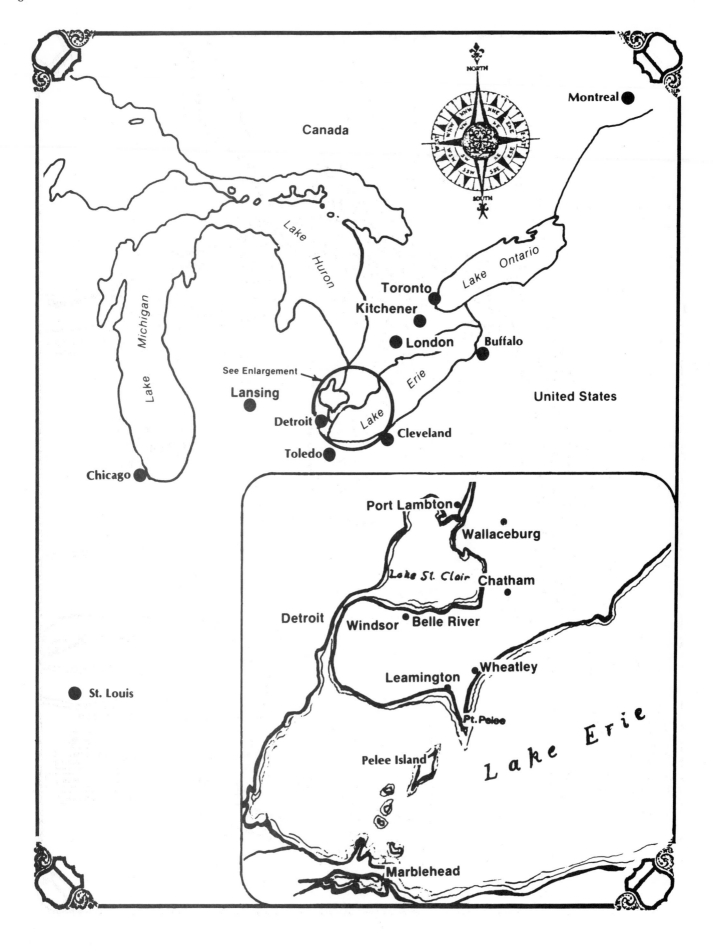

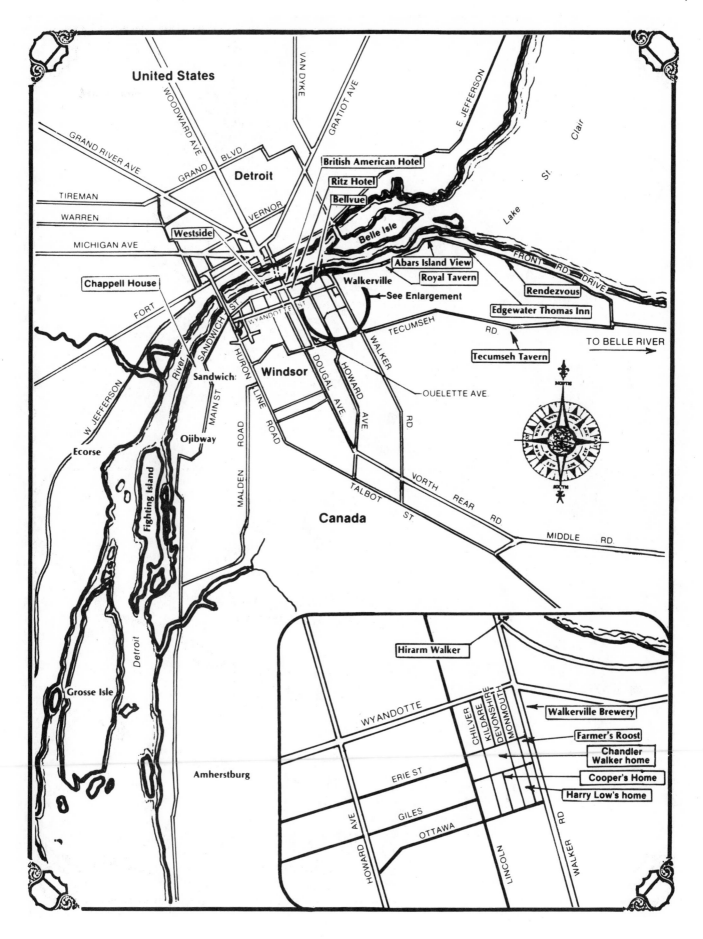

Al Capone. Capone developed most of the rumrunning activities in the United States, and is said to have accumulated up to $100 million per year from contraband beer sales alone. He is said to have engineered countless killings, but when finally sent to prison in 1931, it was for tax evasion.

Foreword

Prohibition, that wild and hysterical age that ushered in speakeasies, flappers, the rumrunner and the color and excitement difficult to match at any other time in history, was something that touched everyone.

If you weren't involved in the actual traffic of liquor, you were buying and drinking it. If you weren't drinking, you were campaigning against it. If you weren't parading and carrying placards you were privately sipping an ale and smirking with cherished delight. But for all of those who lived through Prohibition, it was an era that left its mark on memories.

Some recall it with a smile and a wink. You can almost hear knees being slapped with delight at the telling. And the stories recounted are brimming with exaggeration, a blend of gossip and fact, but blessed with an affinity for the spectacular.

These are the reminiscences of people who guided jalopies across the ice, carting wooden crates of bourbon and good Canadian whiskey to blind pigs and warehouses on the American side; of those wide-eyed bystanders who unobtrusively stood at a counter drinking shots, trying to catch the eye of some giggling gal with kiss curls who kicked and waved on the glistening ballroom floor of a border roadhouse; of the people who paid dearly for the occasional bottle from someone whose reputation associated him with the masterminds behind the liquor trade; of the innocent participants from that era who had an Uncle Jake and Aunt Gertie who kept a healthy supply of booze under the floorboards of the back shed.

All of these characters have an exclusive flag over the territory in their memory they call the Prohibition Era.

The liquor being sold in the United States for the most part was smuggled across the border from Canadian ports. The great majority originated at Windsor, or the Border Cities, as the ports surrounding Windsor were called. Police estimated that nearly four-fifths of all the liquor being sent to the United States was smuggled across the Detroit River. The traffic was so heavy and frenetic that this route came to be known as "The Windsor-Detroit Funnel."

Windsor unquestionably was the stomping ground where small time newspaper vendors and cabbies became exporters and bootleggers going after the fat wallets of Americans.

One would have thought Prohibition would have put an end to the consumption of liquor but it had just the opposite effect. Less than a year after the legislation was enacted, more than 900,000 cases of liquor were shipped to the Border Cities for what was allowed as "private consumption." This was a devastating increase in the per-capita consumption level of a prewar nine gallons to 102 gallons. The liquor, of course, wasn't for private use, but was shipped across the river to blind pigs and warehouses.

One Windsor widow, who lived on Pitt Street, just one street up from the Detroit River, was suspected by the police of selling liquor to smugglers, who took the supplies to the United States. She had purchased forty cases of whiskey and nine barrels of liquor over a six-month period. Upon being brought to court, the protesting woman said she had taken up serious drinking since the war and now downed at least five quarts of whiskey daily. The magistrate was unsympathetic and ordered police to confiscate the remainder of her "household supply."

So, Prohibition failed. At least, it fell short for the temperance societies, churches and fanatic evangelists who authored the legislation.

But for the owners of blind pigs, the bootleggers, the rumrunners, the gangsters, the roadhouse proprietors, the police, the magistrates, the spotters, the boaters and armies of others, it was a roaring success. It meant work. Employment. Easy money. Cash in the pocket. Good times. Shiny new cars. New suits.

But their tales by no means eclipse the recollections of hard-driving temperance soldiers who worked tirelessly to win the battle against strong drink. Prohibition may have slipped out of their grasp, but echoes of those times still resound clearly at conferences of the United Church when old delegates rise with antiquated objections to the present liquor laws and recommend lame protests. They hold back from wanting to marshall that era once more, for they fear ridicule and uproar. They are the ones who campaigned actively to bring in the laws to put liquor under lock and key and to eradicate its ugly effects, which they claimed destroyed not only minds but families. For them — those in the Dominion Alliance, the Woman's Christian Temperance Union (WCTU), the Women's Legion for True Temperance, the staunch and pompous Methodists, the saloon busters and the angry evangelists — Prohibition is something they endured in the past. Lost years. Fatal years. Little did enemies of moonshine and saloons realize that upon creating Prohibition and putting liquor out of the reach of the general population, they had in effect created a monster. For instead of society turning reflectively upon itself to ponder the common good, it reacted by plunging headlong into one of the wildest, most violent and colorful of times — the Roaring Twenties.

It was during this era that North America gave birth to some of the largest crime syndicates and most vicious criminals. Al Capone, Bugs Moran, Johnny Torrio, the Purple Gang, Pete Licavoli, the Little Jewish Navy (sometimes called "Jew Navy") became household names.

Unemployment during this period became a myth of sorts, since there were legions who joined the forces of both the temperance groups and the bootlegging industry.

Prohibition in fact backfired. Instead of eradicating the manufacture and sale of liquor, it sustained and boosted it to the point that its use in both the United States and Canada was even greater and more widespread.

Detroit, for example, boasted that during those years sales related to liquor — profits from smuggling and in blind pigs — made booze the second largest industry in that city, exceeded only by the manufacture of automobiles. The Detroit Board of Commerce speculated that more than 50,000 people were involved in the booze business.

Actual sales of booze over the counter in Detroit amounted to more than $219 million, while wine sales surpassed $30 million.

The numbers of people working in the liquor trade in Canada are much harder to estimate, but in the early days of Prohibition, it was said that twenty-five percent of the population near the Detroit River was involved in smuggling booze to Americans. And nearly a quarter of a million dollars was collected in fines by Windsor courts from boaters illegally possessing liquor during the first seven months of 1920.

One can't help but take note, however, that when the Methodists and anti-saloon leaguers preached about the evils of strong drink, they could never have envisioned what might happen. Could they have conjured up the bizarre and terrible wars among bootleggers, gangsters, roadhouse owners and even squabbles and tragedies among their own over-zealous clerics and temperance leaders? There was no way they could have predicted the St. Valentine's Day massacre in Chicago. Or the shooting of a roadhouse owner in Sandwich, Ontario by a Methodist minister who packed pistols and was accompanied by gun-toting hoodlums.

It was indeed an irony that the Canadian White Ribbon Tidings in 1919 sang:

Then storm the citadel of Wrong
With votes as ammunition
And usher in the welcome dawn
Of Total Prohibition!

Those glad voices at that moment didn't perceive the follies before them. They couldn't have foreseen how legislation against the consumption and sale of liquor would turn out to be the very thing necessary to *bolster* the trade, something very much removed from an era of "Total Prohibition." Far from it.

These same enthusiastic campaigners who declared in editorials that failure to vote for Prohibition could be "the thing that turns homes into hovels," couldn't have anticipated just how Demon Rum was responsible for transforming these hovels into castles. The evidence is staggering when one sees the proliferation of grand homes built in the old Walkerville area in Windsor.

Ironies or no ironies, these advocates of temperance, who declared strong drink to be the cause of "feeblemindedness, idiocy, epilepsy and tendencies to all kinds of moral weaknesses," won the day. In their editorials, slogans and relentless campaigning, meetings and parades, they won the support of churches and government, and eventually the general population. Or at least they succeeded in convincing an overwhelming majority to vote for prohibition on liquor and beer.

But after succeeding, a new battle was thrust upon them: enforcement. Keeping Demon Rum out of the hands of the weak. And this is what spawned an era of deviousness, great ingenuity and color. From it came the rumrunners, the bootleggers, mobsters, tipsters, gamblers, protection rackets — and a never-ending source of booze spilling out casually and uncontrollably across North American towns at exorbitant prices in shot glasses, quarts, gallons, kegs and boat loads.

If anything, this is the quality of Prohibition as we have come to recognize it. We recall the scraps of stories, the bits of history picked up from sketchy newspaper flashbacks, but we have long forgotten the overwrought and somewhat absurd efforts of the church leaders who warned society that strong drink led not just to the obvious — drunkenness, but to wife-beating, broken homes, bad health and vile talk as well.

But the battle waged, however, by these passionate Methodists and anti-saloon, hatchet-carrying women is not something to be ignored by historians. After all, these fierce temperance armies scored an important victory at the polls and raised the flag over a new era. But once the ballots were counted, and the victory announced, the new war had began. It was an underground battle which defeated the prohibitionists and won the day.

The nagging questions however always arise. How did Prohibition take hold? And why did it fail?

First of all, Prohibition was something shared by both the United States and Canada, and by that I mean in terms of legislation. But there is a marked confusion over this, because how could Canadians send shipments of booze across the border to the United States, if legislation was in effect in Canada prohibiting liquor?

To put it simply, the laws were enacted at different times and with loopholes.

In the United States, the Volstead Act went into effect in January 1920 and placed a ban on the manufacture, sale and transportation of all intoxicating beverages.

In Canada, the federal government introduced legislation in March 1918 ending legal importation of liquor into the country, its manufacture in Canada, and transportation of it

Carry Nation. Hatchet carrying Carry Nation, who literally busted open rumshops as early as the turn of the century, symbolized early Prohibition movements. She was famous for leading groups of raiders who wrecked saloons with rocks and hatchets.

to any part of the country where its sale was illegal. All the provinces of Canada, the Yukon and the Dominion of Newfoundland passed prohibitory laws on liquor in the war-time spirit. Quebec was the only one to renege, and after a referendum returned to the sale of light beers, cider and wines.

When the United States had passed its Volstead Act, the temperance forces could actually claim that the entire continent north of the Rio Grande was dry — except for the province of Quebec.

Where the confusion reigns, however, is in the ensuing events. The Canadian federal government repealed its war-time measures at the end of the war, so in December 1919, strong drink could again flow along the recognized trade routes across provincial boundaries. It could also be exported to countries which did not have laws prohibiting liquor. Of course the United States had such laws, but sure-footed suitcase smugglers, fast boatmen and, later, crafty air pilots took their chances and sent the booze across the river. Most carried false export papers.

Billy Sunday. More than 80 million people attended the dramatic evangelical services organised by the baseball player turned preacher who would pull off his coat and vest during a heated sermon to harangue a crowd in a booze sermon, damning "crooks, corkscrews, and whiskey politicians". Sunday left major league baseball to hit the sawdust trail of preaching and was a great force for the temperance cause.

To hamper this liquor activity, the provinces drafted new legislation to fill in the gaps created by the federal government's decision to opt out of Prohibition.

Essentially, the situation in Canada was that some province had prohibition on the sale of liquor, its consumption and its transportation within the province. But no ban existed on the manufacture and export of liquor — and that's how Canadians thwarted the prohibitionists.

How all this came about can be boiled down to about five causes, situations or environments responsible in ushering in Prohibition. They were:

1) The First World War
2) The new authority of women
3) A half-century of campaigning by church leaders, politicians, evangelists and women's groups.
4) The existing moral climate of the time
5) Rural paranoia about urban intrusion

Most blame the First World War, which had a tremendous influence upon the eventual passage of legislation which took away a person's freedom to drink. During the war both the United States and Canada, as already stated, enacted laws that set the groundwork for full bans on liquor and beer. It was believed that money should be diverted from liquor to "war fitness."

All the provinces of Canada and its territories brought new sanctions into effect. As an example, the Ontario Government passed the Ontario Temperance Act (OTA) in 1916, which closed down all bars, clubs and liquor shops for the duration of the war. The federal government's legislation didn't come until later, near the end of the war in March 1918. It put a stop to legal importation of liquor into the country, the manufacture of it in Canada and its transportation to any part of Canada where it might be illegal.

The moral climate in the U.S. brought on by the war, it is said, permitted the easy passage of the Volstead Act. The 18th Amendment to the Constitution banning the manufacture, sale and transportation of all intoxicating beverages breezed right through Congress in December 1917. By January 1919, the required 36 of the 48 states had backed the Amendment, and by October of that same year, despite the veto of President Woodrow Wilson, Congress approved the Volstead Act. On January 16 1920, the new law went into effect. It was named after Congressman Andrew J. Volstead, a Minnesota Republican, who said, "The law does regulate morality and has regulated morality since the Ten Commandments." He was utterly confident the new rules of order would be obeyed.

Another war-time condition which aided prohibitionists in both the United States and Canada was the new authority of women.

Before and during the war, women found voice in numbers. They banded together in exclusive groups. In many cases these were temperance-oriented organizations, such as the Women's Christian Temperance Union and The Dominion Alliance.

Women had also acquired far more responsibility in having to fend for themselves during the war, to find work and feed the families while their husbands were overseas fighting in the trenches. The short absence gave them not only more leverage but more independence, thereby influencing the man of the house to vote for laws to prohibit the use of liquor.

But more importantly this new authority of women took the form of enfranchisement. Women received the right to vote in elections. In Ontario, as an example, the government under William Hearst enfranchised women in 1917 with the result that women suddenly made up half of the electorate. This action by the Ontario Premier was considered one of the main reasons for the overwhelming majority selecting Prohibition in the 1919 referendum in that province. Where women did not get the right to vote, as in Quebec, stiff temperance laws failed to get approval.

Still, it was primarily a half-century of campaigning by groups like the WCTU, the Dominion Alliance, the Anti-Saloon League (U.S.) that helped shape, or tire out, the minds of North Americans and eventually legislate restrictive regulations on the sale of liquor and beer.

By the early 1900s in the United States, the great temperance leaders, who decried the insidious influence of strong drink, urged their forces to use anything to shut down the saloons — even hatchets if necessary. The bible and hatchet carrying Carry Nation and her male counterpart, the iron-fisted Dr. Howard Russell, were the most popular below the border. Rev. Ben Spence, the dogged and determined leader of the Dominion Alliance, and N. W. Rowell, a zealous Methodist and leader of the Ontario Liberal Party, crusaded vigorously through the difficulties of "wet" times in Canada.

Occasionally the two forces joined hands to bombard the common enemy. One of the most dramatic examples occurred when evangelist Billy Sunday castigated and cursed the evils of drink at the Toronto Arena to more than 10,000 frantic supporters. In a barbed, stirring speech, this dynamic purveyor of Prohibition demanded that people march in support of the referendum that would legislate the sale of booze out of existence in Ontario. Staggering across the stage like a man possessed, he argued that if they did not kindle in their hearts the spirit of Prohibition, then "whiskey people could . . . make the old world a puking, spewing, vomiting, maudlin, staggering, bleary-eyed, tottery wreck . . ."

It seems odd in retrospect to believe that such dynamism and groups could attract so many willing and trusting adherents, seize the reins of government, and effect, with relative ease, what they insisted were long sought-after laws. But a glimpse of that era and the moral climate that existed shows us that more than liquor was outlawed.

The period up till 1920 was dominated by prohibitions — on clothing, behavior and even food. In Ontario, especially, the straight-laced Protestant ethic dictated an exclusive code of conduct. It was strictly forbidden in 1919, for example, to purchase a cigar, an ice cream cone, a newspaper or anything vaguely frivolous on a Sunday. And playing sports of any kind was absolutely banned on the Lord's Day.

The United States wasn't exempt from this, either. In Michigan, women weren't allowed to wear high-heeled shoes. It was considered a crime.

Thus, it follows that the population which observed so stringent a set of codes of behavior, should be the same to concoct a ban on intoxicating beverages.

But in addition to all these factors, the impact of the farmer on the polls couldn't be ignored. The farmer was regarded as a kind of silent partner to the movement that spawned the frenetic activity to put a ban on booze. The prohibitionists relied upon the farmer to cast his ballot against the evils of drunkenness and sloth, which he viewed from the safety of his front veranda in the remote and serene countryside, as something urban in nature.

In Ontario, the farmer had an ally when the temperance forces were gearing up for the referendum. *The Farmer's Sun*, the official organ of the United Farmers of Ontario (the UFO Party) told farmers what they already knew — that the sanctuary of their rural peace could only be ensured if they voted to bring cities and towns under the umbrella of Prohibition.

The Farmers' Magazine advocated a similar prescription for good living. During the 1919 campaign, when the referendum was being hotly debated, the magazine declared, "We as farmers can't afford the risk of reckless auto driving, and wild county midnight depradations if liquor people get 'yes' written on the ballot."

In Ontario the politicians cleared the path for Prohibition. The leaders of the three largest political parties — Premier William Hearst of the Conservatives, N. W. Rowell of the Liberals and Ernest C. Drury of the UFOs — were all Methodists, all solidly behind Prohibition. So, Ontario couldn't help but vote the laws in; there really was little choice with a slate like that.

It's only fair to explore the other opinions of the temperance question. The extremes to which the prohibition movement went weren't overlooked by everyone and weren't universally accepted, or regarded as being "normal" for that time.

Stephen Leacock, writing for *The Living Age*, described a prohibitionist as a drunkard who could always be relied on to poll a vote in favor of Prohibition while "in a mood of sentimental remorse."

Leacock was not so ironic when he criticized the manner in which prohibition forces used the war as a vehicle to keep booze locked up. He wrote that during the Great War, Prohibition "masqueraded as the crowning effort of patriotism. The war over, it sits enthroned as a social tyranny."

The famous humorist was deadly serious in his campaign, almost a one-man show, to fight Prohibition. In an address delivered in 1921 at a Toronto meeting of the Citizens' Liberty League, Leacock said, "The attempt to make the consumption of beer criminal is as silly and as futile as if you passed a law to send a man to jail for eating cucumber salad . . ."

Leacock wasn't alone, however. Organizations, groups and newspapers formed a solid front to fight the temperance movement. In Windsor, a new newspaper called *The Plain Dealer* became the official organ of the Border Cities Branch of the Citizens' Liberty League for Moderation, and its sole purpose was to print the facts about fierce, sloganeering prohibitionists.

The anti-prohibitionists weren't without the support of the church either. The temperance movement may have had the unwavering backing of the Methodists, but there was religious sympathy for those who opposed the wave of sentiment in support of regulations on liquor and beer. In 1920, the eccentric and iron-willed Bishop M. F. Fallon of the London Diocese of the Roman Catholic Church furiously argued that Prohibition opposed all the best Catholic traditions of personal conscience. He was supported by Rev. T. C. Street Macklem, Provost of Trinity University in Toronto who considered the new legislation a detriment to health because it only forced people to drink contraband and homemade concoctions, which were probably contaminated or poisonous.

Not enough people listened to the anti-prohibitionists. Prohibition, despite the formation of hard-working counter-leagues and societies, swept in with the force of a tornado. Ontario went "dry forever," in the estimation of some. Other provinces followed suit, including Manitoba, Saskatchewan and the Northwest Territories.

But the center of attention was Ontario, more specifically the Border Cities because these isolated communities became the focal shipping point for illicit booze to the United States.

Why Prohibition fell apart and failed to succeed can be answered by a chronology of events and the background behind them.

— October 20 1919, Ontario went dry by an overwhelming majority of more than 400,000 voting against *repeal* of the OTA (in effect since 1916). The government sale of liquor was also soundly defeated by a majority of 240,000 votes. Ontario had also swept in a new leader, Ernest C. Drury, a Methodist sunday school teacher and avid temperance man. He was leader of a new party in Ontario — the United Farmers of Ontario, a political force dedicated to enforcement of the OTA. Drury appointed William E. Raney, an active Dominion Alliance member as his attorney-general.

YESSIR! I'M HERE ON A LITTLE 'BOOZINESS TRIP'

Wrong impression — Postcards that went into circulation depicting Canada as the barroom for the United States were vehemently opposed by temperance organizations.

The victory both in the referendum and the election was viewed as a momentous one, especially by the Methodists who openly boasted in their *Christian Guardian*, "the liquor traffic's damnable trail (which) has besmirched every aspect of our political and social life," had finally come to an end. The editorial claimed that liquor had "bred crime and harbored criminals . . . mocked at decency and wallowed in violence," and now, it had "run its lurid course . . ."

What irony! What ensued was specifically what the prohibitionists believed would be eradicated. Prohibition created an age of mobsters and boosted crime to new heights . . . all because of overlooked loopholes and the very insult of taking away a man's beer.

The new laws were shortlived.

— In December 1919, the federal government repealed its war-time ban on the manufacture of intoxicating beverages, the importation of liquor into Canada and the transportation of it to any part of the country where the sale was illegal.

This virtually took the wind from the sails of the dry advocates, because once again booze could be manufactured in Canada, and once more Ontario residents or residents of any other province or territory in Canada could import all the liquor and beer they wanted.

Thus began the flow of booze into the homes of Ontario at a phenomenal rate.

People were never prohibited from having a "cellar supply," for personal use, and so now they could stock up on the legal supplies from outside the province. And the area supplying it was the Province of Quebec.

Because the cost of transportation was exorbitant and far too great for the average man, the bootlegging business got its biggest boost. A bootlegger ordered the booze from Quebec and arranged for its transportation to Ontario. Instead of retaining it for his own cellar supply, which was allowed under the regulations, he sold it to the highest bidder. This was illegal, of course, but done nevertheless.

The Ontario Government very quickly realized they had been fooled by the federal authorities.

— Under pressure from temperance groups and provincial authorities, the Dominion Parliament approved Bill 26 before scrapping its war-time Prohibition measures. This bill decreed that the provinces could prevent the importation of liquor by holding a referendum.

In response to this, British Columbia, Alberta, Saskatchewan, Manitoba and Nova Scotia all voted "dry" in their importation referenda, leaving isolated Ontario to debate the question further. The province wanted to turn off the tap of imported Demon Rum into Ontario homes, but temperance leaders were divided over just what drastic actions should be introduced.

The Dominion Alliance hoped for more than just an end to imported booze — its leaders wanted a ban on the sale of native wines, which were still permitted under the law. There were also heated arguments over the transportation of liquor *within* the province, which eventually led to the passage of the Sandy Bill which disallowed the movement of liquor within Ontario except by and under the order of the Board of Licence Commissioners.

The bill, however, could not go into effect until Ontario had voted in favor of Bill 26 which would stop importation.

Ontario voters went to the polls April 18 1921 and passed both pieces of legislation in a referendum, and on July 19 1921, Ontario no longer allowed residents to order whiskey and beer from Quebec or any other province in Canada. At the same time it was no longer permitted for anyone to transport intoxicating beverages from one place to another except under order of licencing officials.

The loophole in this latter law was uncovered by the watchful amiable giant of the illicit liquor trade — Jim Cooper.

Cooper, who built the fashionable Cooper Court, first in Belle River, and then a Walkerville version which had a marble-lined swimming pool and lavish pipe organ, virtually made a million from his clever insight. He set up shop in Detroit and under a bizarre technicality supplied liquor legally to residents in Windsor. Canadians merely had to telephone a Detroit number and order liquor from Cooper. The goods purchased were not brought into the province of Ontario. They already were there in warehouses. But because the booze was not purchased in Ontario, but in Detroit, it was perfectly legal to have it delivered from a Windsor warehouse to Windsorites.

There were other means of acquiring liquor. One was through a permissive doctor's prescription plan, a plan so abused that the Board of Licence Commissioners refused to honor the prescriptions if they believed physicians were not writing them honestly. Some doctors had taken advantage of the law to the extent that people were lining up in the streets outside their offices.

In one month, one doctor had issued 1,244 liquor orders and on one particular day had written out more than 244 prescriptions. It was such a spectacle that Stephen Leacock remarked that if you wanted a drink in Ontario, "it is necessary to go to a drugstore, and lean up against the counter and make a gurgling sigh like apoplexy . . . one often sees these apoplexy cases lined up four deep . . ."

By May 1921, a limit was placed on the family doctor so that he couldn't issue more than fifty prescriptions for one quart of liquor each month.

Another means of buying liquor was from the manufacturer. But this had to be for *export* purposes.

With clearance papers from Canada Customs showing you were exporting liquor to Cuba, South America, or virtually anywhere where Prohibition wasn't in force, you were permitted to take all the booze you could carry and pay for. The only stipulation was that a B-13 clearance document had to be issued from federal customs officials with the destination stamped on it.

The liquor was collected at the export docks which were strung out along the Detroit River shoreline from Amherstburg to Belle River. And the exporter, or rumrunner as he came to be identified, loaded up at night. Armed with the papers, or what Elliot Ness called, "The Canadian Print Job," the rumrunner stole away with his shipments across the lakes and rivers unseen by the watchful Yankee patrol boats. The runners weren't lugging crates of whiskey to South America or Cuba, as was indicated on the clearance documents. They headed for Detroit or Cleveland. So ludicrous was the situation, that one newspaper ran a headline reporting that the same vessel was going to Cuba four times daily.

These bold and brash runners — some of them taking photographs of themselves sitting upon crates of booze on a wind-swept frozen-over river — were a special breed. Getting caught wasn't within their dimension of living. They were rarely caught with the goods.

They carried the supplies on rafts, row boats, canoes, sail boats, speed boats . . . anything that could float and facilitate travel to Cuba or South America or Detroit.

Of course some of the liquor remained right here in Canada. The boats would pull out of the export docks headed for some faraway port across the world, and instead would zoom straight to slips behind the roadhouses, such as the Rendezvous, the Sunnyside Tavern, the Edgewater Thomas Inn. If not there, the liquor ended up in private homes or secret caches where it was later hauled by automobile and truck to blind pigs.

Drury and Raney went to every means to stop the illicit activity, but to no avail. When they contested shipments of beer and liquor going into the United States, a Windsor judge declared that intoxicating beverages could be shipped there, quite legally. The magistrate said that unless Canadian authorities changed the laws, customs authorities were obliged to provide clearance papers.

Raney moved swiftly and harshly to put an end to the traffic of liquor. He enlisted the fanatical Reverend J. O. L. Spracklin, whose story is included in this book, but the scheme collapsed. Spracklin shot and killed a tavern owner in a zealous campaign to eradicate bootlegging in what was termed "The Essex Scandal."

Conservative estimates from the Canadian authorities showed that more than $40 million worth of booze was being shipped across the border. The largest percentage was going through the Windsor-Detroit Funnel.

Booze was going across with skaters on sunny afternoons, tourists crossing on the ferry boats. Bottles were strapped to underclothing, inside brassieres, in stockings, in boots, up coatsleeves, in tires of cars. But this was small time suitcase smuggling. Liquor found its biggest profits in boats and old jalopies.

But there were some ingenious ways. Air rumrunning was perhaps the most dynamic of them all. Aerial smuggling was a novelty, and at first it was something that went unhampered by authorities, who already had their hands full in trying to combat convoys of boats that sneaked across the river at all hours of the day and night.

The aerial rumrunners were big-time and gang-organized, under contract. Al Capone and the Purple Gang were lucratively involved in this, since they needed swift supplies on a daily basis. It was estimated that as much as $100,000 worth of booze left Windsor and neighboring parts each month for American landing strips.

In Ontario the landing strips were farmers' fields, given over to the rumrunners at a flat rate fee. Sometimes they were paid as much in one day as what they would have earned if they had put in a crop. Sometimes the farmers aided the runners by assisting the pilots in landing at night. They would drive their cars to the field and keep their lights on, and often would set up lanterns and build small fires. For this assistance, they were paid as much as $5 a case.

Large cargoes of liquor also made their way to Detroit through the railway tunnel under the

William E. Raney — When the United Farmers of Ontario swept into power in 1919, the new attorney-general, Raney, was determined to enforce Prohibition. Much of his previous public career had been devoted to combatting race track gambling.

Detroit River. Railway cars labelled for Mexico by way of the United States were shunted off the main track and unloaded on the outskirts of Detroit. The *New York Times* in a 1923 exposé of these events claimed that more than 800 cases of beer daily were delivered by mis-labelled boxcar to Detroit. The *Detroit News* claimed in a 1928 story that more than half the shipments of illegal liquor to Detroit came by rail.

The typical scam was that carloads of just about any legal product were shipped across the border from Buffalo through Ontario to Windsor, where upon arrival the Customs seals of these cars were broken and the liquor substituted for the contents. Fraudulent seals were then affixed and the boxcars rumbled right on through into the United States where they never underwent inspection.

There were some bizarre stories from that era including tales of liquor encased in torpedoes shot beneath the river's surface to secret terminals. And there were those who claimed there was a pipeline in the river bed which flowed with whiskey. There are some oldtimers who insist they had seen it.

One true story recounts how a contraption built to haul up to 20 cases of liquor along the river's bottom by means of a 500-foot cable, was uncovered by customs border patrol inspectors in the fall of 1929.

Nothing could stop the flow of booze into the United States, not even the American patrol boats.

At the start of Prohibition, the American forces to combat rumrunning were sadly impotent. Both the Michigan State Police and the Detroit Police had in their possession a single antiquated boat that could barely catch the slowest rumrunner's vessel. In time, however, they built up their potential and by 1922 had a 200 horsepower boat with a top speed of 38 mph. Its crew was a formidable collection of brutes, carrying with them handguns, machine guns, tear gas and rifles.

An ironic twist came when American forces intercepted the *Tennessee II*, which was reputed to be the fastest rumrunning vessel on the river, and began to utilize it to chase after other smugglers.

But in the beginning of Prohibition, the rumrunners nearly drove the police off the waterfront. The runners often fixed a cannon to the bows of their vessels and gave chase to the police. Gangs such as the ''Jew Navy'' openly attacked the police's clean-up operations on the lakes and rivers.

Drury and Raney knew by 1923 their regime had collapsed around them, and that the rumrunner and bootlegger would flourish as long as Prohibition remained in force. All the propaganda about crime and drunkenness being wiped out was just pure puffery.

Rumrunning became big business.

Blind pigs and illicit stills had sprung up everywhere, even within walking distance from Queen's Park, the Parliamentary offices of the Ontario Government. The speakeasies, gambling casinos and bootlegging joints across the province, and especially in the Border Cities, were doing a roaring business.

Even the Canadian Government received handsome benefits from Prohibition. The Canadian taxation system at the time was funnelling money like never before into the government's coffers from smuggled liquor transactions. The Dominion Government levied a nine dollar tax per gallon on all intoxicating beverages. This was refunded upon presentation of a customs receipt from the country to which it

was destined, providing that country was not in the throes of Prohibition. Since most, if not all, of the liquor, landed on the American shores, these receipts were never handed in. The tax dollars as a result piled up in Ottawa, and by 1928 the Canadian government was gathering up to $30 million a year from illegal exports to the United States.

Besides the government, there were officials in the employ of both provincial and federal authorities who garnered tidy sums from the rumrunning activities. Newspapers revealed for example, unhampered delivery of beer to Detroit, Cleveland, St. Louis and Chicago. One United States Border Patrol officer, Daniel Shimel, who was one of the most notorious hard-nosed policemen of the bunch, was offered more than $50,000 to resign. He resigned, not for the money, but because his colleagues, who were taking bribes, threatened his life.

At one point, the entire Yankee Border Patrol force was fired or resigned when it was discovered that most of them were on the take.

One bootlegger, George Remus, who was called ''King of the Bootleggers,'' estimated that he spent more than $20 million on payoffs during his lifetime.

In Canada, the situation was the same. People like Cecil Smith and Harry Low slammed down big bucks to ensure little trouble from the police and warehouse owners. Graft, about as commonplace as smoking in public, shocked some officials, most notably the Canadian Minister of National Revenue, William D. Euler, when he paid a visit to Windsor in 1928. He stood on the riverbank and saw the boats leaving the Canadian side and heading straight to Detroit, and nowhere to be seen were the American patrol boats. Euler decided to ask a man at the export dock who was in the business why these runners didn't get caught, and the reply was simply that the police conveniently took the day off.

As one can see, the wooly and wild days of Prohibition were too much for the prohibitionists. Drury and Raney literally had their hands full. Booze was making its way across the waterways, mostly in the Border Cities, from Amherstburg right over to Stoney Point on Lake St. Clair, sometimes by plane, by rowboat, by speedboat, and later by huge schooners.

At the end of 1923 Drury's government counted its success in that it had ended importation of liquor from other provinces, and it had set controls over prescriptions given by doctors.

But in reality, it had failed to halt the massive export of liquor across the border, and by no means did it succeed in boarding up the blind pigs, bootlegging joints, casinos and roadhouses.

In the election of 1923, the UFO Party was defeated by a new Conservative Government led by Howard G. Ferguson, who promised during his campaign to advance measures to please everyone concerned with the OTA.

Ferguson moved cautiously, not wanting to dismantle the framework set up by Drury immediately, and in 1924 held a referendum to determine whether voters still wanted Prohibition. The huge majority of 400,000 of 1919 dwindled to a mere 33,000 but it passed again.

In 1925, Ferguson's government introduced legislation permitting the sale of 4.4% beer, soon to be called "Fergie's Foam."

In 1926, Premier Ferguson returned to the polls, this time basing his campaign on the reintroduction of liquor through government control. His party was returned without losses.

In June 1927, the Conservative Government introduced the Ontario Liquor Control Act, thereby ending Prohibition in Ontario. Liquor could now be bought through government outlets.

In the United States, Prohibition was still in full swing. It wasn't to be repealed until 1933. Thus, the rumrunners, undaunted by the fall of Drury and unconcerned by the scrapping of the OTA by Ferguson, went right on shooting booze across the border to grateful Americans.

But all of this came to an end in 1930 when the MacKenzie King Government, heeding the pressure of the United States, shut down the export docks and made the shipment of booze illegal from Canadian ports. This was seven years later than Drury would like to have seen. It was too late to be of any use to the prohibitionists, but it did put an abrupt end to the boom years of Prohibition in Canada, especially to those in the Border Cities where fortunes had been made and where the lowly had enjoyed the years of hobnobbing with the wealthy.

As noted earlier, Windsor was certainly the major stomping ground for liquor profiteers. The stories of the giants — Harry Low, Jim Cooper, Cecil Smith, Vital Benoit — are included in this book, but so are the vignettes of those curious and lesser known rumrunners, who manned the boats and stole across the midnight waters. Most of them are in their eighties today and live alone, and some have kept their secret until now. And others, who are quoted anonymously here, are still afraid the tax department or police will break down their doors and catch them fifty years later.

Those days are still fresh in their minds.

My book takes the form of a "scrapbook", which simply means that it is a collection of interviews, tape-recordings, newspaper clippings, drama and miscellaneous bits about the turbulent era of Prohibition. The colorful lives of King Canada, who used to ship liquor daily to Al Capone in Chicago, of Walter Goodchild, who fought for his life in the Battle of Old Crow (not an Indian name, but the brand of bourbon), and the stories of the girls who engaged in the liquor trade at the age of five, of people who lugged iron boxes across the river bottom, of Jake Renaud, who aided his father in operating a speakeasy, of Noel Wild, who witnessed the kidnapping of his father (a newspaper photographer) by rumrunners, and the stories of policemen, customs officials, newsmen — accounts of the incredible escapades of the gun-toting Methodist Minister Spracklin . . . yarns about blind pigs, speakeasies and the crazy, gone-mad era that roared on in the riverfront roadhouses . . . detailed narrations about Detroit's notorious Purple Gang and crime syndicate bosses like Pete Licavoli, who are the people who fashioned the Roaring Twenties. Their stories are told here in magazine and newspaper excerpts, and in their own words. Contraband liquor was what they all had in common. It made their careers, kept them at work, gave them fame and wealth, no matter how short lived.

Section One

ROUNDERS AND RUMRUNNERS

Old jalopies were used to haul liquor across the winter ice in broad daylight. Car doors were left to swing open, so that should the ice break, the driver would be able to jump out quickly.

Blaise Diesbourg

Chapter One

KING CANADA
Blaise Diesbourg's Tales

Blaise's involvement in the liquor traffic soon brought him into contact with the kingpin of the underworld — Al Capone. He met Capone in a cellar in Belle River and struck a deal to supply him with daily shipments of booze by plane. It was then that he adopted the name, King Canada. He soon became a supplier to the Purple Gang in Detroit and to other big dealers in the United States. Instead of carrying a weapon, he carried a tough-minded attitude, which seemed to guide him to success. Blaise made bundles of money, but spent it as fast as he made it.

Blaise Diesbourg's story begins in the early years of prohibition in Ontario when he was bootlegging and serving bar at his brother Charlie's hotel, the Wellington, on the main street of Belle River. He is remembered as a tireless worker when it came to loading liquor and beer into old cars and airplanes.

This spry 83 year old French-Canadian, who was born in the farming area near Belle River, a small town west of Windsor, lives with his dog in a two-room house that he built himself. In his closet, he keeps his choicest home brew — an endless supply of cherry and tomato wines. And in his kitchen, there is always a bottle of whiskey at hand if there is a lull in the conversation. But with Blaise, you needn't worry. He loves to talk, argue, rib and laugh.

Early Bootlegging

My brother was paying me only twenty dollars a week, you know. He said the business was all shot at the hotel — that's the Wellington Hotel and it's still in operation — but he said he'd give me a room and said I could eat here. And I helped him around the place, serving beer and cleaning up. It was during that time (Prohibition). Oh, the police would raid the place. Why sure! But my brother didn't do nothing — he just paid the fine and opened up as soon as they (liquor licence inspectors) left. Nothing to it.

But that twenty dollars — I'd go to the dock (the export dock in Belle River which Art Diesbourg, his brother, owned), buy a case of whiskey and peddle it around, you know. I used to pay, oh about a dollar and a quarter a bottle, and I'd sell it for three dollars, I started up that way. I wasn't selling it across the river (in the United States). No, I was getting rid of it around here. Bootlegging it. That's what I was doing. But then I went on my own in about 1925 or 1926. I went to Stoney Point (east of Belle River on Lake St. Clair) and I kept my own hotel there. I called it Omar Hotel after Omar cigarettes from the other side. I had a partner, and he didn't want to buy my half of the business when I wanted to get out. He was no good . . . he'd drink everything.

We were bootlegging the stuff right from the hotel . . . selling it to anyone, but we also had rooms upstairs. My customers usually had lots of money . . . they were fellows from Chatham who came here with their girlfriends for a good time, and they'd drink in the rooms. We'd hide the booze at the neighbor's or wherever we could.

But we'd get raided. All the time. Jesus Christ, the police were in my place everyday, until I put a stop to it.

I sent a fellow I knew in government to Toronto, and he fixed it for me. I couldn't put up with that shit, no goddam way.

I said to my friend, "I want that son of a bitch fired off the force." He said to me, "Don't worry Blaise, he will be."

Well, he was, you know. I met my friend at a church affair in Stoney Point . . . it was in June. He said, "That guy (the constable) won't be bothering you any more, Blaise."

Yep, he was gone . . . they say he was fired. I think he got a job in London. But you know, before that man got fired, I tried to reason with him. I mean he was raiding my place everyday. I got tired of that, so I decided I had better have a talk with him to fix this up. I decided to go see this constable . . . this is before I talked to my government friend.

So anyway, I went to Leamington, (about thirty five miles east of Windsor) where the police had their office. I saw him there. I went in, and I said, "I don't want you no more to raid me," but he said, "Who the hell are you?"

I said, "Well, I'm just a little guy trying to get along, but I see I can't get along with you."

I had a bottle of whiskey with me. I took it out of my pocket and I put it on his desk.

"Now," I said, "lock me up!"

He said, "I will!" Oh, he was mad.

I said, "Have a drink with me, like a man." He wouldn't take a drink.

He said, "I'm going to call my partner and we're going to put you in jail." But I told him, there was no goddam way he was going to put me in jail. I took the bottle of whiskey and put it into my pocket, and said, "I'll see you later." And when I went out the door, I said one more thing: "You know, you won't be here for very long." And he wasn't. He got fired. And you know, I never got raided after I talked to my friend.

The Export Business

Them fancy people up there at Walkerville and them other places called this rumrunning "the export business." But you know and I know what that meant. It meant you took liquor across the border and sold it. Why sure it was exporting the stuff, but there's no goddamn way it was legal. No way. But I'll tell you, everybody was doing it. Everybody took the stuff across, because it was the best way to make some good, fast money. Take it under your coat on the ferry, a couple of cases in a rowboat, anyway you want. But me, I went into it in a big way. I took it across the ice, 800 cases of whiskey and beer, and it was like a highway out there . . . the cars going back and forth . . . and no one to stop you. Well, they had the law . . . but in the winter it was hard to catch you.

The export docks were the places where you got the stuff. They were open day and night, twenty-four hours. Some guys would buy the stuff, load up the boat and leave it in the slips until night, and then they'd take it across.

I bought the stuff from all different kinds of places. They had export docks all along the river . . . but I never bought it from just one place . . . different ones all the time. And you paid cash for the stuff, maybe $10,000 sometimes. I'd get what I want and load it up.

The biggest outfit at the time was the Mexico Export Company. My brother, Charlie, was the watchman for them when he gave up the hotel. But anyway, they were the biggest. There were also five docks at LaSalle. I couldn't tell you the names of all of them.

But there was also a dock in Amherstburg and in old Sandwich where the boats used to tie in. Coming this way (west) there were others. There was one where the CPR used to pull in on Sandwich Street near the railway bridge. They also had docks at Riverside, Little River and one nearby at Lauzon Road . . . and then at Belle River. A big dock here. My brother, Art, was in that one with another fellow.

Well a guy could come in to these docks and get his whiskey and take it where he wanted. He had to have the papers of course (B-13 papers* from the Canadian Customs indicating destination).

Well some of the bigger outfits from the other side wanted to make sure they get their stuff across. You may have heard of the Jew Navy*. Well they were a gang over there. They had a fleet of boats . . . more than the police . . . and they come over here and they docked and if the law on the other side was on the river, well they chased them away, so they could get their stuff across.

It was a big outfit, this Jew Navy. They had about fifteen boats, and when the law on the other side saw them coming, well, they didn't wait around. When they seen the fleet coming, they just get to the hole, just like a rat. Oh, yeah, they were scared. Well, later the law got themselves some big boats and they weren't so afraid.

In those days, you didn't use the banks. What good is a bank? They're never open when you need them. When I buy a load of whiskey at two o'clock in the morning, I need $12,000 in cash.

*B-13 papers were export permit papers from Canada Customs. Refer to Foreword.

*Jew Navy, also called "Little Jewish Navy" is looked at in chapter 14.

Rumrunners reaching shore. A well dressed man, possibly a tavern owner, helps rumrunners haul a boatload of liquor up to the shore.

So, I'd get the money, but I'd keep it somewhere. Not at a bank. Who's going to open the bank at that time of the morning?

The bank manager here in Belle River asked me one time why I didn't put my money in his bank. I said to him, "Why should I put my money there? Suppose I want $20,000 at two o'clock in the morning, what would you say? You'd say to me, 'Go to hell!'"

You couldn't write a cheque in those days . . . except maybe at Walker's. I used to go to Hiram Walker's and buy a fifty-case load of whiskey. I think at that time a fifty-case load was $1,500. I gave them a cheque. They knew me.

I never was stopped at any of the other places. I always paid cash, and I could get $10,000 worth of whiskey just like that if I wanted. I was never stuck.

But one thing, I never did double-cross anybody. If you double-cross, you're a dead goose. That's what you are with them fellows. They'll get you. And that's what happened with some people. The law got them.

The law only stopped me once here. We had one provincial policeman here in town, and he knew me, and he knew what I was doing. But he didn't bother me. He was all right, a nice fellow, but this Mountie police guy he was the one.

He came around one day asking about me. He said to the provincial, "Do you know this guy?" And of course, the provincial said he did.

Well, the Mountie policeman said, "Well, you know, he's taking stuff to the other side there." But the provincial — he knew I was doing this — said, "Oh no, he'd never do a thing like that. You'll never find a thing going to the other side from him."

"Well," the Mountie said, "look at this plane going up in the air there. He'll be here in fifteen minutes. I'll stop him. He'll be here on the Main Street."

Whiskey shipment on ice. At any time of day, the whiskey dealers and rumrunners would pile up shipments. Sometimes they were left like this in the middle of the lake for American rumrunners to retrieve.

Sure enough, I was. I come up the Main Street, and the provincial said, "Hey, put your car over there, the Mountie wants to search it."

I said, "O.K." But you know, I didn't have a damn thing, only my money. He took all the cushions out of the car. He looked under it, and when he got through, he had all the cushions out and hadn't put them back. I said to the provincial, "You tell that Mountie police to put them cushions back where he got them."

"So," the provincial says, "You know, you heard what he said, eh?"

The Mountie said, "Yes, I heard him!" And he put the cushions where they were in the car. I was never bothered with them any more.

Taking the Booze Across

I used to take it across in old cars, old Ford trucks, on boats . . . but also planes. I was one of the only guys who organized that — putting the stuff on the planes. I would load them up on my own fields. I had five fields . . . some I rented . . . in a way. I just went to the farmer or the fellow with land, and they said it was okay and told me to go ahead. I gave them a case of beer . . . a goddamn case of beer, you know, was a lot . . . they'd pay twenty dollars for a case. Well, they were happy to get it. If they had a wedding, you know, and they wanted a keg of beer . . . well, they'd come to see me, and I'd say it was okay. Or if they wanted a bottle . . . if they were celebrating . . . they could have a bottle of whiskey . . . they didn't pay no money.

So anyway, I had the fields, one was my brother Art's. He had the farm, the place I was born and raised. He had that farm. We had our plant (stash for whiskey and beer) there, too.

Once one of the big guys in Windsor sold me some stuff and the police got wind of it. I had fifteen cases of alcohol . . . all in crates . . . five-gallon cans.

Well, I had a plant that nobody could touch. They tried. The Mountie police come and they walked over it. It was underground . . . in a big soft-water well (cistern) from the eavestroughs. We cut away the eavestroughs, pumped the water out and put the booze in. And it was just like walking in that door there, and it was just under that carpet. The opening to the well was right inside the house.

When the Mounties came, they thought it was in the hay in the barn, but that was a cheap trick.

They were here like a swarm of bees, looking for that goddamn alcohol. But they didn't get it . . . they couldn't find it.

The night I brought it here, it was raining pitchforks. I took the truck and I hauled the alcohol to my plant. The next morning there was about fifteen Mountie police.

I was standing in the window of the hotel. I seen them. One fellow says, "See that hotel there? There's a guy in there that knows where that whiskey is." He was talking on the street and pointing with his finger. I knew where he was pointing. He was pointing at me, because they knew.

Well, anyway, I was the one who had the planes. That was the big business.

The Name "King Canada"

I was called "King Canada", because that's how I wanted to be known in the United States. I gave myself that name, because here in town if the law comes looking for King Canada, well, nobody's going to know who that is. The people in town know me as Blaise Diesbourg but they don't know King Canada. If the law comes to me and asks, I say I don't know. I did this, so the law couldn't keep track of me and what I was doing.

Contract with Al Capone

Al Capone came to see me. He came to the dock, to the Mexico Export Dock, and he asked if there was anybody that could handle that stuff for him. And I was the only one that could. I mean Capone was getting the stuff by boats . . . but he wanted the stuff everyday, by plane. I was the only one that could give 'em that.

So we got in the house of my brother Charlie, in the cellar, and we talked. There was another fellow with him. So we talked.

I said, "Listen, I am King Canada, and you don't fool with me. The first thing you miss, your goose is cooked."

He says he is Al Capone from Chicago.

"Yeah," I says, "I'm the King of Canada, and you know you can't fool around with me. I know every move in Chicago . . . every move you make."

He says, "How?"

I says, "What do you think I am? Don't you think I know something through the government of what's going on in Chicago?"

"Yeah," he said.

"Yeah," I said.

Al Capone

Capone was kind of a tough man . . . but oh, he was a good guy, you know. He was about, oh, I guess, five-foot ten or eleven . . . but smooth. He was never tough with me. I met him only two times . . . once here in Belle River when he came to see me and once more in Chicago when I went down there with his pilots.

But you know when he come down to see me, he had this other fellow with him. I did not tell you this. He wanted me to carry dope. He says it's only a little bundle . . . a little package . . . only twenty-five pounds.

Well, I says, "How much are you gonna pay?"

And he says, "$100,000! You think that's enough? I'll pay you in cash right here if you will handle it."

"No," I said, "I've never killed nobody, and I don't intend to kill nobody. And another thing, if the Mountie police ever got wind what I was handling that stuff you know what they gonna do with me?

He said, "No."

I told him that I'd be going to bed at night, and they'd be sitting in the chair alongside the bed. If they ain't there, the minute I got into my car, they'd follow me. I couldn't make a move... I couldn't operate at all.

So I told Capone's man, all right so a hundred thousand is good, but what in the hell is it good

A typical export dock, Government Wharf #4 on the Windsor waterfront.

for if I go to jail for the next twenty years? I can't use that money, you see.

Well, he says, "Yeah."

Yes, I worked for Capone. He had his own planes . . . old bombers . . . each had a pit on it about long enough to hold twenty-five cases of whiskey. At six o'clock in the morning I'd meet the pilot there in one of the five fields. It didn't matter if it was six below, or ten below, I was there with the load. I loaded the plane up.

Capone would order from the export dock and it would be delivered to my field. I would load up the plane when it landed . . . that was my job. The pilot used to pay me money in a bundle from the bank. And it was stamped on the back how much it was. I never counted no money. He would give me the bundle and I'd throw it on the floor of the car. Never counted it. Never had time to count it. Because I only had five minutes to load in the plane. I used to throw on twenty-five cases every morning . . . 300 bottles of whiskey.

One morning the pilot stopped at Ford's airport in Detroit to get his car fixed . . . something had gone wrong with it. He called me on the phone and said, "I won't be there tomorrow morning. I'm getting my car fixed. It's in the shop. I'm going to be short $200 with the money."

Another time, the pilot said, "Capone wants you to come to Chicago." So, I got in the plane and went with him to Sportsman's Park Racetrack in Chicago. And he was there —

Capone that is — with his big car. I got in with him. We had three motorcycles, all machine guns, three motorcycles in the front and three in the back. And we had nine miles to go to the place they called the Fort.

So, Capone says, "I want to show you a good time tonight." We started drinking, and he had about fifty girls . . . young girls about sixteen, seventeen. Oh a beautiful show! He put on a real show! All dancing and everything! I got drunk and forgot where I was.

Well, the next morning, I had to take the plane because one of the men I had hired was waiting in the field with the load . . . back in Belle River.

The fellow sitting on the chair near me — I was just lying in the bed there — says to me to get up. He was sitting there with a machine gun in his hands and he tapped me on the shoulder.

"Come on," he says, "Put your pants on, the car's warming up, the engine's going in the field. You got to get back. We have to send you back this morning and pick up that load."

So by jeez, I hurried up and put my pants on, and I said, "I want a drink of whiskey." I used to drink a lot you know. So, that fellow reached down on the floor, and says, "Here, take a drink. Here's a glass." So, I took the bottle of whiskey, and I filled up the glass and drank it. I put my pants on, and when I had them on, I took the whiskey and got in the car and I come home to Belle River. Well, first he drives me to the airport, then to Belle River by plane.

Everyday, I send the load to Chicago. I had, you know, a different field here. I never had them land in the same field.

But Capone was a nice fellow. Oh yeah. But they say that you couldn't double-cross him, because you'd be a dead goose.

Well, anyway, I'm the only one, the King of the Airplanes. I was called King Canada or the King of the Airplanes.

The Purple Gang

I had a gang in Detroit I used to deal with. They were called The Purple Gang, you know. Oh, now they were tough. But they didn't bother me.

They had a big bar over there, and you knocked at the door. And there was a guy always there at the door. And when I used to go in there, I would just knock, and he'd say, "Who do you want to see?"

Well, I knew the guys there, and when the bar was running, he'd holler to another fellow to go get my friend. So, when my friend came, he'd say, "Oh, hello, it's King Canada! Let him in! Let him in!" And I'd go in, and they'd bring champagne . . . anything I wanted. Why sure, they knew me, all right.

You know I made a lot of money in those days working for people like Capone, the Purple Gang and a big fellow from Philadelphia. I was rich at one time. I had money, but just like that — it was gone — and you know when you get too big in a business — you become too big of a man — and when that happens, you lose out. I bought an airplane. I paid $12,000 for it. It used to carry fifteen cases.

Well, this guy from the Purple Gang there on the other side, he come and made two trips — I couldn't fly myself — and busted it up on the other side there. He landed in the field where it was rough. They busted up the under-carriage, and then set fire to it. The registration was under my name, so if anything happened, I'd tell them to set fire to it. Get rid of it. I don't want no trouble.

Well, that gang in Detroit says you better buy another one. Well, son of a bitch, we make only one trip on this side, I load them up here in my field at the end of this road here. His engine wasn't working right. So, he just made it right across here at that army base. Just made it over the fence, and he crashed. Just over the fence. Right away he set fire to it . . . before the

soldiers got there. Oh they knew it was whiskey, but they didn't know the number of the plane, or who the plane belonged to, you see.

The Purple Gang had the pilot . . . a good pilot, too, most of the time . . . but I just wasn't lucky. Anyway, I lost $24,000 in there, crashed up two planes, a month apart. Yeah. They were $12,000 apiece.

Other Dealings

I knew a lot of guys, you know. In this business, a lot of the big shots over there would come here to get the stuff. They didn't care who supplied them with the liquor . . . as long as they never got caught . . . and as long as you can do it. I mean, no goddamn way you going to fool them . . . but no goddamn way they going to fool me either . . . I tell them that every time.

I knew the Licavolis . . . now they had a gang over there, too. Now they say they were part of the Purple Gang, but not true.

No, they were worse. There was two of them . . . two Licavolis. Peter and Tom. It was Licavoli who had that big boat, *The Sprite* . . . they called Pete himself "the Sprite" It held 400 cases of whiskey or 800 cases of beer. And the law got it, you know. They had it in the pound in Detroit. Licavoli went down and got the Purple Gang to get it out . . . well they got it out. And they made two trips with it over across — 400 cases of whiskey one trip, 800 cases of beer the second trip. Well, the law was after them. They stored the stuff at Bob-Lo Island over there (near Amherstburg), and the law got them.

I used to supply them with booze sometimes. I loaded them up here.

I also used to have a fellow named Remus. He was a big dealer. He was from Cincinnati. And he used to haul . . . he took 800 cases of whiskey or 800 cases of beer at a time. His load was that big, you know.

Well, I had the job to load 'em up. So we had to go across the lake with it, and he had to be loaded that night. It had to go then — that night. So, I laid on four lifts across with the truck . . . 200 cases at a time . . . four trips . . . and he got his 800 cases.

It was no problem taking it across the ice. The ice was safe. I made the four trips in my truck. Where the channel was open, I built a bridge over it . . . and I'd just drive over that bridge. This channel was like a big crack in the ice. Some days it would be open . . . somedays closed. We took eighteen foot planks and put them one over the top of each other, you see. Then, you hammer a spike through, into the ice so it won't slip. Then you go on it, see, and it would grab

*Peter and Yonnie Licavoli were Detroit gangsters. Their profiles are in Chapter 16.

30

Old Jalopies. Old cars bought for five or ten dollars were used to haul whiskey-laden boats on skids or runners across the ice. A runner would not lose much if such a cheap car fell through the ice.

the ice. Then we added another eighteen foot plank on the top of it. So when you go over with the truck, it went down so far into the water . . . it dipped into the channel and the water would come up to the truck. Well we'd go across, unload the whiskey and have fifteen minutes to drive back. We did that quite a few times. Whiskey and beer...until we got caught...that last time we got caught going to the other side that way for that man in Cincinnati. He was a big dealer...a big fellow.

We just use a regular Ford truck, you know. Two hundred cases is a big load, you know, at a time. That's 200 cases of whiskey. I travelled that lake day after day, and that last trip I made over was a funny thing, you know. I had to take that load across at night to the same fellow, but he was short forty-five, sixty-five or eighty cases of whiskey...I don't remember how much. So we put it in two cars and then started there, and we had that much water on top of the ice here . . . a couple of feet.

But as we went there was more than a couple of feet . . . we had rubber boots (hip-waders) up to here. We walked as far as we could and held an axe and we couldn't touch the bottom where the ice was . . . that's how far down it was . . .

My friend says to me, "We gonna cross?"

"Oh yes, we're going to go across. No goddamn, shit, we'll go to the bottom of the lake, or go across. Number two is what we gotta do, you know."

So, the other fellow with me, he was scared, you know, and he said, "You go first, and if you go in, you go in . . ."

So I put burlap bags around my engine, you know, on the side and, I went around and, I opened her up . . . very wide . . . and I went through that water, and when I got through my engine was just tip-a-tub, tip-a-tub . . . just going. I said to my friend, "Don't stop the son of a bitch, or you'll never start it." So I kept going, and finally got up my speed. Well, the other fellow followed me, when he seen that I went through all right. He followed . . . so we got to the other side . . . oh, maybe, it was two and one-half miles away . . . and we unloaded . . . but we only went two or three miles on that side of the river where we unloaded the stuff.

But when we came back to the lake, the ice was floating on the water . . . the ice had come up . . . it had melted. So this fellow — oh he was stupid — he says to me, "How are we gonna get back?"

I said, "We'll get back with the ferry." Well that night we slept in Detroit, and the next morning, we take the ferry back . . . the Walkerville Ferry.

Another day, one of my dealers, another big dealer, you know, wanted about 1,000 cases of whiskey. He said, "Can you supply me with 1,000 cases?"

I said, "Yeah, 10,000 cases if you want it. That don't mean nothing to me. As long as you pay for it, I'll ship you 10,000 cases."

But he says, "How the hell am I going to get them? I want to take 400 cases at one time."

I told him, "You go to work and buy a whole bunch of cars." At that time, you only paid five, ten, fifteen dollars per car, you know. You didn't want no good car . . . I mean if it fell through the ice . . . it was gone, so you bought old junkers . . . as long as they ran.

Anyway, this fellow says, "How am I going to get them all across?"

"Well," I says, "When you are ready to go, I'll get the truckload here on the ice, a truck four miles out on the ice, you see . . . that's where the shipment will be. So he got the cars, twenty-two cars waiting all in a circle, and we loaded them all up, and I went with them. I sent the truck back, and I went with them. I showed them the road to go.

We got across to the other side all right, twenty-two cars and 400 cases.

Yeah that's what it was like . . . a lot of whiskey went over to the States. A lot of whiskey went over there . . . to be sure. It was any fellow that used to go to the docks with a little boat and take maybe ten or fifteen cases of whiskey, and fifteen or twenty-five cases of beer, and then they go around some place and they used to sell it to the blind pigs there. But that was small, but nobody really got killed. But I was in the big stuff.

I knew one guy who was like Jim Cooper from Walker's . . . he was very rich. But he was crooked, and he paid for it. He could have bought Toronto out. And he could have thrown all the shit-ass out of Toronto . . . had that much money! They put him in a box, and filled the box full of cement and dropped him goodbye John. They never found him. I wouldn't tell you his name. I know him well. And they looked for him and looked for him . . . and they'll never find him. He's maybe 200 feet underground. How the hell are they going to find him? Yeah, he was a big guy. Oh, pretty big. But I know what happened. I'll tell you this. I don't tell you no lie. I dealt with the guy that dealt with him and beat him. I sold this guy whiskey, and he's the one that told me.

There was another guy. He lived in Toledo. He was getting whiskey across for a certain guy, you know. And them guys, they don't fool around. Play them crooked, you're gone. That's it, there's no question asked.

Big bucks in the canals. The intricate system of canals at LaSalle gave easy access to booze on the Canadian side. The canals led to roadhouses (Sunnyside and Chateau LaSalle) and were even close to the Hoffer Brewery. Bullrushes and weeds kept a cache well hidden.

Rumrunners atop a load of booze. Walter Goodchild (left) with Big Mac Randolph sit on a load of contraband liquor before taking it across at Amherstburg.

Chapter Two

The Battle of Old Crow and Other Tales — The Story of Walter Goodchild

Walter Goodchild, 80, still lives in Amherstburg, where he does his own canning and drives a 1938 Ford and drinks bourbon on cold blustery days.

It was July 2 1920. This fellow came around and asked us, "How about going for a ride?" There was a bunch of us, maybe five, and we always had a bottle of whiskey with us. It was hot in July, and so we took a ride up to the River Canard . . . only a few miles away from Amherstburg. We had a few drinks on the way back.

But anyway, as we were passing the Indian Burying Ground, just opposite it, there was a shot. Seemed like it went right through our car, and so to this friend of mine sitting in the back of the car, I said, "What are you doin' with that gun, you crazy fool?"

He said, "I had no gun. That shot came through the car from the ditch." So, we backed up to see what it was, and when we did, we stopped in front of this farmhouse — I believe it's still there — it was gated off. There was an old car in there, and we knew the man who owned it. He used to dicker in whiskey. And in those days, you could send to Montreal and get all the whiskey you wanted, anything from one to a hundred cases. So, anyway, we realized that he was loading some whiskey, and of course, we knew all the men that were in it . . . about eight guys, and they'd all divide up those hundred cases, but this fellow we knew who was dickering in the whiskey he was the one who did all the buying and selling.

So anyway, someone in the car said, "Let's go back and give the boys a hand." So we went, and just as we got in through the gate — we couldn't see much because the hay was high, up to our waist. It was ready to be cut, just about the right time for hay, you know. Anyway, we got about halfway up there, and out of the hay jumped this big tall colored guy, just about six foot three. He was born and raised here, and we knew him real good. He was drunk. Oh, my

God he was drunk! Anyway, he had this gun right to the head of my friend — the guy that drove the car. Right to his head, and he told him to get out of here.

We said, "Lon, please put that gun down. We'll go back and give the boys a hand." But nothin' doin'. He was shaking his head. And he wouldn't put down that gun. So we said all right and we got back into the car. We decided to get our own ammunition. I'll tell you why.

See, at that time everyone was stealing and robbing each other's stuff. I don't say *we* were at that time, because we always had enough . . . mostly because we were hauling the stuff across the river all the time.

Anyway, we got back on our way, and we ran into another friend of ours, who had been out of the army not too long. He had brought with him about three revolvers. He asked us where we were going, so we said, "Well, come on." His name was Rubber Hamilton.

I said, "Come'n Rubber. Bring your gun with you." We went and got ours, then went back up that lane. There was a wagon with a farmer there . . . a gentleman sitting on the wagon with a load of whiskey. There was also a load of whiskey right on the river bank, close to us. So when we come back, the only one sittin' there was this farmer with the load on the wagon.

We said, "Now, you don't have to move." And we still wondered where all the men had gone. We figured if they took off — if that's the way that colored boy was going to act — then we'd take some of this whiskey.

Quite a while passed and no one showed up. Two of the boys went back to Amherstburg and got one of our friends — he's dead now — anyway, he had a boat and was the only man around here at the time that had a fairly good-sized boat.

34

Well by the time they got him out of bed and got back down here, a lot of time had gone by, and still no one had shown up. It was just breaking day now when we heard someone comin'. Funny part was that it was one of the men that had an interest in this whiskey. He was one of the guys that combined all the whiskey together. So, just about the time he got to the riverbank, just like a bunch of Indians, seven other guys were comin' with him, all shooting.

We were down at the bank with the first load of whiskey ready to go. It was piled so high, and it was all in those straight pine boxes or crates. So they came down upon us, shooting. So, gee, when they started shooting, we got behind all the whiskey and their bullets were going right through the crates at us. Well, to tell you the truth, we shot back. But I didn't shoot to kill nobody. I don't think the other boys did either 'cause we knew every man that was in that group, and we were all friends, you know — all born and raised together around here. But it was this colored man who caused the grievance, you see. We got a little peeved about it. So after my revolver ran out, I ran up the beach. There was about an eight or ten foot wide beach there. And the man who lived across from the Burying Grounds, he had a rifle. You know, he told me afterwards that he knew who I was. But as I said, it was just breaking day, and he shot on one side of me and then on the other side. The bullets were hitting the sand, and the old sand was flying like that. He told me afterwards that he could've killed me, which he could've.

At the north end of this beach, there was an old hotel by the name of Zebb — I don't know exactly how to spell it. It was there long before I was born even. But it was an old dilapidated thing. But in between the place where we were shooting and this hotel, it was quite a piece . . . and there was all this wild lettuce, about so high. At that time they used to pile it up like a farmer piled hay. Well, it was all piled there but it had dried out and rotted a little. So anyway, it was early in the morning by now, and the dew was on this lettuce and I ran through this lettuce and was going for the highway. I was heading for the road where our car was.

But then I found this dried lettuce piled up and because I was wet running through the leaves, I stopped here for a while, and I laid on top of this stuff. I went to sleep on it. Yeah, I never woke up in fact until the sun woke me up. Blazing down upon me, it was.

I heard some people hollering my name when I finally woke. I got a nickname — Goody's the name. I heard them hollering it, and I wasn't sure just who it was, and I thought it was the other guys who were still after us.

So anyway, I woke up — I don't know exactly what time it was, because I didn't have a watch. I took the streetcar down. It was five or six hours probably after all this happened, and everyone thought I was either drowned or dead. They were looking all over town for me. People were hollering to see if I was still around, see.

When I hit Amherstburg, they were all dumbfounded because they saw me gettin' off the streetcar. They had thought I was dead. And I guess it was a pretty close call, anyway, what with the guns firing off like they were. And I suppose they could've killed us if they'd have really wanted to.

And you know this other fellow by the name of Rubber Hamilton, well, let me tell you about him. The streetcars were running then, and there's a little gully in there just right where the Indian Burying Grounds is. It goes to the river... and at that time there used to be a trestle went across made of big heavy timbers. So anyway, the guys started chasing some of our boys, and Rubber fell in between them big trestles. And my God, they kicked the devil out of him. Oh God. They really kicked him. I would say there were seven guys.

But you know after that feud — if that's what they want to call it — everybody was friendly again. But it was just this colored chap that caused all the damn grievances. It was all over this stuff — Old Crow. I don't even know whether they still sell the stuff. That's why people 'round here call it the battle of Old Crow. It was over that brand of whiskey.

Anyway, that colored guy left town (Amherstburg), because, as we told him, when he wouldn't put that gun down, "Lon, we will get you." So, he left town. He never did come back.

When I was taking care of the slot machines and pin tables on the corner of Louis and Wyandotte in Windsor, there was a railing in front of the store, and who was sitting on it but this Lon Taylor. But now, this is years and years afterwards, and we really held no grudge against him.

I hollered to him, "Hello, Lon," and I started walking toward him just to talk. He took off down Wyandotte street, and I haven't seen him or heard of him since. He must have had it in his mind that we were after him. He must have thought we intended to hurt him. We were a little mad, because he pulled that gun on us at first, you know, but he wouldn't put that gun down. I was afraid he was so drunk that he would shoot this guy, you know, and he had it

(above) The rumrunners. In the winter, rumrunners put sled runners under their boats and towed them across the ice. Here Big Mac Randolph and Walter Goodchild wait for a car.

(below) Shorty England and Big Mac Randolph with hundreds of sacks of liquor.

right up to his head . . . so that's why we might have sounded tough with him.

Anyway, the battle was over that Old Crow whiskey. It was old bourbon.

Before the battle of Old Crow, we used to go to Toledo. You see Ontario was dry at that time. (1918) We used to go to Toledo to get it . . . in gallon jugs out of a barrelhouse. You know what a barrelhouse is? That's where they have forty or fifty gallon barrels and sell it from the spigot. Originally they used to have one in Amherstburg. The building is still there. There were three barrels on a bottom rack . . . each with a different kind of whiskey. And he had these wooden spigots, and if you wanted a shot of whiskey he'd open a spigot and fill it for you.

thup, thup, the sides would be going like an old cow breathing.

This was in the end of March, or first of April. Cold, yeah! We were almost to Monroe. This was when everyone was bootlegging out of Ohio. Ohio was wet at that time. Michigan was dry, and if you got caught, you'd never know what they'd give you. Anyway, we were almost to Monroe — that's just about the borderline. It's four o'clock in the afternoon and all the fishermen as a rule are out of the lakes one or two o'clock at the most. From the east was comin' this blackest cloud I'd ever seen. A storm comin'. Of course we weren't too far from shore, and these fishermen fished what they call "trap nets." It's the same as a prawn net only you

Walter Goodchild on the boat he took across Lake Erie to Cleveland.

A shot glass then sold for ten cents. But anyway we used to buy the stuff out of the barrelhouse in Toledo a dollar a quart. Just fill up a jug. We knew the chap that was bartender there, and he'd open these spigots and fill. He didn't fall smart for a while because we were taking Canadian measures in our jugs. We were gaining a quart on each gallon.

The first trip we made, we had my uncle's old lifeboat — I don't know where in the world he got it. It was a big one, about that deep and about as long as this room. It was dilapidated and the gunwales were all shot and he had a one-lung motor in it. Every time the motor'd go

don't use stakes, you use floats. Well, the water was getting a little rough, and you couldn't see these little wooden buoys. And we ran into one of these nets. Got caught in our wheel, and we didn't have a knife to cut ourselves loose. We didn't have nothin'. We never even had a life preserver. Besides that, we had taken my uncle's boat without permission. So, we didn't know what in the world to do, and that storm was comin' in from the east. She started to blow, and I don't know, but I think the Lord was with us. I turned around and looked toward Toledo and here's a fish boat comin'. There were three men in it, and when they got to us, they cursed us and told us, "What in hell you kids doin' out here in this storm?"

We said we were caught in the nets. So this one guy said, "We see you are." And it was their nets. Well, they didn't care about that, but you see, fishermen in those days were prepared. Their boats were almost all flat bottom, and if they got caught in the nets . . . you know what a corn scythe is? Well they had one with a broom handle on it, so they could go underneath the propeller and cut it off. Well they cut us loose, and said, "You damned kids get into Monroe." Well we were only about one half a mile from Monroe then, and that's where lots of fishermen were working out of. In fact, I knew three or four there because their uncles used to fish with my dad near Colchester (on Lake Erie's shoreline).

Well at that time Monroe pier was quite long. I would say you'd go from twice as long as here to the highway before you'd hit any part of the town. But the fishermen were living down there on the bank. So we pulled into the piers. They said, "You get to hell in that pier," so we did. But when we pulled in there, we just pulled in halfway. We didn't want nobody to know that we had this liquor, cause we were in Michigan now. We stayed there all night. And the storm, oh it blew, and it was cold. We didn't have nothing but a couple of rain coats, and slept on the piers all night.

The next morning was the first of three mornings that we were there. The storm lasted three days, and we stayed at the cabin with the fishermen for all that time. They had invited us there the morning after the night we came in. Well, anyway, when we went in there first, the channel that is, we took this net, filled with the gallon jugs in it, and lowered it into the water between the boat and the dock. The wind changed, came around and threw waves up this river every once in a while. So when everything had calmed down and we were ready to go, we went down and pulled up our nets. The whiskey! We had nothing but broken glass. The swells, you see, ran the glass back up against the rocks that were down there and broke every bit we had. So we had nothing but a few chunks of broken glass.

We headed back to Amherstburg, and I remember it was nice and calm when we come in. My uncle was sittin' on my dad's boat, and he was quite deaf, but anyway he saw us comin' in and he hollered, "Where you damned kids been?" He talked in a squeaky voice.

Well I made every excuse I could . . . and he wasn't all that mad and didn't say much. About two days afterwards, we took the boat again.

Yeah, we took it again, but darned if we were going to get caught again, so this time we went prepared. I got a hold of one of those scythes and put a handle on it. We also took some extra clothes with us in case. So we went out and, this time we didn't hit Monroe on the way back. We brought back about fifteen gallons. Would you believe I got ten to twelve a quart? And each time we went, we were gaining a quart, and hell it was only costing us maybe seven or eight gallons on a one-lung motor, just one cylinder.

We had all kinds of ways of taking the stuff across to the other side. We used to haul it across the ice, too. This was during when the docks were open . . . about 1925.

This friend of mine used to pick up whiskey at the docks . . . the export docks, and he got me a job on one of the beer docks at Park Street here in Amherstburg, right at the foot of the street. So for about two years I went in it for myself, hauling from across the river myself.

For a while, too, I was buying out of Montreal. But I did not go there myself. There was five or six gentlemen around here that were pulling it, and I would buy off them. I had two chaps bringing it from Montreal. They would take my orders, and they would pull it, because you see I would have to take it across the river and deliver it over there. That meant I didn't have time to go to Montreal myself and pick it up. So I paid these guys so much per case to deliver it here, and then I would take it across to the States. And as far as export papers . . . I never filled out one in my life. "Cuba"* was too close.

When the river was open, I used my rowboat. But when there was ice, well, yeah, I put runners under the boat, and pulled it with a car. I have hauled as much as twenty-five cases. I had a big boat, my Dad built it, and it could hold maybe 300 bottles . . . it was a deep boat . . . my Dad built six of them for the bootleggers.

Taking the stuff across usually took a little while, because you had to listen and watch for the law. Usually I never pulled in daylight, but for about a year I did. I pulled in broad daylight at seven o'clock in the morning, between seven o'clock and eight. And the law never caught me. Nope. I had some close calls. That's why some of these instances I could tell of would surprise you.

Let me tell you about this one hour in which we pulled the stuff across. We had to work one hour — that's all the time we had. From seven to eight, because the Immigration Office on East Jefferson in Detroit would change shifts at that

*Cuba was a commonly used destination on the export papers.

time. The guys would have to leave Grosse Isle, go there and relieve the other guys to go to work. That took them more than an hour. So from the time they left the other crew and came back it was in that hour right in broad daylight that we'd unload.

At that time, we knew about where the law was, too, because when we used to come over on this bridge, we used to give the guys a case of beer a week to tell us if the law was on or off.

I seen the Immigration one time look in a fellow's boat and chop it apart. One guy I knew had two boats he had bought from Dad, and we were standing there talking to him, when all of a sudden the Immigration went down the hill where we were and looked in his boat.

We kept the bottles in jute bags. And you know when a new jute bag sheds, it leaves this fuzz-like stuff around and it will drop in the boat. Well the Immigration saw this stuff and took that boat and chopped it right in the centre with a fireman's axe. The man had bought it only two weeks before. But these guys knew he was hauling the stuff, so they chopped it up. Boy that made me sick — a brand new boat. Chopped it right down the centre like a "V" on both sides and kicked it out into the river. The front end and the back end . . .

You know during these days when you took orders for liquor from people, you would have to remember all the brands by number and letter. I could do that, and I did. Not only that, I'd always memorize my customers' phone numbers too. I had to 'cause if I got caught with anything that they thought was connected with liquor, the law would pinch me . . . and these fellows would be pinched for it, too.

Just how much I hauled really depended on the orders I got. Sometimes two times a week, sometimes five, maybe four, really it all depended upon the orders.

American Border Police disposing of seized liquor after a raid.

Chapter Three

Assorted Stories — Whiskey Slides, Starting in the Business at Five, Iron Boxes Under the River

With a few exceptions, the people telling these stories asked to remain anonymous. They called in response to an advertisement run in The Windsor Star. Many of those who gave me their story wanted to remain unknown because they felt that even after all these years, it was better to keep quiet. These are glimpses into the bizarre ways in which people struggled to get booze across the river.

Housekeeper from LaSalle: On the Fringe

They had to watch for hijackers and one of those hijackers was Cecil Smith.* There was a gang of them. I know 'cause I lived across from them when I was five years old. I got punched in the nose many a time 'cause I was a tomboy. Another group would bring it to their homes, and they'd hide it in the barn or in the greenery. Then they'd make contact with the Americans to meet them at a given place, and they'd have to turn around and haul it from their home to there. So Cecil and the Brophy gang — it wasn't only just them, there was quite a few other gangs, you know what I mean? — went where they were meeting and waylaid them on the roads and take the loads away from them. Oh, you don't know the racket!

How they operated the roadhouses was — I can tell *some* tales out of school. These people are dead now. They used to pay off these Provincials. They didn't go by names. The Provincial might call and say "number nine", and he'd hang up. You knew to get the heck out. You'd grab the stuff you had in the house and put it in the boat and get out in the middle of the river. That's why the roadhouses were practically all on the river. You could get a meal in these places, and if you were known, you could get into the back room and get a drink.

Mushrat La Framboise was a real character. I think his name was Art. They called him Mushrat because he used to go muskrat hunting. Him and Pete his brother are both dead now. But anyway, Mushrat used to run up and down the river with his boat, and sometimes he was with a Mountie and sometimes he was with bootleggers. He was riding both sides of the fence. Muskrat meat was very, very lean, but they used to put on muskrat suppers up there, and if you wanted to put on a muskrat supper you got ahold of Mushrat and tell him how many you needed. He went both sides, I was told. How could they run that way? They used to be able to do it, because they were in with this one officer, and they'd pay him off, not so much in money as in favors, you know what I mean. If he wanted a party, well you gave him a party. Or else.

Another thing too, I got acquainted with some people that lived around Wardsville. (about sixty-five miles east of Windsor) There used to be a marsh there. In between Wardsville and this Glencoe, on the number 2 highway — see it wasn't paved then — and these young fellows that showed up in daytime, they'd bring a bunch of water there in barrels and they'd make a real mud hole and then at night, they'd hitch up their team and wait. The bootleggers would get stuck

*Cecil Smith, a bootlegger and hijacker, is profiled on page 81.

*Mushrat La Framboise and his brother, Pete (Whiskey Jack) are profiled on page 56.

there and they'd pay them to haul them out.

Then they'd turn around — and at that time the oil wells were working — so they charged the people who wanted to go see what the oil wells was like. They charged fifty cents apiece to bring them to the oil wells, but it cost them a dollar and a half to get back. 'Cause they'd be stuck over there. Well, sure. They didn't want to walk back, they had to pay a dollar and a half to get back. Well, leave it to these young farmers, you know, they talk about how bad the kids are today, but, you know, you stop and think about all the pranks some of these others played. Sure, just as bad or worse. They played it maybe not in destructful ways as destroying property, but they used to do an awful lot of pranks. If they got mad at a farmer, the next morning he would get up and maybe his wagon would be on top of the barn.

A Five-year-old Girl Watches Over Daddy

I'm fifty-four and my dad has been dead for awhile. But my dad was mixed up in bootlegging, but I don't think he was notorious.

Now, he used to run with a fellow named Sticks Washbroke. I think he used to smuggle Chinese and dump them in the river. Dad used to talk about it once in a while when he was drunk. And they are all dead now, so it's okay to talk about it. But I can remember I was only about six years old and it was *Big Moosh and Little Moosh. They were brothers, and I don't know what their real names were. I was just a little kid. But I know they both went to jail. They were at my house when I was a little kid and my mother was a churchgoing woman and there was always trouble about this. My Dad was a real rounder and then I grew up to be kind of a rounder too in a way but I'm okay now.

My father was running the stuff out in Riverside around Little River. These fellows had boats see, and I remember as a little kid, just started school, and the police bringing my dad home all full of blood.

He had crashed through a bridge, and the car was full of booze. He darn near got killed, and there were bullet holes in the car. And my mother told lies to me, but I could see all this blood.

And my mother always maintained that these people took Chinese people over to LaSalle (still on the Canadian side) and told them they were

*Big Moosh and Little Moosh were two French Canadian rumrunners.

in the United States. It's funny in a way, but not really. You know, they'd get a hundred dollars from them.

There was also Dinny Dinan. He used to run a blind pig, you know where the wool shop is on University? Across from the Capital Theatre on Ouellette Avenue in Windsor. Up the back stairs, up those stairs they used to have a game going. My mother would make my dad take me from Riverside, because he worked on the Wabash Railway. And when he picked up his pay cheque she figured that he'd get home with some money if I was with him 'cause I was a little kid.

I can remember sitting around and watching these people gambling and I started to drink beer when I was about five years old. And I did become an alcoholic incidentally. Well, it's okay now, I haven't had a drink for seventeen years. Things got so bad once, in the basement of the Metropolitan store I put an iron under my coat and I started to walk away slowly and I thought, "That's good for a couple of dollars anyway." But they had it chained down and I could have got nailed for shoplifting.

And another time I was with a gang that had a whole bunch of stolen stuff in cars and the police raided them at the Pilette docks, and I pretended that I was necking with a fellow, and I watched them get arrested and I never got touched.

Rounder from LaSalle

We got liquor from Montreal, and sold it and bought a farm with the profits. That's how well we did with the liquor. That's what it was like for the rumrunners, as you call them. Oh, there was a lot of money to be made, to be sure. American dollars were about 15% less then. A lot different than now.

I had brothers keeping the beer docks in Amherstburg, and I was there everyday with them. I was hauling for blind pigs in those days. Some of them got raided, I remember, but I never got caught. Anyway, I was taking the stuff to three or four places. I used to haul ten cases of beer in the car with one case of whiskey. I never was caught. I did it for three or four years. Well, we'd pay for the fine stuff maybe twenty dollars per case. And we had 200 cases last time and that paid $4,000. We made over $8,000 clear. Then bought a farm.

In those days I helped out my Dad. Then he died, and I kept on for a few years, and I quit. These runners, they used to cross over the river with a boat. In the winter time they used to have a car and they'd have two great big planks on each side of the car. If they saw a crack in the river, they'd put the plank across the hole. They

Blind pig raided by vigilantes. Windsor wasn't the only place for blind pigs. In Elk Lake barrels of the best Canadian whiskey were destroyed when a blind pig was discovered. Most of the contraband alcohol originated in Ontario.

were risking their life. They were desperate and it was never too much trouble.

I can't count all the blind pigs there were in LaSalle. I'd say about seven or eight up there, but they had quite a bit from MacGregor to Amherstburg.

When these beer docks were open in LaSalle and Amherstburg, you know they'd wait until dark, then they'd cross over. Even hauled it in planes — they had a plane that landed not far from here, and it had a bullet hole in it. The pilot had time to unload, and he just flew back.

You know, I used to be at the beer docks pret' near every night, every day pret' near, when it rained — that's when all kinds of guys were coming over. Each one had a big gun. The last load we sold here, the guy came in, and he had two great big revolvers. He put one on each side of him, and then he took out a roll of bills, large enough to choke a cow. You know we had to keep that money in the house all night. It was kind of risky. But you get used to it. They were tough days but . . . there was quite a bit stolen too. People going around stealing loads of liquor. And if you didn't want to hold it yourself, they'd

give you money. They'd give you a thousand or two to get a load and send it to your name. Quite a few around here that done that.

Be better to haul the load ourselves. I wouldn't go back to it. But those days, when we had the load here, the police would come every day. We'd put a bottle and a glass on the table and they'd take a drink and go down and see if the load was in the basement. If you didn't do this they'd seize every damn thing.

The law wasn't so strict as it is now. As long as you had the stuff in your house it was all right. We got the last load from Windsor . . . used to be on the box car, we had 200 cases, we had two wagon loads. We came up the Malden Road with no gun or nothing. We could have been held up right there.

Airplanes and Wooden Boxes: Walter Johnston's Adventures as told by his son

They had money coming out of their ears at times, they were smuggling so much. They were filling deflated spare tires and false gas tanks and running back and forth from Windsor to Ecorse (Mich.). They also took it over from LaSalle to the other side under water. They rigged up two cables and pulleys at each end, attached a wooden case to the cable, and pulled it across, not letting it touch bottom.

My father had an airplane at that time, and they were flying from here to California with liquor, but they lost the plane. They had to drop in a plowed field one night, and they lost the plane and a load of whiskey.

They were also supposed to be smuggling Chinese across to Detroit. But they weren't. They were taking them down to LaSalle and dropping them on the Canadian side. They were getting about fifty dollars each for doing that, though they were supposed to be bringing them to the United States. Sometimes they were. But when they didn't they were just taking them for a ride and dropping them off in the same place. The Chinese didn't know any better. That was all in the game at the time.

The Whiskey Slide — Francis Chappus

The following is told by Bert Chappus before he died in September 1979. He was the son of Francis Chappus, a former conductor of the streetcar that went into LaSalle. Francis Chappus was also a wheeler-dealer in the whiskey business.

There's a whiskey slide on the side of this house. It's a ramp, and you'll notice all the basement windows are barred. And that house next door — it was built on pilings in the bay, on big long pilings. Half of the house was a boat house with a big door that opened up to let the boats in. And the only thing that house was used for was to store liquor. It would sit right on the bay of the Detroit River . . . it was owned by my dad, Francis Chappus. That's all that it was used for at that time. I moved it back and rented it after the bootlegging days.

Anyway, they used to come in with the boat, which was a big tug. There was a cannon mounted on the bow. The boys would sleep in our house and put all the arms and ammunition on the porch. And they had everything you can think of — from machine guns to handguns. There's one revolver I used to like, a .38 with a long barrel. And I used to go out there every morning and throw a can out on the water and shoot at it. I wouldn't miss often.

These people who came worked for my dad would come in a boat. They transported the booze from Montreal through the waterways. But oh it was nice to watch. They used to come with that boat and throw the stuff into the house.

Nobody could see them, and they'd just throw the whiskey crates down the whiskey slide, and they'd go right into the basement. Of course, the guys used to put the stuff into the boat house too, because the boat house was only half the house. The other half was open so they'd pile the whiskey up and keep piling it up.

My job was to count the money. It was all American bills . . . mostly fifty and hundred-dollar bills . . . and some bigger ones. Every night it was $75,000 to $125,000 . . . and I'd have to count all that. Well, it didn't take long to count with thousand dollar bills. I stuffed it into the stove, an old Moffat Electric with a warming oven on top . . . just stuffed it in there. I guess that's why there were people around with guns . . . to protect against a raid. But dad never fired a gun. He had other people to do that.

They hijacked him a few times. That's why these guys had a cannon on the bow of that boat. That's why they had machine guns. They worried but, as you can see, the house is barred, and we had a good dog. That dog used to take me across the river to the island in my cabin, my fishing cabin over there on Fighting Island. Yeah, we used to be able to cross there by foot on the ice. And that dog, well my dad fixed up a harness for him just like a horse, and he pulled me across on the sleigh. Just like a horse.

On the road in the front here (Old Front Road) they used to have to get the horses out to get the cars out of the mud. It got so mucky out there with the Whiskey Six Studebakers and all those cars . . .

Anyway, my dad stored whiskey here, and then the boat would come across the river and pick it up. They would come over every night, as I said. My dad never went with them. I guess at that time, I was about twelve.

At that time, my dad was a streetcar conductor. There was a switch right in front of our house here, and he would go to Amherstburg and around the river, all the way along the Detroit River . . . all the way to Tecumseh and then back. They'd switch right here in front of our house and change cars.

The Sunnyside Tavern was operating in those days. They were serving liquor — it was run by my uncles, Albemie and Alberic. They got raided, but they used to have guys at Turkey Creek and down at the other end, and they would flash their signal lights . . . so everything was put away out of sight from the police. They had a big gambling casino upstairs.

The hotel was finally sold to Ray Booker. The place had screen stars coming there. Jean Harlow used to come down here, and Mae Murray had her speedboat down here.

Loading up a speedboat from an export dock on the Canadian side of the river.

Running the Rum from Pelee Island — the Story of Edward James Betts

A rugged and broad 73-year-old, who has a great sense of humor and still works part time in the harvest months for Canadian Canners, remembers the times when he hauled whiskey and beer from Pelee Island. Betts has been living in Windsor since 1951 and worked for twenty years for Ontario Hydro.

I was thirteen years old and that's when they used to run the whiskey . . . down from Waterloo, they used to bring it through here in Reo Speeds and Whiskey Six Studebakers.

And the man at that time I knew, I'd ride with him at different times, was Cecil Smith. If you look back in the records you'll find his name. He had a sister down there by the name of McCall, and I used to go to school with her kids. That's how I first met him.

He got to know me, and he used to pick me up on the road. He used to be driving a Cadillac then. I hardly ever saw him with the liquor himself. But he had Whiskey Six Studebakers and Reo Speed Riders running from a distillery in Waterloo. They used to go out from that part of the country and bring it through here.

I lived down just the other side of Wheatley. My dad was a fisherman. But we moved from there when I was sixteen to Pelee Island. As you know Pelee Island is the most southern part of Canada except for Middle Island.

Well, at the time, rumrunning was really going, there was a little harbor on the south part of Pelee Island. There was an export station there and another one at the north end of the island.

Well the rumrunners used to come from Amherstburg down from the river going across over to Cleveland and all that. They used to lay over at the bay at south end of Pelee Island until night, see?

There was an export station run by Ted Rocheleau and a Jewish family by the name of Kovinsky.

All this rumrunning business, you know I never saw any cheques, it was all done in cash. Oh yes. All the dealings I ever saw, them guys used to unroll the money in . . . thousand dollar bills, five hundred, that was just common stuff.

My dad and I used to work for a man as fishermen . . . and sometimes we used to go across to Ohio in the fishboat. We used to get a hundred dollars a trip. Ross used to take fifty dollars and Dad and I would get twenty-five dollars.

Well, then the Coast Guard got tough. When we first started, hell, they didn't bother. We used to run liquor back and forth there like nobody's business.

We used to take over about 220 cases of beer. But then the Coast Guard got tough. They mounted one pounder guns on the Coast Guard boats, and they had their .50 calibre machine guns. Well, Dad and I didn't go out anymore after that. We didn't get shot at, but they had shot at other people. We didn't know.

We brought the beer to Marble Head. That's over on the higher side on the other side of Carol's Isle. It was about a two hour run at night. Yeah, we used to go there after dark and come back. We took a pretty good load for the boat we had. That's what we got. One hundred dollars. He took fifty dollars for the boat and dad and I got twenty-five dollars apiece.

Now that export station run by Fred Rocheleau — he's dead now — didn't have no name. It was just a little harbor on the south end of the island. It's so little just small boats can get in it. Runners used to come in there. As a matter of fact, there used to be a Deputy Sheriff on the other side who'd come over and load up. Yep, from Port Clinton. Guy Tiddle his name was. He used to bring a fishing party to the east side of Pelee Island, and on the way back he used to stop in at the export station and load up with whiskey and put it down under the deck, see.

And these other guys used to come in and pick up loads in speedboats, and they'd have twenty or thirty cases, all this stuff was done up in burlap bags, you know. It was sewed in burlap bags, the whiskey was, but all the imported whiskey came from Scotland, and all that, they came in wooden boxes. But our Canadian whiskey was done up in burlap bags.

So if you had to throw it overboard, it would sink. Wooden crate would float, cause you used to sometimes get chased, you know.

Well, then there were big boats that used to run out of Amherstburg. The *Shark* was one of them, I remember she used to carry 1,400 cases of beer. She was a big schooner. I'd say she was a rich man's yacht at one time.

They were nice guys — these guys — they were nice, but they were tough too. If you got them in a corner, they weren't afraid to use a gun. They had them to use too.

I got married when I was 22; I was still working as a fisherman. They had a little trouble in the lakes with boats being hijacked. Well, they came down here one time, this boat came in one afternoon. We knew it was a strange boat — to us anyway in the harbor. So we went down there and there were five or six guys. Oh, they were tough buggers, and they wore handguns, Tommy guns and shotguns and high-powered rifles and they were in the export station talking to Rocheleau.

We asked what the hell are they doing around here? Fred said they've had trouble with boats being hijacked out here in the lake. So these guys wanted to talk to these fellows see? They were back the next morning and we asked Fred Rocheleau did they get the fellow that was doing this job? He said I guess they did.

We heard through the grapevine afterwards about the fish boat that used to come and pick up our fish. They'd found the boat out in the lake with nobody aboard. She'd been all shot up.

One of my second wife's relations got shot up down the river, got killed. American Coast Guard. They were being chased by the Coast Guard down the mouth of the river here someplace going over probably to Monroe — that used to be quite a place over in that way, where they used to land.

And the Coast Guard chased them and shot them up. Sunk the boat. He got killed anyway. I guess he had a hole in his back.

You know that brewery down in LaSalle, Hoffer's, that was built in the rumrunning days, just for rumrunning. That Calvert's Distillery in Amherstburg was just for that too, you know. They used to bottle Old Kentucky and everything all out of the same vat. Old Crow would knock your hat off in them days, I know. About one hundred proof. I guess it's made in the States. Whiskey or whatever, you'd take a drink, and your hair would stand up on end.

A guy worked there and he said they used to bottle it just right out of the same vat and all the difference was the label on it. At Hoffer's — they used to make beer, but I don't know . . . it never went on the market that I knew of in Canada.

Well one of my friends in this rumrunning business was Leon from Erieau. Running across there, going across in the fall with a brand new boat. She had two Liberty engines on her and she wasn't ironed off (strengthened with sheet iron over the wood hull.) Brand new boat, first trip across and they run into windowpane ice — that's thin ice, and she got cut open.

Well, that's what they figure happened because another boat went the same night. She was ironed off and they run into the same ice; and Leon, they still don't know what happened. They never found that boat.

No, never found the body. But they don't know what happened 'cause that was getting late in the fall when the ice was forming on the lake. The other boat was ironed off; you see, so the ice couldn't cut through. That's the only thing they can figure what happened. First trip, brand new. Never come back, no trace or nothing.

A Pram, A Baby and Bottles of Booze — Norman "Yorky" Haworth

I used to do it all the time — smuggle booze that is — I'd take my daughter over (to the States) in her pram. But underneath her, there was a false floor and I'd put the bottles in there. Then I'd give her a sucker, and off we'd go. And just as we got to Customs, I'd pull the sucker out of her mouth, and she'd howl. The Customs man, not wanting to put up with a screaming baby would just look at me and say, "Get out of here." And off we'd go. And of course, as soon as we were through, I'd give her another sucker.

Taking Bottles Across Easy Like — Two Stories

One time, we were going across at Buffalo and I had a bottle. I turned to my girlfriend and said, "I bet I can go up to the Customs man, tell him I've got this jug and walk right through . . . untouched.

And she said, "No way!"

So halfway across, I stopped the car and got out and she drove. When we got close to the Customs booth, I started lurching, and when I got there, the Customs official said, "Anything to declare?"

And I said, "Yeah, officer. I got twenty-six ounces of the finest Canadian whiskey, right here," all the time slurring my words and patting my stomach, which is where I had the bottle, tucked into my belt. And the officer just said, "Get out of here." And I did.

Carrying liquor at the time was a greater offence than drinking it. The London Advertiser observed in 1919 that "the $200 fine for the bottle ON you can scarcely be matched up with the ten dollar fine for the bottle IN you."

We used to take bottles across. Not a lot. But sometimes quite a few. And my lady had a rig she could put a lot of bottles in. She had these belts and she'd strapped them to her body,

Casks of liquor worn under a dress. Bottles were stuffed in stockings, specially tailored pockets, coat sleeves, pant legs, lunchboxes, hats, spare tires — anywhere.

beneath her dress. One time, we got to the border and they asked us to get out. She got out her side and I got out mine and we were looking at each other over the roof of the car while the customs men searched the car, when all of a sudden she got this terrified look on her face and smash smash smash smash . . . one of the belts let go . . .

Old Ford City, Whiskey from Montreal and the Blue Top Brewery — Jake Renaud

My father (Joe Renaud) used to have a bar at that time. It was called the Ford City Pool Room . . . on Drouillard Road. They had a couple of pool tables and a bar. That's in the OTA (Ontario Temperance Act) days as they used to call it. My dad served the stuff right over the bar, but he was supposed to serve that 4.4 beer. But they had 4.4 on tap and reversible taps that held the other stronger stuff that wasn't legal. They had the pipes running to the same outfit that dispensed the other 4.4 beer, but you could switch it over. The copper pipes were underneath the floor, so when the law would come, my dad would just reach some place and flip the taps over.

There were only two bars like that in East Windsor at that time. My dad had another bar later on when things were legal. He started that one on Drouillard Road, too. It was called The Renaud House. The building's still there.

But before this, my dad, with my three uncles, used to haul whiskey from Montreal in suitcases. They'd bring them into Windsor and down to the docks and load them up there for others — Americans — to take it across. My dad never took the stuff across himself.

How it worked was that I had three uncles in Montreal who put the whiskey in suitcases on the train . . . in the baggage car . . . then they'd ride the load back to Windsor. Their destination ultimately would have been the Michigan Central Depot, but before they got there, they'd pay the conductor to stop at the Banwell Road (outskirts of Windsor), which is where my grandfather's farm was. Anyway, they'd stop the train and throw the suitcases off. My dad would be there waiting with the horse and wagon, and he'd bring the load into the barn where the cars were waiting to take the whiskey to Windsor. And of course the train, once the suitcases had been thrown off, would continue its merry way to Windsor.

They used to say Mushrat had one of those boats with a plug in it like a bathtub. When the police spotted him, he'd just pull the plug and the boat would sink. He'd go back to where it was later on when no one was around, and he'd dive for the stuff. He was really good at this, and anyway with the whiskey being in these jute bags and tied together at the top, the bags had these ears on them. Well, when they were dumped over board, you could dive down and pick them up by the ears and haul them to the surface. It wasn't heavy bringing them up until you got to the surface of the water, but then there'd be a guy there in a boat to pull it up and out of the water.

My dad never actually hauled any stuff across the river, though, that was for the other guys to do. But he did sell liquor in his Drouillard Road place . . . from the pool room . . . he just had a beer licence for the 4.4 beer, but he sold liquor by the shot if you wanted it. But he had to hide it, that was on the side . . . fifty cents a shot as I remember . . . beer at that time was twenty-five cents a shooper. A shooper was like a big glass. Did he ever get caught? Well, let's put it this way, he paid his dues. When Mousseau was going to raid us, well, we knew. We were notified ahead of time. We knew because it was his driver — Mousseau's driver who told us. Today might be East Windsor's turn (Ford City) and tomorrow someplace else, but today it was our turn, so everything was on the up and up.

But after he came so often and didn't find anything, he'd say, "Well, look, we know you're doing it," so my dad would go out and pay somebody off, so the police would leave us alone. But one time I remember Mousseau telling my dad — my dad knew him real well — "Joe, I know what you're doing. This time you gave us the slip, but there's always next time . . ."

Oh they knew what was going on. You could go into my dad's place and get a bottle of whiskey, wrapped in newspaper. But anyway, my dad never got caught, he always made arrangements. There was a Provincial (policeman) that lived across the alley from us. I used to have to bring a package over there every week. I'd run across to the house — I can only surmise what was in the parcel — to keep him quiet.

The way it was in the Ford City Pool Room was that if you came in for a bottle of whiskey — it wasn't sold over the bar — my dad would say, "Jake, go to the house and get a package." My dad would then call my mother on the telephone so she'd get a couple of bottles of whiskey and wrap them in newspaper and put it into a bag. I'd bring the whiskey back to the pool room and my dad would sell it to the guy. I was the runner. I was always in the pool room because I was a shoeshine boy after school.

We were kids then — that's the very beginning of Prohibition when you had to get all your stuff outside of Ontario — and Montreal was where you could get it. Well we didn't know what was going on. We'd sit on the whiskey in the cars. They were all touring cars at that time, and we used to ride to LaSalle, going the back way of course to avoid the law. We'd bring the whiskey

Sandwich, Ontario, police posing with still after raiding a blind pig.

down to the docks and unload it. The Americans, or whoever was buying the stuff would be there to pay for it . . . then it was their business. You see, these were the guys who'd contact my dad to prepare a load, and he'd prepare one and deliver it right to the dock.

One time, I remember him saying, the train didn't stop at the Banwell Road — it couldn't make the connection or whatever — so then it went right into the depot. Inspector Mousseau,* the liquor licence inspector was waiting there to inspect the loads coming in. He was standing on one side of the train at the baggage car, but instead of opening the baggage car on that side, this guy opened it on the other side, the side *not* facing the station. So all the suitcases were put on these four-wheel trucks and there's an elevator that takes them underneath the tracks and to a ramp where the stuff goes out to Wellington Street, well my father loaded the stuff into cars there and was gone. Meanwhile Inspector Mousseau's watching the rest of the baggage going into the baggage room, and he seizes all the stuff thinking he's got the goods, well he does, but it's only clothing . . .

These touring cars held a lot, you know. There used to be the Studebaker Sixes or Whiskey Sixes. My dad put the stuff in the back seat, or where the back seat would've been, but he'd

*Inspector Mousseau was a liquor licence inspector. He is featured predominantly in chapter   on Reverend Spracklin.

taken it out. The whiskey used to be in these jute bags. Mushrat La Fromboise and all those guys used to dive for them whenever they had to dump them in the water when the law spotted them taking it across.

Then, of course, later on when I was older I was a driver for the Blue Top Brewery in Kitchener. It was owned by my Uncle Bill Renaud and Art Diesbourg, Blaise's brother.* We were driving beer in trucks down to the Brewer's Retail warehouses in Windsor, or it was *supposed* to be. It was re-routed someplace else sometime. Well, some of the time, once a week anyway. I stopped when I got to Belle River . . . I'd go there for supper, or at least that was the excuse . . . I mean I really did stop for supper, but I never had any beer when I left Belle River, so I'd go back to Kitchener. I would stop at Art's farm and park beside the barn, and then I went into the house for supper. When I came out the truck was emptied. I mean who knows where it went.

My uncle was really in the business though. I remember he had a big yacht that was supposed to be for export purposes. He called it "Miss Liberty," Well, the story was that he used to load up at the export dock and head out to the lake or some doggone thing and somebody'd come and unload the stuff from his boat and put it on their own — and then they'd be gone.

*Blaise Diesbourg or "King Canada," was featured in Chapter I.

(above) Waiting for the go-ahead signal. As soon as it is given, the rumrunner will race across the narrow river to Detroit in his speedboat.

(below) Scout cars and decoys make it easy for a quick transfer of the whiskey to waiting fast cars at the riverside.

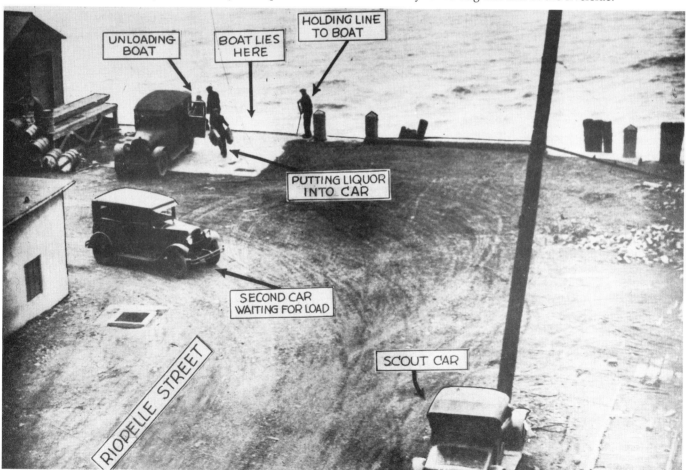

Section Two

BYLINES ABOUT THE BAD OLD DAYS

The book industry appears to have ignored Prohibition, but newspapers and magazines continually lure writers to compile information about the era. Most of these pieces are sketchy, but some show brilliant flashes. The following includes excerpts from background articles on rumrunning; an interview with Noel Wild, son of Horace Wild, a *Border Cities Star* photographer who was kidnapped by rumrunners; and, a third item, a dramatization about the rumrunning days written for radio by Ron Scott.

Chapter Four

Boozing in the Dry Days — Clippings About That Era

Detroit Skyline. The Ambassador Bridge was still under construction when large U.S. border patrols were organised to catch rumrunners crossing the river. Until that time, runners with cannon on their boats could turn on lone patrol boats and sink them.

Gayle Holman's "The Dry Era," a piece which appeared in Windsor This Month *(June 1974), points out that rumrunning wasn't done exclusively with convoys of cars and boats. The railroad played a major role:*

A resident of one of the busiest rumrunning areas at that time was working for a family who was into the trade. She didn't want to be identified, but shared some stories of that era.

"They would bring it on the trains by the carload. Men would be in the cars before the train even stopped, throwing cases out to men in horse-drawn wagons riding alongside of the train. The Americans would come over and pick it up most of the time. They would bring it across the river in small boats, the whiskey in burlap bags, and if the law got close they would dump it over the side."

The crazy excitement was widespread. The money flowed in as the whiskey was run out.

"There was a lot of money made, some wouldn't bother to count it. They would keep it in cracker barrels then dump it into bags and take it to the bank. If the people at the bank had been crooked, they could have made a bundle."

As Holman found out, the police weren't naive about what was taking place. The export docks and warehouses which covered the waterfront for miles were the clearing houses for illicit booze — and Carl Farrow, former chief of the Windsor Police, who was a provincial constable from 1928 to 1934 in Amherstburg, remembers what it was like:

"This was the export area here, in other parts of Canada they were doing the same thing, but this area was very active. They used to clear loads from Canada on what they called B-13s, a Customs form. All along the river and lakes they had warehouses and export docks. Americans would come over in rowboats, motorboats and luggers and load up at these docks. When the coast was clear they would head back across to the States. The only time we would bother with them was if they tried to come back into Canada.

"Nearly every time they would list their destinations as Cuba and quite often you would see a fellow come in with a rowboat, rowing in, load up with ten cases of beer, and clear for Cuba. You knew very well he wasn't going there, he'd never make it. Well, away he would go and in a couple of hours he would be back, the same

Rumrunners in car dragging a boatload of whiskey across the frozen lake.

guy in the same boat. He would clear another load for Cuba, but this time he might take twenty cases of beer. You could watch them build their business up, and I say them because there was more than one, until they quit beer and started running the hard stuff. Then they would move to bigger boats and shipments and the guy would go from rolling his own cigarettes to smoking cigars. Then you wouldn't see them for a while until one day he would be back with a rowboat again. He was either knocked off over there by the Border Patrol, or maybe hijacked. Later on they used to ship by plane. They would land back in the country some place and bring it back that way.

"They used so many ways to get it across. They filled the inner tubes of spare tires with liquor and had false bottoms in their cars and boats. Quite often they would wear a special belt and the bottles would be hanging down the man's pant legs or under the woman's skirts. As long as the bottles didn't clink together, they were okay. They even had false gasoline tanks and instead of filling up with gas they would fill up with whiskey.

"In the wintertime when the water was covered with ice, they used to come over pulling big luggers, which are like huge rowboats, and sometimes they would put an inboard motor in it. Runners would be put on the bottom of these boats and several men wearing spiked shoes would pull it across the ice. When they came to open water they would lower the boat into the

water and row to the next piece of ice, pull it out, and so on.

"Another thing they used to do was come over and buy up all the old cars they could get hold of, as long as they would run. If they were touring cars fine, if they were sedans, they would just chop off the tops and load them up with liquor. This was done when it was really cold out and there wasn't too many cracks in the ice. You could watch them from the shore in Amherstburg and they were just like ants. They would do it right in the daytime, open for anyone to see. I don't know what it was like on the other side, but it didn't seem like they worred about it too much. A lot of them went through the ice.

"In June 1928, we fished out of the Detroit River and Lake Erie, about twenty-eight bodies. They weren't all rumrunners but I would venture to say a large percentage of them were. They had either fallen through the ice into the water, or out of their boats, or they had been hijacked by someone else. Of course, that was a bad area for bodies as far as we were concerned. If they had gone into the Detroit River up around the Windsor end, by the time they could be recovered they would be around Amherstburg or out a little further in the lake. It got to be quite a job pulling them out and it wasn't very pleasant.

"There wasn't too much trouble associated with this. I was right on top of what was happening because we covered four townships, Anderdon, Malden, Colchester North, and

Colchester South (in Essex County, Ontario). This was also the area where most of the export docks were. We had very little trouble with the people coming over but we had some real characters. I met Al Capone once and some of his people. They came into Amherstburg in a big speedboat and stayed for a while. Also Bugs Moran who was a rival chieftain from Chicago and in competition with Capone. They were just here to look over the export docks or pay some of their debts. I'm not sure. They didn't throw their weight around here though.

"In the later part of the twenties and thirties, the gangs got quite active in the Detroit area. There was the Purple Gang and a few others fighting for control, hijacking, shooting and so on. However, there wasn't any gang fights here. Here they were just concerned with keeping the supply coming and what they were doing was legal.

"It wasn't a very popular law in Amherstburg. For instance, there was an awful lot of people who made their money through that, and they paid good wages. Nearly every family in that area had somebody connected with the family involved in the rumrunning business. They didn't feel too bad about it. The stores and restaurants did good business from the people who came over with their boats and in the course of a day there would be quite a few of them.

"Many of them were caught, but a lot of people got through and made a lot of money although, unfortunately, they didn't hang on to it. It was a great time for made-to-measure shirts, silk with monograms, and they paid exorbitant prices for them.

"I was in Windsor for one-and-a-half years before I went to Amherstburg. We (provincial constables) had two raiding squads going night and day. We used to raid blind pigs, gambling joints, and bawdy houses. There was less rowdyism in blind pigs at that time than you find in hotels now. They had to be careful, because it was against the law and they didn't want to draw too much attention to themselves. A lot of hotels were running as just hotels, but they were doing bootlegging on the side and they were very careful."

In an article in The Windsor Star* *(January 31, 1953), Farrow is quoted again about the era, calling it "amusing, and ridiculous:*

"They even operated in the winter around Amherstburg. They'd take an old sedan, put chains on it, cut the top off it and load it up with whiskey.

Then called the Windsor Daily Star.

"They crossed the ice on Lake Erie. They carried planks to help them across cracks in the ice. You'd look out over the ice, and it would be black with cars — just like ants — heading for the States . . . the highways all along the riverfront were just black with trucks carting liquor to export docks."

Holman in her Windsor This Month *article makes the point that it became "almost fashionable for the young men to become involved in the goings-on."*

"The first time we tried selling whiskey we went to Montreal and got a load of about 150 cases. You could buy it, but it had to be for your own use. They never asked any questions either, when a guy would order 200 cases. If it was for his own use, he'd be 1,000 years old and still be drinking.

"They would bring the order in by train and unload it into wagons pulled by horses. The day we got ours home some Americans came for it at about four o'clock in the morning. The next day the police said we had to pay a ten dollar fine on every case because they knew we had sold it. We would have been in a lot more trouble if they had showed up at the same time as the Americans.

"People used to sell their names to a guy so he could go to Quebec and get a load because it always had to be under a different name. The whiskey could be bought for about thirty dollars to thirty-five dollars a case for good stuff and sell for about $175 to $180 a case. It had to be good, though, if you bought cheap rye you wouldn't get that much for it.

"We only got two loads and I went into bootlegging selling to four or five blind pigs, then after about two years I quit. There were a lot of blind pigs, especially in LaSalle and Amherstburg. They were well run. You could go in to get a beer but if they thought you had enough, you were cut off. I had a Model T Ford I used to carry the stuff in. They would call me when they needed some and I would go out with maybe ten cases of beer and a case of whiskey and drop it off. The blind pigs were in ordinary homes. There would be some people in the living room and some in the kitchen. You would have to be a friend of a friend of a friend before they would sell you a drink.

"You had to be tough. You'd go into a blind pig and they would try to push you around but you'd have to make your own way. You couldn't give a damn about anybody.

"I would sell by the bottle too. I'd buy the flat bottles because the women would stick them down their dresses to take back across the border. I had this old stove and I used to put the

Unloading beer from the Tecumseh Brewery under Customs supervision. Provincial Police often supervised the unloading to prevent hijacking of supplies and to ensure that whole loads were not diverted to Canadian hotels.

bottles on it for a few minutes to warm them up for the ladies.

"If you had the nerve, you made a lot of money. But money? What's money? You'd spend it as fast as you could get it. Easy come, easy go. I'd go into a blind pig and buy a drink for everyone there, maybe twenty or thirty people, and it would come to a lot of money, but you didn't care. But the blind pigs were run well. They didn't allow any riff-raff, they were good clean people. Some were run a lot better than some of the hotels now. There was one blind pig that sold over 100 cases of beer and five or six cases of whiskey on Friday, Saturday and Sunday. It was well run.

"There wasn't much trouble and if there was it usually had to do with someone hijacking. After we got our second big load and had sold it these men came to the house with guns. They said that we had better let them in so we did because there was nothing there. They had come to steal it and if we hadn't sold it we would have lost it all.

"You had to watch for the police all the time. When I knew where the police were going to be, that's when I took out a load. If a person found out there was going to be a raid, he would let everybody know so they could get rid of everything. They usually knew ahead of time what was going to happen.

"The last time I was going to get some stuff, I was just driving out of this garage with it when a provincial policeman went by on a motoocycle. If he had looked at my car he would have known I was carrying a load because the back of my car was almost touching the ground. But he kept going on and I got out of there fast. I went home, had a party and that was enough for me.

"People risked a lot for a few dollars. I would never do it again. There were some people who would bring it over to Detroit themselves. If that river ever dried up the things they would find on the bottom. Some even used to drive it across in the winter and carry long planks with them. When they would come to a crack in the ice they would put the planks across it, drive over it, pick them up and go on. I never had any real trouble and never had anything stolen. And I never locked my door."

Another article in The Windsor Star *(October 29 1960) focuses specifically on the rumrunning vessels:*

Pipelines, underwater cable tramways and even the employment of a diver towing a sled on a river bottom were all used (to get liquor across the border to the United States), but it is safe to hazard a guess that ninety per cent of all liquor illegally imported into Michigan came in surface vessels.

These vessels differed widely in size, type, shape and appearance. Steamers, tugs, fast motorboats, sailboats, rowboats and even canoes were employed. All had one purpose: using high speed, evasive tactics, camouflage and surprise to dodge the United States Revenue cutters and police boats waiting on the far shore.

While most boat owners depended on speed and darkness to conceal their operations, others decided to use refitted steamers for the haul. They reasoned that these old craft would be above suspicion and they had the capacity to carry a profitable cargo.

One of the old steamers, retired to the scrapyard after years of service, was the *City of Dresden*, an old wooden ship which had run for years out of Dresden to Great Lakes ports. It was taken out of the "boneyard" at Amherstburg, refitted with the powerful engines which had been in the equally famous Wallaceburg-built *Energy*, and sent out with a full cargo of liquor.

The Dresden, rotting in the bottom, was a fast ship as a result of the engine switch. So it was natural when a revenue cutter gave chase in Lake Erie that her skipper elected to run for the Canadian shore.

He was winning the race when there was a sudden jolt and a crash and the old *Dresden* ran hard aground just off Morpeth dock. Her rotten

timbers gave way and she filled quickly and sank, although the crew made it safely ashore.

A similar, but not quite so exciting fate met the Wallaceburg tug *Maude*, which had been rebuilt out of the old *Grace Darling*, a familiar waterfront sight for many years. Originally, an eighteen-ton steam tug, she was built by William Taylor at Wallaceburg in 1884 for J. W. Taylor and Hiram Little.

The *Maude* made one or two trips across Lake St. Clair with comparatively small cargoes and returned in safety. The owners finally decided to send her out with a real payload and 800 cases were jammed aboard the little craft.

October 5 1922, was a typical fall day, with a fresh wind blowing up chop on the shallow lake and the chill of fall in the air. Crew members of the *Maude*, still living in the area, recall they were apprehensive, but financial considerations persuaded them to make the trip.

The little tug made the downriver run from Port Lambton safely, but below the islands of the St. Clair Delta, she felt the full force of wind and wave. She struggled out into the ship channel, though, and proceeded on her way.

Out in the open lake, however, the waves began to wash over the heavily-loaded little tug

Destinations labelled. When shipping out booze from Canadian ports, in many cases the crates carried the customers' names or destination. None of these places or companies were American, of course, but in fact much of the liquor, such as this shipment slated for "Agostini Brothers, Trinidad" went "astray".

and the wave action worked the caulking out of her seams. The *Maude* finally filled up with water and nosed under, several miles from land and into twenty-five feet of water.

By good fortune, lookouts on the ore freighter *Wilpen* of the old Shenago Furnace Company Line spotted the sinking, and within minutes the soaked but otherwise unhurt tugmen were wrapped in blankets and drinking hot coffee in the galley.

Toronto Star *writer and well-known author Frank Rasky probably wrote the most colorful piece on Prohibition in* Weekend Magazine*. In speaking to old rumrunners and people who survived the era of flappers, speakeasies and jazz, he wrote:*

They remember the hip flasks of bathtub gin that used to be called rattlesnake juice and jackass lightning; and the F. Scott Fitzgerald flappers making whoopie in the bootlegging joints — the speakeasies and blind pigs.

They remember the fleets of rumrunning schooners sailing out of Canadian ports, purportedly carrying codfish to Cuba, but actually bearing caseloads of booze to parched Americans; and the international fuss raised when a United States Coast Guard cutter had the audacity to sink the *I'm Alone,* a rumrunning ship from Lunenburg, Nova Scotia, 200 miles off the United States coast.

They remember the wisecrack of mobster Al Capone, who stopped chewing gum long enough to tell reports, "Do I do business with Canadian racketeers? Why, I don't even know what street Canada is on!" They remember, too, the tan spats and natty suits of Rocco Perri, Canada's self-styled King of the Bootleggers, long since dethroned and reputedly wearing a cement overcoat on the bottom of Hamilton Bay.

One "Windsor imbiber" told Rasky it was easy then to buy whiskey. You simply had "(to) make out a six dollar cheque for twelve quarts of Golden Wedding Whiskey and send it, along with a two dollars and sixty-five cents express order, to a supply house in Montreal. If he felt like assuaging the thirst of neighboring Detroiters, he would slip bottles into the pockets of a carpenter's apron, and, with the bottle concealed under a coat, cross the river on the ferry, then sell the caseload at a tidy profit of $120."

The most ludicrous aspect of Canada's liquor regulations, Rasky cites, was the bunghole of freedom they (the federal government) left open to Canadian breweries and distilleries. *While alcoholic beverages were banned in Ontario, for example, it was perfectly legal to manufacture and export booze.*

Weekend magazine has been replaced by *Today.*

Manufacturers got around this slight restriction by forging the receipts and paying bribes to Customs officials. Since Canada's 132 part-time customs officers earned salaries of fifty dollars to $400 a year, this wasn't difficult. The Windsor-Detroit area — known as Rum Alley, because the two border cities were separated only by the mile-wide Detroit River — was easily the most lucrative funnel of graft. During the height of Prohibition, the marshy Canadian shore was lined with at least fifty floating "export docks," and it was estimated that Customs payoffs averaging $2,000,000 a week bought immunity for liquor exporters. With a poker face, the Customs men billed out barrels of hooch to destinations like Peru, or St. Pierre and Miquelon, the French islands off Newfoundland. When a rowboat cleared for Peru in the morning and returned from Detroit one hour later to clear another cargo of liquor to St. Pierre, nobody asked questions.

Few Canadians questioned the propriety of the professional rumrunners. They were romanticized as buccaneers — Captain Kidds who outsmarted the patrol boats of the United States Coast Guard's "Dry Navy" to maintain freedom of the high seas and a friendly neighbor's right to liquid refreshment. Their schooners usually pulled out of Lunenburg, Nova Scotia or Victoria, British Columbia, their gunnysacks of booze frequently camouflaged as cargoes of lobsters, canned peaches, or coal.

In some lonely cove off Maine or Seattle, the skipper unloaded his cargo into high-powered speedboats. He made certain the purchasing agent properly identified himself; the ripped half of playing cards or corresponding torn dollar bills were commonly used.

The fleet of little boats would then wait at Rum Row — the nickname given to the line of ships anchored in international waters, three miles off United States coastal cities. At a pre-arranged signal, they'd dart off in different directions. One empty boat served as decoy, trying to lure the Coast Guard cutter astray so that the others could slip ashore unmolested.

One notorious rumrunner from Lunenburg, William F. McCoy, became somewhat of a hero. He was so nimble at dodging the revenue cutters that his name passed into the language. His yacht, *Arethusa,* was equipped with armor plate and bulletproof glass, and in New Jersey speakeasies, his Canadian whiskey was reverently guaranteed to be the "real McCoy".

56

Rasky's article recounts how rumrunning was done by plane. He interviewed Charles Walter Wood, a Torontonian who is now retired from the Ontario Provincial Police and who "used to match wits with sky racketeers picking up liquor consignments on the Niagara Peninsula."

Rasky writes:

Wood still possesses a photo of himself and a fellow constable, posing triumphantly after they'd seized thirty cases of whiskey and champagne which a racketeer tried to smuggle out of a private airfield at St. Catharines, Ontario. "It was like one of those Keystone Cops comedies," he says. "When we broke cover, we surprised the gang with half of their gunnysack bags already loaded in the plane. The pilot stood with one leg in the open cockpit, the other on the wing strut. He shoved the throttle to make a fast getaway. But I grabbed the wing, so he couldn't fly away."

Rocco Perri was the one rumrunner who commanded Wood's greatest respect. "You could never catch Rocco actually handling his wet goods," Wood says. "He was too smart an operator for that. And his mistress, Bessie — a charming, good-looking, but brainy woman — had a mind like a steel trap when it came to organizing the business side of their deals."

Perri was a seemingly amiable, five-foot-four booze baron who looked like a sawed-off Mussolini; he had a weakness for sporty $200 suits, exclamatory neckties, and high polish on fingernails. Yet the immigrant from Reggio Calabria in Italy started his career as a construction laborer on the Welland Canal. He opened up a grocery shop on Hess Street in Hamilton, specializing in olive oil and macaroni, but soon began bootlegging whiskey at fifty cents a shot.

His prices went up considerably when he was joined by Mrs. Bessie Starkman, an auburn-haired Polish woman seven years his senior. She deserted her two small children and her husband, a Toronto bakery wagon driver, to expand Perri's small operation into the biggest rumrunning business on the Great Lakes — one with a $940,000 a year turnover. She did all the bookkeeping herself and kept more than $500,000 available in eight Hamilton banks (under assumed names) in case of emergency.

Perri and Bessie directed their fleet of fifteen-horsepower cruisers and forty souped up Reo trucks from a nineteen-room house on Hamilton's then-fashionable Bay Street south. The place was the envy of the neighborhood, with its Oriental rugs, $2,000 piano, billiard room, and secret subterranean room where

Sicilian "alky cookers" distilled highballs for visiting socialites and cabinet ministers. Perri was invariably accompanied by a couple of bodyguards, William (Bill the Butcher) Leuchter or John (The Mad Gunman) Brown, who despite their tough nicknames were later rubbed out in gangland wars.

Most people agreed with Perri when he laughed scornfully to a *Toronto Daily Star* interviewer in 1924, "the law, what is the law?... Am I a criminal because I violate a law which the people do not want? . . . I have a right to violate it if I can get away with it."

Chasing rumrunners sometimes had an ironic twist. Rasky interviewed former Windsor Deputy Chief Christopher Paget, who recounted how he and his fellow officers didn't mind "lending a helping hand to a liquor dealer in distress," even if that meant rowing their booze ashore in their own boats. Of course that was usually when they were off duty.

"Once, he and a fellow officer were out duck hunting in the inlet between Fighting Island and Turkey Island — two islands on the Canadian side that were a favorite rendezvous for rumrunners. They came across a United States cruiser (with the proper legal export papers) that had run aground in a shallow; it was stuck in the mud because it was overloaded with 150 cases of beer. Paget and his friend readily agreed to lighten its load by rowing individual cases of beer ashore in their small duck boat.

But it was a laborious process and Paget was glad to see Arthur (Mushrat) La Framboise, a celebrated Windsor muskrat-trapper and rumrunner, come chugging up in his speedboat, *"The Joan of Arc."* Paget will never forget how Mushrat yelled out, "As soon as I give this fellow a bath, I'll be back to give you a hand."

Mushrat meant that his motorboat was dragging a corpse — a victim, evidently who'd been taken for a ride by Detroit mobsters and heaved into the river. After depositing the body with the local coroner, Mushrat returned to hook the *"Joan of Ark"* to the big cruiser and yank her free.

"We got five dollars each for our trouble and a free case of beer," Paget says. "Then my buddy and I continued our duck shooting."

Mushrat La Fromboise was a legend. So was his brother "Whiskey Jack." The two were hard working rumrunners. Rasky writes:

By day, he'd (Whiskey Jack) get $190 for rowing eight loads of fifty cases of beer across to Ecorse — the Detroit suburb known as The Gold Coast because it claimed the world's largest number of blind pigs. His customers would flash green lights or hang out white blankets to signal

Submerged houseboat filled with liquor. Looking from a boatwell on the Ecorse side, this scene shows the submarine operations of rumrunners. The dotted line shows the location of the cable along which the houseboat carrying Canadian liquor was drawn under water.

when the coast was clear of police patrol boats.

By night, he was paid twenty dollars — ''Plus all the Old Crow Whiskey I could drink'' — for guarding as much as 1,500 cases of smuggled booze cached in a clubhouse on Fighting Island. His employers, who called themselves the Fighting Island Gun Club, were a dozen liquor brokers from Detroit and Windsor, constantly worried about hijackers.

Mushrat was more daring. Rasky describes one night when the hard-bitten LaSalle rumrunner delivered 500 cases of booze across the river ice in a Model T Ford. Hijackers nabbed his load and shot a bullet into his skull. Mushrat spent only three days in the jail, and his brother told Rasky, ''They pried the bullet out, and it didn't affect him at all.''

Mushrat, his brother said, squandered his money in the stock market by investing more than $25,000 in a gold mine ''that had as much gold in it as I have teeth in my mouth.''

Whiskey Jack told Rasky he believed ''Ninety-five per cent of them (rumrunners) died as poor as church mice.''

A Windsor Star *article in the 1950s recounts some of the more bizarre methods used in transporting liquor across the border during Prohibition. One of the most ingenious methods was the ''submarine tramway'' used by whiskey dealers to channel whiskey from Courtright to St. Clair, Michigan.*

The Canadian terminal of the operation was well-concealed in a private home. From that point, a heavy cable ran under the river to the rear of a gasoline service station in St. Clair.

When finally located, it was the service station which proved the undoing of the enterprise. The station operators were too busy to service cars and trucks, thereby causing suspicion by the authorities and an inevitable checkup and crackdown.

The tramway was powered by a heavy electric motor to drive the cable and its cargo. This was carried in a ''tank'', a metal container about eight feet long by four feet square.

In operation, the ''tank'' was loaded with at least forty cases of whiskey, a cargo found by experiment to have the right weight to hold the container well below the surface yet not allow it to drop to the bottom. On the return trip, an equal weight of water was used to hold down the container.

The first tank was lost, and is still on the bottom of the river. Enterprising scuba divers needn't make plans for salvage, though, since the tank was lost on the return trip and had no whiskey aboard.

A subsequent tank was fitted with a different attachment and survived until the operation was terminated.

A newsman who worked for the Border Cities Star *on a part-time basis during Prohibition was the slight and dapper dean of Windsor newsmen — Angus Munro. Although he didn't join the staff of the Windsor newspaper until 1938, he was a correspondent for it in Detroit. It wasn't until his retirement in 1969 however that he began to reflect upon that era, and in his weekly column, "The Way Things Were," he recounted the tales from that time.*

Munro described this area as "North America's largest non-commercial beer cooler," because "snugly tucked into the mud at the bottom of the river is a fortune in booze of various kinds, tossed overboard by rumrunners or dumped after seizure by the river patrol."

Munro was referring to the practice of rumrunners dumping cargoes into the river, most often in the LaSalle and St. Clair River areas in order to avoid being caught by the heavily-armed border patrols organized by the Michigan police.

"Coast Guard authorities have estimated," he wrote in his column of March 15 1969, "that thousands of bottles of choice liquors are there in the dark depths. Most of it is at least thirty-five to forty years old."

This cache is "Canada's off-shore wealth," Munro concluded with some amusement.

In a September 5 1970 column he recounts a quirky story about smuggling booze:

Smuggling of one sort or another always has been associated with any border community. Windsor and Detroit are no exception. Particularly was the case in the 1920s when liquor was the chief form of contraband.

The stories are numerous of the means employed by so-called "smart" smugglers. Liquor was poured into the inner tubes of auto tires, then the tubes were sealed and carried as spares. Women smugglers carried special containers under their voluminous skirts. The cans of liquor were suspended by cord dangling from a belt worn around the waist.

A story has come down through the years that indicates the lengths to which the liquor smugglers would go. It concerns a report by Customs officers who noted an increase in the importation of eggs from Windsor to Detroit, but

thought little about it until one day in May, 1920, when a man carrying a large market basket and just off a boat from Windsor, was hit by a taxicab near the foot of Woodward Avenue in Detroit.

A crowd gathered. There was an unmistakeable aroma of whiskey in the air. Several dozen eggs were spread out on the pavement. The man, not seriously hurt, obviously was ill at ease. As soon as the crowd gathered and a police officer approached, he took off.

The market basket, with some of the eggs intact, remained in the middle of the pavement. The fleeing smuggler wanted no handicap during his sprint for freedom.

Upon examination, the basket contents revealed eggs filled with liquor and carefully sealed. It was then that the Customs officers came forward to testify they had noted increasing numbers of shoppers bringing "eggs" from Windsor to Detroit. From that day on, all baskets of eggs were suspect.

In reporting the incident, the *Border Cities Star* of May 18 1920, described the operation in the form of an advertisement:

Fresh Canadian eggs $2 a dozen. Laid by Canadian-Club hens; Scotch Plymouth Rocks; Brandy Pullets; Martini Leghorns; Bronx Minorcas and Gin Bantams.

The report went on to explain that the whole smuggling package might be described as "Eggs Diable".

There was no explanation of how the original hen's eggs were tapped for their new contents. This could mean long and tedious work, but apparently nothing was too great a task for the bootleggers of the day — not even pricking holes in hen's eggs and draining them, or carefully breaking them, emptying their yolks and whites, then carefully filling and sealing them for the journey across the river.

Eggs and whiskey still mix. Today we call it eggnog.

Another event recalled by Munro is the famous one of William E. "Pussyfoot" Johnson, the crusading dry leader, whom he says was "literally taken from the platform" at the Windsor Armories, where he attempted to speak.

In a piece which appeared May 8 1971, Munro wrote:

Reports of the incident vary, but it appears that the internationally known prohibitionist was brought here under auspices of the Ontario Referendum Committee. It was the end of an exciting province-wide tour. One account of the meeting describes it thus:

Mr. Johnson, from the start of the meeting, faced a howling mob. They set up a continuous chorus of booing that effectively prevented any attempt at speaking.

The crowd was not ugly. It just didn't want to hear any prohibitionist talk. But a few ugly incidents developed later. These happened when Police Inspector M. S. Wigle, with two patrolmen, decided the dry crusader was in danger and spirited him out the side door. They formed an escort and marched him down Ouellette Avenue, shepherding him onto a ferry.

Realizing the move by police was going to deprive them of further heckling, some of the crowd began tossing missiles of various sorts. There were rocks and an egg or two. All missed their target, but some policemen were hit, although not seriously hurt.

The crowd of several hundred followed the policemen and their charge all the way to the ferry dock to the accompaniment of boos and catcalls. "Pussyfoot" stood on the deck as the boat pulled away and waved a smiling goodbye to the crowd.

Johnson lived a remarkable life. For fifty years he waged war on drinking in every major country in Europe and America. (He died in Binghampton, New York, in 1945 at the age of 82.)

He became an international figure when he went abroad to represent the American Anti-Saloon League. He was credited with obtaining a more than ninety-seven per cent conviction's record in nearly 6,000 bootlegging cases from 1906 to 1908. Eight of his deputies were killed during this period — one of them because he resembled Johnson.

In England in 1919, "Pussyfoot" was mobbed by an angry crowd and lost the sight of his eye. He acquired his nickname while enforcing dry laws in Oklahoma. An Oklahoma newspaper reporter, referring to Johnson, once wrote: "The booze hunter strikes like lightning, even if he is a pussyfoot."

In his later years, he is reported to have pondered his experience in these words:

I regret that the United States ever tried prohibition without the support of public opinion. It will return some day, but not in our time.

Some who recall the Windsor visit say it was one of the most exciting nights in the city's history. Only prompt police action prevented more and perhaps wilder demonstrations.

A *Border Cities Star* reporter wrote: "It was merely a demonstration of mob psychology."

The "prescription plan" was considered one of the many farces of Prohibition. In a May 29 1971 account, Munro focused on "what was known in those

Pussyfoot Johnson — He once confessed that he had to lie and bribe and even drink to bring about national Prohibition.

days as a 'script' or a 'per' which actually meant a signed prescription from the doctor" that liquor would be of some aid to the patient.

The system was rather loosely enforced, especially after the first few weeks. Some were "sick" at regular intervals — say, every week or so. They appeared in sound health, but they were able to get prescriptions. These were filled by presenting them to a licenced vendor or, later on, a government store. The banner year for scripts was 1919.

As many as 222 in one day were issued. The same doctor, according to court testimony, dispensed 1,244 in the month of December. A vendor who handed out the liquor could testify to the steady progress of "sick" people. In August he testified, 619 were issued by doctors; in September 1,095; in October 3,259; in November 6,827 and in December 8,512.

The same reports indicated that more than ninety per cent of all Ontario doctors were not involved in the excess dispensation of scripts. This meant that most doctors, anxious to follow the ethics of their profession, declined to issue scripts unless there were indications of real need. As a result, they lost patients and families who might otherwise have become their patients, while the less-ethical doctors gained patients.

Within a few months violations became so flagrant that the issuing of pers for liquor was cut to thirty in any one month by any one doctor. This still left room for abuses, but they were cut to a minimum.

The average fell from hundreds per month to about twenty-five or thirty — some fewer. Oldtime Windsor residents who recall the script era, tell stories of going to a doctor and complaining of a cold or upset stomach or even remote ailments and having no trouble getting their prescription.

It was still the judgment of the vendor whether or not he should fill the doctor's order. If too many from the same doctor were presented by the same customer, the incident was reported and government inspectors moved in and checked the circumstance.

There was at the time a rash of what was known as Spanish influenza. It is still the contention of many who lived through this malady that liquor of one sort or another was responsible for saving lives. Doctors won't agree, but there is no question that liquor was not the sole means of treatment. Conscientious medical men took other measures and provided the patient obeyed orders, many got over their problem.

However, because of virulent effects, the "flu" took many hundreds of lives and would have taken many more had not liquor been made available, if one can believe so-called expert opinion.

There is no problem in getting liquor today, but oldtime doctors will verify that it was a difficult period for them and their profession.

Noel Wild

Chapter Five

Being Kidnapped By Rumrunners — Horace Wild

In the course of their activity, rumrunners were accustomed to being chased by United States patrol boats, being fired upon with "tommies," battling off hijackers, virtually anything, but not having their work documented by news photographers who wanted to blaze their faces across the provincial dailies.

Angus Munro was right when he said newspaper photographers from that era were noted "for their sheer crust in getting the pictures" they wanted. This was particularly true in the case of Horace Wild, a Border Cities Star *employee, who took his son, Noel, with him on assignment to photograph rumrunners in action.*

Noel Wild recalls those events of June 29 1929 vividly.

In 1929 the *Border Cities Star* decided to do a feature on this rumrunning business. A friend of the paper had a big speedboat out here on Riverside Drive, just down the road from where I live now. My dad and I and two reporters went down to Amherstburg where we knew there was some running going on from the dock.

We made our way down there. It was a nice, calm day. When we got down to Amherstburg, we went back and forth along the river. There were men loading the boats, and cases of the stuff piled up. They were putting them on the boats to take across the border.

So anyway, when they saw us taking photographs, they got really upset, so we turned around and tried to get away.

As we were coming back, they loaded about four carloads of fellows and some others got into a couple of boats to give us chase, but their boats weren't as fast as ours.

But the cars they had followed the road along from Amherstburg. We decided the best way would be to let them catch the boat, so we decided to get off. We pulled over just about where Calverts is today, and we put in at that point and jumped off. My dad and I grabbed our cameras, got off and ducked into the woods. But these boys weren't so dumb. They came along the road and caught sight of us. They wheeled

around and came back to get us. We tried running, but they got ahold of us. They grabbed dad and me and smashed his cameras. They didn't find the film dad had hidden, but they smashed everything else.

We had thought if we had got off on the land, we'd fool them. We had been coming around this bend in the river, and we figured if we hid along the shore, they'd still chase the boat, but that didn't fool them at all . . . and of course they got us.

They took my father away and headed back to Amherstburg. They left me, because I was only sixteen years old. I informed the Provincials when they came along the highway a little later. Quite a few hours were involved in between the time these rumrunners got us and picked up my father and took him back to town.

They had taken my father and bound him in chains and were going to throw him into the water. These kidnappers weren't from Amherstburg. I think they were from the States. I'm sure they were Americans . . . there must have been forty of these guys.

The Provincials managed to stop them from doing away with dad. They got there just in time, apparently. Dad was a little upset . . . I know he was, because he told me afterwards. And of course the *Star* really blew up the story about him being kidnapped by rumrunners.

In those days, these were regular export docks we were on. They were allowed to export out there . . . well they were supposed to be exporting the liquor to South America or to Europe or somewhere . . . but not to Detroit. But we were photographing all these guys . . . you could see every one of them in our pictures. If those had appeared in the paper, every cop in the States would have been after them, that's why they came after us.

I managed to get a few pictures out, but they didn't use any of them. In those days we were using the Speed Graphics. They were awfully heavy to carry, but we were used to them, and besides, that's all we had in those days.

Old style breathalyser test.

Chapter Six

Prohibition: The Water Highway — By Ron Scott

The following is a dramatic presentation of the tales of Prohibition that was done for CBE Radio in Windsor. It brings together many of the old stories set against historical background.

* * *

Two rumrunners reminisce:

It was three fellas, the first guys that ever went to Montreal to get some whiskey. They worked at this United States Steel over here. That's at the shipyards in Ecorse. They took their pays, those three fellas, know them very well, they took their pays and they went to Montreal and between the three of them they bought twenty-five cases of whiskey. They came back over here and my brother took that across in a rowboat, in a duckboat. He made two trips that night. He came back and those fellas were really in it then and my brother got in with them, see? And within a week they were buying a thousand cases.

Money was scarce in those days. Now you take four or five of the neighbors would get together and they would order a load of whiskey. Of course they made quite a bit of money you know, that was the reason. But it was all common people. They weren't gangsters. The majority of the guys that were buying the whiskey were all people like us that would go out and buy, invest their money, try to make a little bit on it. It was all common people and neighbors, together and one neighbor would land at another neighbor's place and so forth. They never thought there was nothing criminal about it.

Oh, there was women in it. Oh yes, there was women in it. Everybody and his brothers and sisters and aunts I guess. Anybody that had fourteen dollars and his train fare to Montreal could go over there and buy a case of whiskey and that was forty ounce, that was no pocket pints. You'd buy it for eight dollars to fourteen dollars a case and sell it for a hundred and forty.

People from every walk of life turned to the new occupation. They even had a new word for it: rumrunning. To most, it was like a game — profitable, exciting and only slightly illegal. Liquor could not be sold in Ontario, but companies could legally export. The market come up to expectations: by 1920, Windsor's Border Cities Star gives a conservative estimate of legal shipments of 2,000 cases a day. Illegal shipments, difficult to determine. On January 16th 1920, the market broke wide open: The Volstead Act came into effect.

And so the blues era had really begun. The drought had spread across the land. In the bars of New York City, tables were draped in purple cloth. But the mourning period was shortlived. In Michigan, it was a mere question of upping Canadian imports.

Canadians were on their toes. They hurried to and from Quebec with every type of receptacle and by every means of transport. The road to Montreal became a conveyor belt for booze.

They were hauling whiskey from Montreal in cans, in gallons cans, it came in suitcases, horse and wagon, trucks of all description. While I was hauling over the river, me and a couple of brothers, there was three cars between here and Montreal, one going, one coming and one in Montreal. Those fellas would come in Studebakers, Whiskey Sixes, Hudson Super Sixes, Buicks, Chandlers. They'd carry fifty cases of whiskey. They'd take all the cushions out — all that was left was your seat, and that's all, and they'd put fifty cases of whiskey in there and they'd make a load in twelve hours. There was always four cars, three, four, five cars between here and Montreal going and coming for the one guy.''

They had railroad tracks here, if you remember, running right in front of the house and the guys would order their liquor from Montreal by the carloads."

There was boxcars of it coming one after another like that, CN, CP, and they'd take a car on the way down to Amherstburg to get an order of limestone and stuff. And this whiskey car was the last one at the rear end. So they'd drop it here and that car had to be unloaded before the train came back here from Amherstburg to pick that car up again. So they'd get over there with a bunch of trucks and unload the car which, there was a thousand cases in those cars."

Police kept an eye on large rail shipments, but the use of camouflage was frequent, often ingenious. Two ex-policemen:

There was different times that I know where different shipments would come in for prominent men in Windsor and it would probably go to Tecumseh or Belle River and with their names, prominent men of Windsor, well we'd figure, it's their own liquor, so we just wouldn't bother with it. But it was the bootleggers were doing it all the time, they were outsmarting us."

Like this racehorse that came from Montreal, it was supposed to be a thousand dollar horse that was coming and they had blocked each end of the boxcar, like. The horse was right between the two doors. And the horse was in there with his hay and stuff and on each side of that horse was probably four or five hundred cases of whiskey. You'd get clearance for that horse that you were going to get out of that car — you didn't give a damn what happened to that horse. You'd break down those two bulkheads in there and get your whiskey out.

An arrival of liquor was of interest to both police and hijackers. There was no time lost removing it from public view.

You take eight or ten guys with two or three trucks, you know, you'd unload a car in a hurry like that. Oh yes, everybody was in a hurry and looking behind him to see it anyone was chasing him and you knew that the law was close in somewhere so you'd hurry. You'd get it out and you were allowed to go over there and get that. That was yours. But after you got it home you weren't allowed to have it so you had to get rid of it somehow.

If they wanted to hide it where those hijackers wouldn't find it they'd find a ditch somewhere and they line their whiskey in there two or three cases high, like, and then they'd just pass with the plow, fill up the ditch. Or in the marsh, in the bull rushes, cattails. Cattails grows seven or eight feet high you know.

Unloading liquor from CP rail car. Booze shipped from Montreal to the Border Cities was the starting point for much rumrunning. Here Old Log Cabin "Bourbon" and Pedigree Whiskey start their long journey, though it was really meant for home use.

Well they had a shack on Fighting Island and they'd take a load of liquor and they'd put it in this certain shack here and they'd hold it there until the American boys were ready to pick it up.

They had hidden places in stairways, attics, in the basement. There was one man on the front was a millionaire and he had over a million dollars worth of whiskey in his place, which was perfectly legal and he built a big home on Riverside and he had a regular vault and he had a million dollars worth of liquor in there.

And sometimes it just didn't pay to help a neighbor.

I remember this time right in this marsh in back of my house here. I got on to a load of whiskey there, a hundred and fifty cases to be exact. I went out on the ice and I seen tracks coming ashore like. It had snowed and drifted and I seen those tracks coming towards the cattails through the marsh and I followed them and I got into the cattails. Mister, there was a platform there just as smooth as this floor here and twice as big as this floor, four or five cases high. The snow had drifted off the tops of those cases so I come to this fella here, which he was quick on the draw. I told him, I says, "You'd better go down to the marsh there and get your whiskey out of the marsh over there." I says,

"Anybody that goes by will see it. I just found it there I was a hundred and fifty feet away from it." He says, "That's right, that's right, I can't leave the stuff there." And I found out afterwards that it wasn't his at all — I just gave it to him.

Ontario had nothing like the vicious gang wars soon to plague the American side, but shots were fired at night in the shacks along the river and people were getting killed.

Two rumrunners

There was lots of shooting all along the shore here. Most of them were hijackers. Like this time here in Martin Lane when they went to rob this stuff out of this barn. There was at least one hundred rounds fired at that time, how come nobody got hit, nobody knows. But it was rough, it was rough. Like my brother there, he was shot in the head and this other fella here, he was the mayor of LaSalle at the time, he got shot in the leg. Oh, there were guys that got shot and were thrown in the river and never came up again, never did find them.

I seen a thousand cases of booze I'd have to pretty well defend with my life. That was pretty near every night. I'd guard them myself on Fighting Island, lots of times. There was another shanty. It used to be a clubhouse on Fighting Island over there and I'd go over there and watch every night. The clubhouse was about the size of these two rooms here and you'd just pile them up in there, case after case, right up to the ceiling. Then you'd make partitions with the cases and you'd be in the center of it and if anyone come along to steal it you'd be well hidden, where you could also look at the door or the window, see if anybody was comin' in. You'd do your best to stop them.

And this was the first time I'd ever taken a pistol in my hand, any kind of pistol and they gave me this .45 or .48 I guess. It had a barrel on it the size of a lemon and I tried it on the Island over there to see if anything come along if I'd be able to shoot with it. So I took one of those forty ounce bottles, after it was empty, naturally, and I threw it in the water in front of me, maybe thirty feet, and I took that pistol and I was shooting at it like that. Every time I'd shoot that thing would fly over my head again and at no time did I see my bullet hit the water and then I seen this fella coming from shore over here in a duckboat and he told me to quit shooting cause I was planting those bullets all over along the shore here.

The people that owned the whiskey came over there at three o'clock in the morning to find out what we'd do if ever hijackers would come around in there. And full of whiskey ourselves,

naturally, all the time, Old Crow mostly, we didn't drink the weaker stuff. And when I heard them they were about a hundred and fifty feet from shore, two boats coming at this clubhouse again, so I prepared myself that they weren't going to get in there. And the door was a door that we'd made ourselves. It was three inches thick and the door knob and keyhole and all that was taken out and there was a hole there six inches in diameter. And I seen one of the guys passing in front of that hole and I told him, I says, "If you pass in front of that door again I'm going to shoot right in that hole." So he passed again but he run and I fired and then they came to the door. They hollered first to tell me who they were. They were the guys that actually owned the whiskey.

I seen one time in a farm in Martin Lane over here there was a barn over there and we had just unloaded a boxcar of liquor there that afternoon. There was 500 cases of whiskey in that barn and the gangsters came to get it. They started to tell everybody that they wanted help over there because the gangsters was comin' — a lot of times you'd know ahead of time when they would come in.

And I remember this time this fella's hiding underneath an old Maxwell touring car right in the gateway of this yard and he was laying down on the ground and he was gonna just shoot at that bunch of fellas in that car comin' down and they opened up. They put ten bullets in that car — never hit him!

*In Michigan, meanwhile, how were the people adapting to total Prohibition? Former Detroit Police Commissioner, Ray Girardin, a crime reporter during Prohibition.**

This noble experiment was not a popular law and the people who drank, broke the law by buying the stuff, using it, really didn't think that they were morally or legally doing anything wrong and I suppose the bootlegger felt the same way, I don't know, he was supplying this demand and the demand was pretty great. Now a lot of people started drinking during that time, probably there was a challenge to it.

Jack Carlisle, old-time reporter with the Detroit News:

It was a game, it was fun to go and look in a peephole and have a fella say, "Who sent ya?: and you told him and you went in. The steaks were good. There were slot machines. No, it was

*Ray Girardin died in 1971.

wide open. At a place belonging to Sammy Kurt & Cohen, the doors were wide open. "Canadian beer right on the wall," they said. It was made in the basement.

Saloon keepers defied the Volstead Act in two ways: some openly, by bribing police. Others, more cautious, turned to the speakeasy. All in all, then, how tough was it to get a drink in Detroit?

Two rumrunners:

Just about as easy as buying a package of cigarettes.

Wouldn't be as hard as a bowl of custard without enough thickening in it.

That's an exaggeration but there were countless blind pigs, speakeasies.

And there were people to steer you into them before you could find one. I was there.

Of course it was better if one were known, you could get in, but many of them took chances on people who just looked all right. Some of the bars operated just as if it were legal except that they had near-beer on tap and if a stranger came in they'd sell him the near-beer.

A total stranger could also become a very old friend — instant friendship service provided by the corner newsboy.

Walt never was at the newsstand very much but it was his stand. He'd be out helping people to know different places to go and what to do when they got there. He might leave the stand and take the stranger and come back with more than he had when he started out with the stranger. Sometimes he'd go right with them, have a drink with them so he could inform the people that he brought them a very nice man. And when he gave them the wink they'd know what he meant.

Canadians made valiant efforts to keep supply lines moving. Ample stocks were coming into Ontario and, if necessary, being stored. As to crossing the border, every device was used: surface craft, from canoes to fishing trawlers, airplanes. From the attempted construction of an underwater pipeline down to the wild, desperate expedient of a man in a diving suit pulling a sled along the bottom.

Even the small jobber, on foot, had a fair chance with the customs:

Two rumrunners:

If he picked his time, picked the right time. Otherwise he had to wear it around his waist. Have a little harness and fix it around his waist and wear a different coat. Wear one of them box back coats.

People used to cross the river with a strap around their stomach and they'd hold about

Man wearing harness to be hidden under jacket. One could easily pack 8 quart bottles of whiskey across the river on a winter afternoon on the Windsor Ferry.

eight bottles of whiskey and every one of them when they walked through the customs you'd swear up and down they were about eight months pregnant.

But ninety percent of the liquor was moved by surface craft.

Three rumrunners:

When they first started we'd take it across by rowboat and duckboat, ten cases, fifteen cases at a time. You didn't want to make too much noise over there because you didn't have outboard motors at that time and if you had an inboard motor that would make a bit of noise, everybody was jittery about smuggling. It was done mostly at night. You'd make two or three loads a night like that. As soon as dark started then we'd start until the law got too hot. We'd go by signals then, lights during the night, flashlights — some used their cars. And flags during the day. So if this fella here gave us a red light that meant that the law was out you see so we'd go to that blue light. They'd flash a blue light over there. We'd flash a blue light over here and then we'd shoot across.

Down at the foot of — for instance Alter Road and some of those places on the east side of Detroit — there was a lot of liquor that came in. If a stranger was there that the people on this side thought was law, they would hang up a bed sheet on the clothesline, which would be visible from across the river. So they'd just delay until the sheet was taken down and that meant the coast was clear and boom they'd come in.

But that took at least forty-five minutes just to row across there and lots of times, by the time you pretty near hit the American shore they gave you a red light and then you'd have to hurry back.

You had no Coast Guard on the river. Now you'd get murdered on that river, try anything like that. You wouldn't get too far. Hell in those days there were no boats on the river. Now how many boats have you got?

Meanwhile the U.S. economy was growing by leaps and bounds: there was money everywhere. In Detroit and Windsor they learned how to make a million and how to spend it.

Four rumrunners:

I seen a dining room table in a house over there had a foot thick of hundred dollar bills on there, all American money.

Well, one guy he made so much money that he had bushel baskets of it. He put it in bushel baskets and just slid it under his bed.

Newsboys was runnin' around town with thousand dollar bills in their pockets for watchin' a certain spot to see that nobody bothered it. It was delicious.

There was a lot of good sport, a lot of good times. The wages weren't very high but as you know the stuff was way low also. You could buy a pair of shoes for a dollar and a quarter. Two, three dollars, that was a real good pair of shoes. A suit for thirty, great living, great living, real good days. You'd buy a car, you'd buy a brand new car, a Model T. sedan, for around nine hundred dollars.

I recall some of the characters — probably the best known was the Lowell Brothers, Jim Cooper, Shotsy Shugard probably he was the most flashiest one because he liked to flash his money — a night's business he wasn't afraid of flashing

better'n a hundred thousand dollars in money. Lay it on the counter in a well known spot called Stoakes Cigar Store down in the neighborhood of the British American Hotel now. That was the meetin' place that and around the corner at Gibson Brothers, the cigar store.

Well we had to wear vests then and I had a real gold fob, it belonged to my mother. It was a locket but it was just right for a fob. Them days we wore spats. I did a lot of copying off of, ah, I'll tell you his name in a minute — Adolphe Menjou.

Oh, he was the best dressed man in Hollywood.

He wasn't dressed a hell of a lot better than me.

Everybody was interested in enjoying themselves, whether it was along the river or back in through the City, the speakeasies, where they all enjoyed a bottle of beer and whiskey and so forth. Windsor as it was, while it was dry it was wet. They had more fine saloons and bars that you could get a drink in than probably any place in the United States.

From time to time, pacing the export docks of Windsor in business suits were men who gave no inkling of their activities across the river.

A rumrunner remembers Al Capone:

He was in Windsor at the export docks and he seemed a good enough fella. Down at Dave Caplan's export dock and Lou Harris - they were both in it together: two Jewish boys and they were good fellas too. And we had quite a conversation. As a matter of fact I was introduced to him and that wasn't the only occasion that I had talked to him. They used to come over every now and again and he used to *kibbitz* around and have a little conversation and what not, probably crack a bottle in the export docks, have a few drinks. Well dressed and all, you couldn't tell him from a business man. But when they came to this country they were gentlemen, you wouldn't want to meet better people.

Jack Carlisle:

Capone had a definite big part in Windsor and Detroit, but mostly through uncut whiskey coming off the export docks in Riverside, Ont. and transplanted over here by a well known mob. And then the other part of it, he had to do with terrible things that happened in Detroit because his execution squad sometimes didn't have anything to do and they came to Detroit to relax and their method of relaxation led to the kidnapping of all the top gamblers in Detroit and gave us our first machine gun killing, which we had never had before.

By 1927, Detroit had become a tough town. Bootlegging, the state's second-largest industry, now grossed an annual 215 million dollars. For this kind of money, the competition was fierce.

Three rumrunners:

There was an Irish gang there and there was also what they used to call the Jewish Navy and there was also the Black Hand squad.

There was about five or six Italian gangs, you see, but among the Jewish element, the Purples had that all locked up.

The Purples? That was a loosely knit organization. I don't think it was ever more than at most eighteen to twenty people. Kids that grew up together. By loosely knit, I mean three or four of them might have a racket going here, three or four another one. Sometimes they'd work together. Sometimes individually. So it wasn't a cohesive group.

In these tough days, this was a young man's racket. The real boss, of course, of the Purple Gang, he looked like he might be a professional dancer. He was a very handsome fellow who had a perpetual youth of 18 or 19 years on his face. Very dapper and very tough. Even the other gangsters of different nationality were afraid of him. And until he went away to jail the Purple mob was very powerful.

Canadian whiskey was far from the only thirst-quencher in 1927.

Ray Girardin:

There were a couple of characters named Sammy Kurt and Sammy Cohen who were written up in Collier's magazine as the multi-million dollar bootleggers. They got notorious because they made beer underground in the basement of a blind pig on Orchestra Place, right on the fringe of downtown Detroit, on Woodward. And the only people that caused these bootleggers any trouble were the federals who came in and padlocked it. And the thing that got them so much notoriety, they padlocked one place so they leased the store next door and continued to make the beer underneath and they ran seven of these one right after another.

Also busy were the alky cookers, do-it-yourself distillers armed with home-made equipment:

Three rumrunners:

They used to call it lightning. I've even heard them mention different places about where to get good lightning and where to get bad lightning —

as if it wasn't all bad. You could get it as low as ten cents a gill and a gill would be a half of a pint, one of those little cream bottles and if there was about two of you, you'd get a real good spark. Pretty near every other house was an alley cooker. They used those, like we call those oil drums and coils. Very crude, and mind you they didn't make that out of the valuable part of any vegetable or fruit. They made it out of the skins because they had to use the other to eat. And potatoes were very well known to be used, the peelings, that meant the sprouts and everything that was in them went in there to ferment.

Well one had to have confidence in the person he was patronizing, to know whether the stuff would be lethal or not.

Fuel oil and that would mix in with their alcohol and unless it was properly removed, why that was rank poison. Well wood alcohol, it wasn't too bad, although there was fuel oil into it.

This product, as well as Canadian uncut whiskey, was close to pure alcohol. Diluted and prepared, it would pass as a beverage. In homes throughout the city, citizens were busy mixing up the now-famous bathtub gin.

And believe it or not it was made in bathtubs. That's what they poured it out in so they could serve it and bottle it. The bathtub didn't necessarily have to be washed out. The whiskey would take care of the rings in the tub. I've seen them do it but not wanting it very bad I didn't — I was scared to look at it, especially when I knew I was going to have to taste it. I don't know how many times I could have been killed with guys that drank too much of that stuff, only it wasn't good like it is now, so you know I had some bad cats on my back. They had to put a certain something in there to kind of heal it up, cause it was really sore. They had to put something in there. They would put maybe a quarter of the good stuff and the rest they'd get their color from burnt sugar. They could burn the sugar and put a certain amount of that burnt syrup in there and it would even help give it a little flavor, but a burnt flavor and shake that up and you had your color. And they had flavors to put in it, so if you didn't want some of that lightning they could put a corn flavor in a little vial and that would fix up a gallon very nicely for you of corn flavor, the same with rye, the same with a Greek drink called Mystika. It tastes something like licorice. It would make you hate your friends, after you got loaded. It was powerful. They put something awful in it for about eight drams to fix up a whole gallon and they had all the labels and everything.

(above) The Walkerville Brewery on the outside...
(below)...and inside, where men are busily turning out as much beer as they can.

I can remember one time I had a bunch of labels that I could put on some different stuff after I had taken off the original labels and cleaned up the bottles. Put the good labels on it and even the stickers with numbers across it and I'd be afraid that the party that I sold it to would ask me to have a drink. Cause I had something better at home.

St. Valentine's Day, 1929 — a garage on North Clark Street, Chicago. A few machine gun bursts and Al Capone eliminates seven henchmen of his last major rival, George "Bugs" Moran. Capone is now king. One of his first chores — to insure his liquor supply line through the Windsor-Detroit funnel.

Jack Carlisle:

"We heard that he had a suite of rooms at the top floor of the Fort Shelby Hotel. So we took his picture around. We didn't have any trouble finding out that this nice quiet gentleman that everybody thought was from Battle Creek, Michigan was Al Capone of Chicago. And he apparently stayed here three days and apparently he had a series of conferences with very notorious gangsters of Italian extraction, about five different bootleg gangs, not only in Detroit but from Ecorse and River Rouge and from Hamtramck. He had found a market for uncut whiskey and it didn't make any difference what the price was; the problem he had was getting it out of Michigan and he would bring in his trucks and he would bring in his bodyguards — because if you recall those days, they were very violent days where a lot of money was involved.

A case of whiskey, uncut was worth a tremendous amount of money and the thing that an organized bootlegging mob had to worry about were these wild hijackers who, after they invested their money in buying this booze and while they were en route with their trucks, would come up with machine guns and shoot everybody and take the whiskey.

Detroit mobsters, apparently happy over the deal with Capone, kept their end of the bargain. Methods of pickup and delivery had already been perfected.

Ray Girardin:

The idea of the bootlegger, they'd have the highest speedboats possible that would at the same time be carrying a big load so they could outrun the others. But they knew the shallow spots along the river. They'd dump it. They could then be stopped, they wouldn't have anything aboard. Then they'd go back with grappling hooks after the law had left and put it aboard and land it on this side. Now in the Detroit Press Club there's a very large blowup of a photograph, of an actual photograph. It was

taken of bootleggers unloading a boat right downtown at the river and you'll notice two things in this photograph: the speed with which they are loading a car and also two other automobiles parked there. They were the block cars. They were designed to get in front of any pursuing vehicle, any vehicle, enforcement vehicle that was pursuing the bootlegger, these other cars would get in front of and sort of run interference to block him off so the man driving the load of liquor could get away.

Warehouses dotted the back streets and alleys of Detroit's lower East Side, but were usually empty and deserted:

Ray Girardin

They'd have warehouses but they wouldn't keep a large store on hand because the financial risk would be too great if it was found. They'd try to deliver it to the retailers as soon as possible and this, of course was a job that was done pretty openly. I've seen it. I've seen deliveries made just as if they were delivering bread to a grocery store and it would be whiskey for the blind pig.

The signs of prosperity in Windsor and Detroit, that summer of 1929, were everywhere. Plans for a tunnel to link the cities, replacing the old ferry service. The

Unloading liquor in sacks at a warehouse.

splendid Ambassador Bridge — almost completed. Industry at a new peak — workers investing their savings in the stock market. Across the United States the picture was the same. Great money to be made — wild stock speculation. Those without savings — buy on margin. America is riding a boom that will never stop. Then, on October 23, on Wall Street, the nation's electro-cardiograph, a jagged line flickers across the screen. Stocks are falling. Diagnosis — a very mild heart attack. October 29, Black Tuesday — panic selling on the market.

Nothing to worry about — temporary fluctuation. Wednesday, October 30, no buyers for anything. The market is dead. Economic paralysis begins to spread across the nation and the world.

And so America entered upon the Dirty Thirties. By the spring of 1930 in Detroit there were lay-offs, reduction in the work week, over 12,000 families on relief. The only prosperous industry was crime. An apathetic public now drank to forget.

Jack Carlisle:

The public wouldn't convict anybody cause all you had to do if you were a bootlegger and you got caught was ask for a jury trial. One of the biggest scandals in Detroit was unearthed by a former reporter on the *News*, the great Barrisford, Victor Charles Barrisford was his name. He went to Montreal on a case one time and came back with an English accent and a cane. But he went over to Recorders Court and the entire basement was made up of exhibits and bottles. See, if you went into a place, if you were a policeman you had to order a drink. Then you had to confiscate it, show your badge and get that drink out of there. Well Barrisford discovered that a couple of thousand of the exhibits had all been drunk up. You can imagine what a scandal that was. The bootleggers and the gamblers, they didn't bother ordinary people. They catered to them. They served them champagne. They served them booze in fancy labels. Nobody got hurt.

Yes, the man in the street was safe, but he had his instructions: Mind your own business.
Two rumrunners:

Well, yes, if you got nose trouble, they would take you for a one way ride. If someone disappeared maybe someone will recognize the name, Brother Wilson. Brother Wilson, fine fellow, stately gentleman. Nevertheless Brother Wilson seemed like he did something was contrary to the code and they found him in an isolated spot in the swamp.

Some of the nicest fellas you ever seen when they weren't working, good spenders, good tippers, best in town. They dressed so much

fancier in much more expensive clothes than some business magnates would dress in. Well I know one, very well — we call him a nice gentleman. I don't know whether I should bring his name up or not. He's a legitimate businessman. But he used to take the whole second floor of the Prince Edward Hotel and use one of us, one of our bellmen, to just watch and see who came in and stop them first to announce their names. They were protected, in case it was the wrong one. And this fella was such a good sport — he must have had a lot of money cause none of the fellas he had in there had a hat on worth less than about twenty or twenty-five dollars, and in his jovial moods he'd throw all those hats out and give each one of his boys a hundred dollars and somebody on the street would be able to pick up a hat worth twenty or twenty-five dollars for nothing.

But the Great Depression was closing in. Soon there would be no money, even for the underworld. This fear drove the gangs to frenzied killing. The mobs were at each others throats.
Jack Carlisle:

On January 2nd, 1930, the gangsters of Italian extraction attempted to assassinate Inspector Henry J. Garvin and they shot up his car on the East Side of Detroit and accidently shot an eleven-year-old girl bystander. Garvin survived. There was a fellow who was the boss of all these mobs in Detroit of Italian descent. His name was Sam Cantilonotti and he had a wonderful nickname called, "Singing-In-the-Night-Time Sam." He died in bed and they gave him a twenty thousand dollar funeral with an airplane flying overhead. Airplanes weren't as popular then as they are now. Right down in the lower East Side of Detroit. Right around near Greektown, the church where they had the services was St. Antoine and Monroe — right on the fringe of Greektown.

After he died, a fellow by the name of Chester LaMarre who was so powerful in those days as an underworld character that he had all the food concessions at the Ford Motor Company, and that was given to him so that he would not kidnap the grandchildren of Henry Ford I. He decided that he wanted to be boss so he invited all the top leaders of these five, six, seven different mobs to a place called the Fish Market on Vernor Highway on May 31 1930. The boys got a little suspicious and they sent a man by the name of Gaspare Scabilia who was known as the 'Peacemaker' among the mobs. And three fellas walked in and shot Gaspare with eighty shots and killed him and his partner, a fellow named Pariso and then of course a lot of trouble broke loose, then a real fight began in the biggest gang war we've ever had in this town.

And here again, Ray Girardin, newsman at the time and later Detroit Police Commissioner:

Now this was all over gang wars as to who would control certain territories in Detroit, certain territories down river, certain parts of the Detroit River were parcelled off. One gang would use one part, another, another. They would not intrude on one another's territory and if they did there would be trouble. We had a great many gang murders. I remember for a while when I was on the paper *(Detroit Times)* that the phone would ring in the morning next to my bed and it got so that when the phone rang it was just getting to be daylight and I would almost know what the call was about. It would be my office telling me that they had just found another body. That was in the days of the One Way Ride when a gangster would be taken for a ride, shot, dumped out of the car and the body left there. The gangsters were very determined to eliminate competition and a lot of people died as a result. Considering the size of this city I think percentage-wise for a while it did pretty well. Chicago probably, and New York might have been ahead of us, but I would say that we were pretty close up there because in one year we had something like twenty-five gang murders in thirty-one days. We had a lot of them.

Self-extermination by the gangsters was also a breakdown in law and order, foolishly allowed to continue. The American public forgot its overwhelming power — that of a hundred and forty million people against a handful of hoodlums. Newsmen and commentators cried out for an end to underworld rule. Jerry Buckley, of Detroit's WMBC, proved by his own death that society was even losing its voice.

Three reporters:

I covered that story. That was in a very busy hotel at Adelaide and Woodward.

Jerry Buckley was sitting in the lobby of the LaSalle Hotel reading the morning paper, at 2:23 A.M., the morning of July 23, 1930.

Buckley was just there resting, probably waiting for someone to pick him up.

Gangsters came up behind him and shot him six times in the back of the head. Buckley had threatened to expose the wide open running of everything in Hamtramck so it was obvious that the underworld had assassinated him.

A colored boy, bellhop seen this, this killing but he wasn't around there long after. He ducked out of there because they'd want to know who seen. Life wouldn't be worth a quarter.

Three persons were tried in Recorders Court and acquitted. Two of the three were later convicted of another murder that occurred right at that very corner but it had nothing to do with the Buckley shooting. Because the same two were convicted a lot of people were under the impression they were convicted of the Buckley thing but that murder was never officially solved.

The number of killings in the streets, hotel lobbies, restaurants in 1930 and '31 finally produced a mild public outcry. Criminals found at last that killing, even among rival gangs, was frowned on by the law. The liquidation of a rival mob could put the seal on their own fate. The Collingwood Massacre, 1931 . . . Two rumrunners:

The Purples got in a fight with the Little Jewish Navy Gang and exterminated three of them. The three Purple people went to jail for life.

The shooting of the Collingwood Massacre was over a debt. The Little Jewish Navy Gang, which was nothing much at all, had bought a lot of alcohol from the Purple Gang because there was a huge convention in Detroit (American Legion Convention) and they sold it to the conventioneers, cut it, made whiskey out of it and sold it. But they didn't pay the Purple Gang and it amounted to a great deal of money, way

Bulletin: Jerry Buckley assassinated. See also page 144.

up in the thousands. So the Purples couldn't collect — so they shot them.

And the leader of the Purple Mob at that time, (Ray Bernstein) stayed thirty-two years in prison in Michigan for killing these three people.

Three were convicted and went to prison. But there wasn't anything from the Purple Gang after that. Prison, death or a new life accounted for all of its one-time members.

Crime, of course, would never be wiped out. But forces were gathering to bring it under control. Detroit, acting on the findings of a grand jury, began a clean-up. In Chicago, Capone had been dethroned in '31 by the federal government and was serving eight years in Alcatraz. By 1933, J. Edgar Hoover was directing a full-scale war on crime. Meanwhile, an impoverished nation decided the people would always pay money for booze and they might just as well pay it to the government.

It was December 5 1933, almost fourteen years after that other winter's day in 1920, when it all started. At 3:32 P.M., word came from a convention in Utah. The state had become the last one required to ratify the 21st amendment, repealing the Volstead Act. Prohibition was at an end.

Of course, the people had been drinking right along, but there was a short and memorable celebration. They repaired to the saloons for the first legal drink in twenty years. Stocks were soon exhausted.

The new liquor was heavily taxed, so bootlegging, at a reduced rate, would continue. But the stock market crash and repeal had brought an era to an end. The big money was gone. The vast bootlegging market was gone. The Roaring Twenties were gone. It was all over.

Harry Low in his heyday. He built an empire with illicit booze, but died penniless.

Section 3

THE BAD AND THE BRASH:
Harry Low, Cecil Smith,
Whitey Benoit and James Cooper

Chapter Seven

Harry Low's Millions

Of the hundreds of rumrunners, bootleggers, blind pig owners and whiskey exporters, there were few giants. Harry Low was one of the few. He amassed a fortune in so little time, but lost it just as quickly. He was the epitome of extravagancy and eccentricity.

Harry Low was a man of vision. Limitless and foolish vision. In the fashionable old town of Walkerville, now incorporated into Windsor, stands a magnificent symbol of his dreams — the grand Tudor home now occupied by Paul Martin, former External Affairs Minister in the Pearson Government and former High Commissioner to England. The mansion was built and paid for by huge rumrunning profits. It was lost because of poor investments, ill-fated judgments and unnecessary risks. It was lost because of the boundless vision Low had during the Roaring Twenties, a vision that couldn't sustain him following Prohibition. Just as Harry Low had become the author of his fortunes, he also caused his misfortunes. The mansion is the simple representation of dreams turning to excess.

Harry Low, a man who had raised himself from toolmaker to millionaire, made his fortune in Prohibition. He had stumbled upon a winning formula, — something that he gravitated to more than machine shop work. Selling whiskey. Exporting it on a massive scale. But his luck ran out after Prohibition and could no longer sustain that unrestrained vision. He died penniless. Vision had made him wealthy during the rumrunning days, but following it, it was this

same far-reaching vision that resulted in the squandering of large investments in extravagant projects far ahead of their time. Like the ingenious auto carburetor that was supposed to use so little gasoline — an idea automakers are still struggling with today. But in the thirties fuel efficiency wasn't a problem, and his idea was scoffed at and rejected . . . and his financial resources dried up. By the end of the Thirties and the beginning of the Forties, Low was virtually broke. And when he died in 1955, he was living on the shabby fringe of Windsor's downtown. He had been living alone, a saddened recluse who no longer wanted to see anyone.

Born the son of a machinist in Ottawa in 1888, he adopted his father's trade and, soon earned himself a reputation as an excellent toolmaker. The advent of the auto industry in Detroit and Windsor attracted him and he soon found himself working as a machinist there. But Low wasn't content with such rudimentary employment. He forsook the trade to open a poolroom on Sandwich Street. Low didn't realize it at the time, but the poolroom was the first step toward rumrunning and the fortunes he had always dreamed of.

When Prohibition came into full force in the United States and Ontario, Harry Low saw a chance to make some easy money. He borrowed $300 from a friend and set himself up in the bootleg business selling liquor to poolroom enthusiasts. But the poolroom was soon abandoned when profits from the $300 spurred him on to engage in the lucrative whiskey export business. Low threw his energies into waybilling liquor from a Detroit River dock in fast speedboats, ostensibly headed for Cuba and West Indian ports, — but, in fact, shooting like bullets to Michigan destinations and Yankee blind pigs. In no time, Low's genius was responsible for the formation of a network running booze shipments from Windsor docks to Detroit, St. Louis, Chicago and places throughout the States.

But Low's rumrunning wasn't confined to speedboats. He invested his profits in large ocean vessels — the *Geronimo* and the *Vedas*.

Aware of their activities, the United States border patrol agents attempted to seize the *Geronimo*. They moored it to a Michigan dock and locked it up, but a storm set the vessel free and dumped it back on the Canadian side where it resumed its rumrunning.

The World War I minesweeper, The *Vedas,* was also bought and used by Low. After the war it had been used as a banana boat, a sealer and general trader, and when Low purchased it, he refurbished the old ship and put it to work hauling cargoes of liquor from Montreal to Windsor, and sometimes boldly crossing Lake Erie to the States for deliveries. But most often, the *Vedas* would transport its shipments from Quebec and rest offshore just outside the territorial limits of the United States. During the night, swift cruisers would steal out and load up with cargoes and ferry them to shore.

Harry Low was veritably a self-made man. He had engineered success from that initial $300 investment. He had gone from bootlegger to businessman. He was soon the head of the largest export firm in the Border Cities — Low, Leon and Burns. That business virtually controlled the movement of liquor on the waterfront in Detroit and Windsor. It took over an entire railroad depot for its headquarters and from there shipments of booze sped to speakeasies and blind pigs in Detroit, Chicago, Cleveland and even to the infamous Rum Row on the Atlantic Coast.

But success didn't come easy. Low went through the hectic, frenetic bootlegging apprenticeship like anyone else. He was coerced into devising some of the most bizarre ruses to get booze across the border. Once workers at a Riverside plant were astonished to see a Model T Ford hurtling down a street and drive off the end of a dock into the river. The plan was to divert attention and send the police into action to drag for "bodies," while Low and his racketeering rumrunners rushed three truckloads of liquor along a main street, into boats and across the river.

On another occasion, Low asked a friend to accompany him to Comber (about thirty-five miles west of Windsor) to pick up a load of

The *Vedas,* Harry Low's pride and joy, put him in a different class of rumrunners. His use of huge steamers made Low a liquor baron in the Border Cities.

The Walkerville Mansion. Low's grand mansion, where he consorted with high society is now owned by former Cabinet Minister, Paul Martin.

booze. Upon arrival, Low was arrested and handcuffed to the wheel of his car. The police had wanted to hold him while they searched for more suspects who were expected to arrive nearby. Low's friend however, wasn't manacled, and when the police left momentarily, he turned on the car's ignition and the two took off to Windsor. They had also loaded up with the cargo of liquor left behind by the police.

But bootlegging was small time compared to the whiskey export business with its large ocean-going vessels and railroad yards of booze. The money Low accumulated led to great extravagancies like his Walkerville home, his pride and joy. It boasted a cloister for reflection and meditation. The windows were leaded, the floors tiled. It cost him more than $130,000 to build and it was regarded as the snooty showpiece of Walkerville. One room's excesses included gold-tipped icicles. In poetic fashion Low had ordered a slate roof to be made "like the waves of the sea."

Low's money also built the multi-million dollar Dominion Square in Montreal, a towering office building that at one time was the tallest in that city. But his vision far exceeded reality and, the excess to which he had gone with the building finally led to losing ownership of the structure.

At the time, Low was a partner in the export firm with Charles Burns and Marco Leon, one of the principals of the old Carling Brewery. Although the three were successful, they suffered a major blow in 1928 when the company was sued by the federal government for $21,000

which authorities claimed was owed in sales and gallonage taxes.

It was during the hearings that some of the dodges used by Low and his associates came to light. On one occasion it was revealed how a large quantity of illegal liquor was seized on a railroad siding at London, Ontario. It had been waybilled as "canned meat."

Low and his associates were also linked to the gangland murder of one of their employees — John Allen Kennedy, who was discovered bludgeoned and shot through the skull in the woods near the Ohio-Michigan State line.

Low was the vice-president of the Carling Brewery at the time, and Kennedy was a bookkeeper for the company.

The Royal Customs Commission had wanted Kennedy to testify at its hearings on the liquor trade, but the bookkeeper had been whisked away to Cuba where he remained for several months. He returned to Windsor only after the heat was off him and, worked for a short time at the Federal Warehouse. He was killed shortly after he had been fired from that job.

Investigators, probing his death, claimed Kennedy had been a go-between for the export docks and customers on the American side of the Detroit River. They suspected, but could never prove, that Kennedy knew too much about the operation and was prepared to confess all to the federal commission. Police believed it was for this reason that he had been lured to a wooded area in Monroe Township in Michigan, where he was slugged at the base of the skull, shot twice and

Harry Low in 1953, shortly before his death.

then dragged into the bush. The spot where Kennedy was murdered was the site of other gangland assassinations. No fewer than seven other murders occurred there, five of them apparently done by the same gang.

For weeks police attempted to link the Kennedy murder to Low, but failed. In fact police were never able to charge anyone, and the case never went to trial.

There were many stories circulating at the time, one linking the actual slaying to some well-known Windsor hoodlums who had consorted with Kennedy just before he was killed, and another which led the police to trace the victim's activities to a mysterious west side Detroit house where he apparently met someone who drove him to Monroe. But police theorized that Kennedy had probably gone willingly to Monroe because he thought the business involved a large "still" known to have operated for months from this area.

The period following this is fragmented and feverish. Low began dabbling, investing, trying desperately to broaden his wealth. First he

turned promoter and helped found the Old Comrade Brewery in Tecumseh, later taken over by O'Keefe's. He then was lured to oil wells in Petrolia, sinking his money into searching out non-existent huge oil reserves. He then bought real estate on speculation, only to find the properties were worthless.

At one point Low, believing one of Toronto's largest department stores was going to relocate, paid thousands of dollars on options for several potential sites. When the department store didn't move, Low lost his money. He also lost thousands when he rushed to buy up properties at inflated prices in Windsor just before the Depression set in.

His "gas saver" device was perhaps his most extravagant investment. Low believed he had uncovered a new gadget that would significantly reduce the consumption of gasoline used in automobiles. After it failed to attract interest, Low bitterly claimed the reason he had backed off was because an oil company had paid him a bundle fearing it would have been put out of business if the device had been marketed.

Low had even gone to the extent of providing public demonstrations of his new carburetor and "gas saver." He rigged up two identical Dodge motors — one with the gadget and one without — and attempted to prove its efficiency. The results were impressive, but according to engineers and observers his tests were still inconclusive.

Low's glory had faded with the end of Prohibition. He had failed miserably as a promoter, invested unwisely and virtually crippled himself financially due to misdirected ventures. In addition to this he was plagued by the police. Following the 1928 hearings and the death of Kennedy, he was arrested in 1931 on a charge of trying to bribe an RCMP officer. But soon after, Low battled extradition to the United States to face a similar charge. He had been accused of offering a Customs officer $450 in a vain attempt to smuggle 285 cases of beer over the border. He won the extradition fight but his troubles didn't cease.

By 1934 Low's fortune had dwindled to next to nothing. He had tried unsuccessfully to regain it with stock market investments. An attempt to seize the contents of his plush Walkerville home to pay bad debts was blocked by Low when he proved the $40,000 worth of antiques were not his property but his wife's.

It was in 1934 that Low and some associates started the Trenton Valley promotions in Michigan. He resigned as its president in 1936. In 1939, however, faced with a United States indictment charging him and Walter H. Hardie, a vice-president of Trenton Valley, with stock swindling, Low vanished from Detroit, where he had been living. The indictment said that he had falsely advertised stock in the corporation and had caused investors to lose more than $1,500,000. He was finally arrested in 1953 in Detroit when he was recognized from a 15-year-old photograph. Besides being charged with swindling, he was also charged with evading income tax payments in 1935 and 1936.

On the income tax evasion charge, Low, it was claimed, had only paid $437 for the two years, although his income in 1935 had been $30,193 and in 1936, $23,239. Low received a sentence of a year and a day in prison, but it was suspended when Low was deported to Canada.

By the time the swindling case arose in court, the statute of limitations had crumpled the fraud charge laid under the Securities and Exchange Act, and Low was free.

An interesting sidelight to this story, however, is that when Low had been arrested early one morning in his Detroit apartment by Sam O'Connell, an Internal Revenue Service agent, he had been living under the name "Harry Love."

He pleaded to authorities that he had informed federal authorities in 1939 of his intention to return to Canada. (It was that year that he had been indicted for using the mails to defraud in connection with Trenton Valley stocks.) Low claimed he wasn't stopped from returning to Windsor, and since he had received no word from the United States authorities regarding the so-called swindle, he never bothered to follow it up.

From Windsor, Low moved to Sorel, Quebec, and worked there in the shipyards, again as a toolmaker. He returned to Detroit in 1949 and worked as a toolmaker, but when he attempted to set up his own machinist shop, his identity was uncovered.

He returned to Windsor and became a jobless drifter, living in a home on McKay Avenue on the fringe of the downtown. He avoided the bars. He kept to himself, and when he died at Hotel Dieu Hospital in Windsor, it was two days before the police or newspapers realized which Harry Low had passed away.

Low had been a tireless dreamer, forever risking money and time on new-fangled schemes and ventures, hoping to recapture the glitter of the Twenties. But these had been false hopes. His luck had withered with the end of Prohibition and, the far-reaching vision of those early years had been replaced by weak excuses and subterfuge to fend off police and tax collectors.

Cecil Smith. A pathetic, forlorn figure in his last days in the Fifties, Smith was still entangled in bootlegging. He claimed that a Windsor police officer had accepted bribes to protect Smith from further convictions...but the policeman hadn't kept his promise.

Chapter Eight

Brains behind the bootleggers
— Fat Cecil Smith

Cecil Smith's story epitomizes the small-time hood on the Canadian side who thwarted the law and the lawless. He was a hood of a different class. He made it big, but lost everything, even self-respect. His name literally swamps the police files, and his stories clog the court clippings in the *Windsor Star*. His story begins in 1919 when he sold his first two bottles of booze, and it ends in 1953 when he was tried for perjury.

As late as the 1950's Cecil Smith still carried with him a black book containing the names of regular clients to whom he sold liquor. A bootlegger all his life, this thumbworn book with curled edges and cigarette burns held a history of its own. He relied upon it, just as much as the winos and diehards leaned upon him.

Bootlegging was second nature to Cecil. It was an integral part of his life, and a bemused Windsor Police department could easily claim that whenever this hulking figure was stopped on the street for a routine search, invariably a few mickeys were discovered tucked away within his deep coat pockets.

But if a jail sentence rarely frightened Cecil, it certainly never deterred him in the business of booze. Bootlegging was his art, his essence, his livelihood. He once told a magistrate that peddling booze was probably far more respectable than selling brushes door to door.

Brash, daring, rarely boisterous, Cecil Smith was known as "the brains behind the bootleggers." But his tragic flaw was this luckless quality. Cecil's path forever crossed the path of the police in characteristic hapless fashion. But spending time behind bars wasn't a deterrent — he was never there long enough to be coerced into ending this illicit liquor activity.

Cecil Smith wasn't a theatrical gang leader. Just a hood. Not a Jimmy Cagney tough guy, just a bootlegger. Overweight and hard as nails. Lacking in personality, tact, charisma. Slick, and always prepared for a new scam. Nothing obstructed Cecil Smith. Not convictions for theft, smuggling aliens, obtaining money in narcotics rackets, perjury . . . and certainly not rumrunning. None of these halted Smith in his lengthy sordid career.

The day he swaggered into the Windsor Police Commission hearing accusing a Windsor police constable of extorting money from him, Smith was confident, calm, smug. It was the end of March 1953. He ambled into the meeting wearing a large, droopy hat, a loud silk tie and a tent-like overcoat. He was unshaven. And unshaken. He delivered his charges that Constable Gilbert Robitaille had been paid $700 on two occasions to protect Smith from liquor convictions. But a recent charge against Smith for bootlegging, accompanied by more demands for money, angered him, even to the point that Smith was prepared to tell the commission everything.

But the unlucky Smith saw the hearing clear the charge against the police officer, and now watched the focus swing to a charge of perjury. Two months later, the swagbelly bootlegger returned for trial and skillfully beat the charge. His large, mournful eyes, according to reporters covering the trial, were full of tears upon acquittal.

That story gives us an insight into the surly, unpredictable nature of Cecil Smith. It also serves as an example of the methods that aided him in amassing a fortune during Prohibition.

During the Roaring Twenties, Smith caught the

easy ride to wealth in the liquor racket. But his road to crime didn't start with booze. It actually predated the temperance laws in Ontario.

Cecil Smith's name first appeared in newspapers in April 1919 when he was caught with two other men smuggling a Chinese alien across the border into the United States. His fine was a mere $100 and court costs. In those times, it may have been a stiff penalty, but by comparison to what he would be forced to dole out in the future, it was nothing. Smith had been the driver in the escapade to smuggle the man into Detroit.

During Prohibition, the undaunted Smith was caught again for the same offence. In July 1929, he was sentenced to serve fifteen months in Leavenworth Penitentiary for conspiracy to violate immigration laws. This time Smith had been caught trying to smuggle three Chinese aliens into Michigan.

Picked up at River Rouge, he admitted under questioning to running a liquor dock at Sandwich near Windsor, but denied he had anything to do with smuggling aliens.

In the courtroom, he went to great length to convince the judge that, to be sure, the dock where he smuggled liquor, was also a favorite spot for "coralling" aliens just before shipping them across the Detroit River. But he said in utmost sincerity, that he regarded the scheme as something against his own better judgment.

In sentencing him, the Detroit judge listed the numerous offences on Smith's record and observed that Canadian authorities "would doubtless be glad to see him go to Leavenworth."

But alien smuggling wasn't where Smith shone. He exhibited his prowess with liquor. Besides it was far more lucrative. So much so, in fact, the Canadian tax officials attempted in 1925 to collect on his alleged illegal earnings.

Ottawa wanted some $28,632 of Smith's $92,020 earnings from bootlegging during 1920. Smith's own tax return differed greatly from the tax department's, thus touching off a legal and bureaucratic war.

First, the intrepid Smith appealed to the Exchequer Court. But he found no sympathy there. According to Justice Audette's review of Smith's file, the profits gathered from bootlegging were not exempt. Failing that, Smith appealed to the Supreme Court of Canada and won his case. The court overturned the previous decision.

One of the Supreme Court judges, Justice Idington, in summary declared the Ontario Temperance Act "explicity (says) that all private liquor transactions are illegal under the provincial law and that a bootlegger is not entitled to compensation."

He went on: "I can't believe Parliament ever had in its serious contemplation . . . the conception of taxing any profits or money raised from such a criminal source."

The *Border Cities Star* was quick to respond suggesting "it now looks as though it may be

One of the larger export docks at Windsor.

necessary for Parliament to amend the income tax act of 1917 and make express provision for taxing bootlegging profits."

While all this was taking place, Smith was ensconced in Kingston Penitentiary for theft of goods from a boxcar in Windsor. From the isolation of his cell, he had been carrying on a headline-making legal battle.

The bootlegger's formative years of crime were never better described than by W. H. Furlong in October 1921 when Smith was indicted on a charge of bribing a police officer.

Furlong, a well-known Windsor criminal lawyer, recounted how Cecil Smith started "as an express driver at nine dollars a week . . . and managed to save enough money to operate a taxicab, but at the beginning of Prohibition his taxi licence was cancelled when he was convicted under the OTA for alleged possession of liquor. At that time Smith claimed the liquor which was found in a travelling bag was left by a man who hired his taxi.

"With no means of earning a livelihood, Smith in November 1919 began dealing in liquor and since that time he has made a comfortable amount of money."

Comfortable enough to afford him a grand home on Sunset Avenue near the river in Windsor. And comfortable enough to provide him with servants, new suits and cars. But as one can see from the court files, Smith lacked class.

In the bribery case, where he was defended by Furlong, it was revealed that Smith had gone to the Canadian Pacific Railway yards at Sandwich with seven trucks and five touring cars to haul away more than 750 cases of liquor. But he was nabbed by Constable William Allen who attempted to seize the freight car containing shipments of whiskey consigned to various persons other than Smith.

Disregarding the officer altogether, Smith pushed past him, handing him a thousand dollars and ordering him "to go up the hill."

Smith had gone through this scenario so often, he didn't expect opposition or honesty. But Allen refused and went ahead with his effort to impound the freight.

Not being completely unreasonable, but obviously stung, angered and holding back his agression, Smith waved two thousand dollars in Constable Allen's face and told him he had better take "a walk." When the obstinate constable wouldn't back off, Smith's thugs were called in to assist, and within a few minutes the unloading operations had begun in earnest in the freight yard.

Constable Allen had been handcuffed, beaten up and placed in a nearby boxcar.

Later in the court, Smith snidely remarked to a witness, "the next time I offer Allen two thousand dollars, he will prefer it to being beaten up."

It was this characteristic brashness and swagger that astounded the police, lawyers and courtroom spectators. And it was in this particular case that Smith earned himself the tough-guy reputation.

In the Essex County Assizes in Sandwich October 13, 1921 Smith explained it had been his custom to pay off express agents at a rate of five dollars a case in order to remove his liquor before liquor licence officers arrived upon the scene. The astounded magistrate queried if bootlegging was his only means of work. Smith laughed.

"I do not call myself a bootlegger, but other people do . . . on good grounds," Smith replied.

He then went on to elaborate for the judge that he never sold "a drop of liquor in Ontario," and that he considered himself a bona fide exporter. With regard to bribing a police officer, the roly-poly hoodlum scoffed at the charge. Sure he had. To date, he revealed to the court, he had peeled off more than $96,000 in bribes, or as he described it, "I've paid that much to the Canadian government."

Smith was sentenced to serve five years in the penitentiary, but he asked for a second trial and won his case on a technicality.

In 1930, Smith was still dabbling in whiskey and again it was booze that got him into trouble. Booze and that unblessed nature he wore like an old overcoat. This time he was shackled with a six-month sentence, having been convicted when another man claimed that Smith had hired him at fifteen dollars a week plus board to serve liquor at the Shawnee Club with the guarantee that he would also pay the man twenty-five dollars a week for any time he spent in jail as a result.

Probably the most bizarre incident was the 1932 narcotics case in which Smith was sentenced to serve seven years in prison after he was convicted of obtaining money by false pretenses. The cunning scam, revealed in the court, described how Smith with another man sold "candy" to Detroit buyers who thought they were buying morphine. The witnesses confessed how they had paid Smith and another man in advance, but were furnished only with packages of peppermints. One indignant man complained he had paid Smith $350 only to be handed a bag of candy, not the promised morphine.

Shrugging these claims off, Smith replied he had no interest whatsoever in smuggling dope —

Cecil Smith attending the Police Commission meeting on the bribery charge. He died a few years later.

bootlegging was his business. Bootlegging beer and liquor, not narcotics. And besides, perhaps he had helped the Canadian authorities by exposing these addicts, he pondered in a bemused tone. Nonetheless, he showed no interest in the case at all, evidenced by how he slouched while his attorney attempted to defend him from the mounting facts against him. He was sentenced to serve seven years, but only served five.

Soon after his release in 1937 the bootlegger was again under arrest, this time for injuring Constable Jack Clark of Woodstock. Smith had been stopped by the Ontario Provincial Police constable who wanted merely to question him about an extortion ring in that town. But Smith turned aside those questions. He told Constable Clark to mind his own business, then promptly lurched away in his car. The over-zealous officer, as hard-nosed as Smith, leaped upon the running board to argue the point, but instead of conversing found himself hanging on for his life as Smith wheeled through the streets of Woodstock and out to the highway. Finally at a speed of seventy miles per hour, Constable Clark was hurled from the swerving vehicle and was thrown into a ditch.

Smith was later caught by the police, but only after a police cruiser rammed into his car and shoved Smith's battered vehicle into a ditch.

Upon being sentenced to five years, an astonished Smith, feeling unfairly treated, turned to a nearby police officer and remarked, "Lots of men get less than that for murder."

In Windsor the oldtimers remember Smith as brash and hard-assed, but he was never one to hold a grudge.

According to former Staff Sergeant Charles Johnson of the Windsor Police, Cecil Smith was "just unlucky . . . other than that, he was okay. He was just always getting caught."

Johnson recalls how Smith worked as an express agent and was responsible for picking up large amounts of cash that came in nightly by the Michigan Central Railway in an iron box.

"The box didn't even have a big lock on it — just a padlock, and Cecil would pick this up and take the money out and bring it home with him. It was $50,000 to $100,000 in cash, spot cash . . . it was the bank pool, and it would have to be delivered to all the banks the next morning.

"Well, Cecil would take it home with him, because they couldn't leave it there, and he'd bring it down to the express company the next morning, and then it would be taken to the banks.

"Well, Cecil was no crook, if you see what I mean. I mean he could've just taken the money. I know this, because my brother used to relieve Cecil when he couldn't make it."

He said it was only later that Cecil Smith became a bootlegger. "In the beginning he was just a small guy . . . but then he made millions . . . oh he was stealing whiskey from other guys, but so were they.

"I remember him as a quiet, easy-going guy... never cantankerous, but when he wanted to be in a fighting mood, watch out . . . but you know I think when he got caught, he was like a big baby."

Johnson said the last thing he heard, Smith was running a blind pig on St. Luke Road in East Windsor, "and he didn't have a nickel."

Smith is an interesting criminal study. He never ceased bootlegging to his regular customers, and the brashness and bravado acquired during Prohibition clung to him like a shadow. It was nothing for him to perjure himself. He had nothing to lose . . . and if he had won, then he had only the court to thank... or the jurors who failed to see through his slick manner. But for the most part Cecil Smith was unlucky. He was one of the few who got caught time and time again. And even though some may have suspected his crying in the court room after he was cleared of the perjury indictment was poor theatrics, perhaps it wasn't. Perhaps at long last he was tired of all the sham.

Milton "Whitey" Benoit, the eccentric son of Vital Benoit, LaSalle's first mayor, sitting in his one-room apartment. By his teens he was already passing hot diamonds for Detroit's Purple Gang. His father poured money into hotels and breweries and was considered one of the giants of bootlegging in the Border Cities area.

Chapter Nine

In the Bad Old Days — Vital and Whitey Benoit

Milton "Whitey" Benoit, now 72 and still living on his beloved Pitt Street, a dumpy hardcore city street in Windsor, is a product of Prohibition. He hauled whiskey across the river in small boats and in old cars. He worked for the Purple Gang, and for a time, Whitey was a bouncer in the speakeasies and whorehouses in Windsor. But he was also the son of Vital Benoit, one of the wealthiest men in Essex County, Ontario. Whitey's father made his money before and during Prohibition. And because his father was rich, Whitey was sent off to the best schools . . . but to no avail. Whitey chose to continue the illicit activities he had picked up during the rumrunning years . . . and even today bootlegs on the side.

He stands at Pitt and Mercer Streets in Windsor smoking a rolly and wearing a sleeveless undershirt. His greeting is gruff and raspy. He shakes a fist at a nearby German shepherd which is barking insanely. He says there's nothing to worry about — "I'm the only mad dog around here."

This white-haired man — his hair has been that color since he was twenty-two — is the last of the old Pitt Street gang, when there were hotels on every corner and blind pigs and "cathouses" in between. The 72-year old remembers it all. He was a part of it for more than twenty-five years between being in jail and on the run. Whitey made a bundle on this street in the Thirties when nothing shut down until dawn.

"It was like the Old West — now it's like walking up the middle aisle at St. Alphonsus Church (in Windsor) — nothing's happening."

This is the same Whitey that Maclean's magazine in the Fifties called "King of the forgers." He had organized a ring writing worthless cheques on non-existent companies.

The ring covered Ontario from Windsor to Kirkland Lake and operated as far east as Ste. Agathe, Quebec. It ultimately took an estimated $150,000 from the Canadian public.

It was the biggest forgery scam in Canada's history and assured Benoit of $30,000 to $40,000 a year, "and I spent every nickel of it because I knew there was more from where it came."

Today, he lives in a two-room flat at the back of a building on Pitt Street East. His place is furnished ascetically with a bed, refrigerator, stove, tables and chairs.

He usually sits at the table drinking beer and reading newspapers while the television set babbles away. His wallet sitting beside the beer is stuffed with big bills.

Outside, along the fence, is a long narrow stretch of garden "which my girlfriend down the street takes care of — she also fixes me meals every day, so I don't complain."

The garden is his pride and joy. He says the winos and other Pitt Streeters take his tomatoes but Whitey doesn't mind because there is enough for everyone.

This attitude had guided Whitey through his long career, always on the other side of the law, "close to the edge at all times."

At twelve, he stole liquor from some rumrunners to party with friends. Later he accompanied "river rats" in old jalopies on the ice taking whiskey across to Detroit.

"I was just going for the ride and one day had the lens of my glasses knocked out by a bullet and also got hit in the leg."

"I escaped the police there (the United States) and went back on foot across the ice — I nearly froze to death."

The papers reported him missing until he surfaced in LaSalle at his father's place.

Vital Benoit

His father, Vital Benoit, one of the richest bootleggers in the border region, owned hotels throughout the area including the Chateau LaSalle.

"It used to be the old Wellington . . . oh, about 1898. We were raised there, and when Prohibition came, my father sold it, then he built the big house further down the road.

"Everyone thinks these people, like my father, were bootleggers, but they weren't because every time one of these guys came from Detroit with a canoe, with a speedboat or a launch, and brought ten cases of whiskey back with him. He had to sign a declaration and had to pay duty, so those guys weren't bootleggers, they were exporters.

"You see my dad had the sole agency of all the Corbey's whiskey at this end . . . he had all the Labatt's beer at one time too.

"We had a big tug at one time, and they used to pull in at Port Stanley (Ontario) and put 1,500 cases of beer on this tug and come around and land at my dad's slip at LaSalle. As I said he was the sole outlet for Labatt's beer at this end. This was during Prohibition . . . this would be about 1921, 1922.

"Then we built Hoffer Brewery in LaSalle about '24 or '25 . . . my dad was in that . . . he owned about sixty per cent of that at that time...

"But my dad made a lot of money in real estate long before all this, you know. He bought all those farms around where the steel plant (Canadian Steel Corporation) was going to be...

and he sold it to the steel company. My dad's the one who built what they call the Seven Mile Road . . . he was in with three others and built that road. (It's the main thoroughfare from Windsor to LaSalle and Amherstburg.)

"You know my dad was the one who had LaSalle incorporated . . . he was the first mayor of LaSalle . . . At one time the street cars only went as far as the Wellington Hotel and then they went back to Windsor . . . this is long before the bootlegging business . . . my dad built those streetcar lines.

Vital Benoit, born in Pain Court, Ontario, was a giant in the hotel business. He not only owned the Wellington (or Chateau LaSalle) but he owned the Royal Oak, which burned to the ground, the one-time Farmer's Roost (now 917 Walker Road), the Bridge House for about three years, and, of course, he owned the former Windsor Hotel on Pitt Street.

"I remember his general store . . . and he had a post office. Then, Vital Benoit's was the only outlet at that time. They used to bring whiskey from the basement of the hotel in barrels, and my dad's hotel was the only whiskey outlet from Windsor to Amherstburg. All these farmers used to have to come to the Wellington to get a gallon of whiskey . . .

"My dad was the one who built up LaSalle. You know, the streets there are named after us kids . . . my brothers and sisters . . . there's Elseworth, Allan, Robert, Nora, May, Violet . . . and of course me, Milton . . ."

When Vital Benoit came to LaSalle in 1898, he purchased the Wellington Hotel and all the property right to the channel for $1,400. He put in the first channel behind the hotel, "and the people would come in with their launches . . . boy, my mother cooked many a thousand fish, frog and chicken dinners for seventy-five cents..."

During Prohibition, Whitey remembers his father purchasing whiskey for people in LaSalle.

"He could buy up to 100 cases of whiskey for personal use — that's during Prohibition . . . my dad would give these people the money to buy it, and it would naturally be his, and he would give them a couple of dollars for buying it. The stuff used to come from Quebec at that time . . .

"And these people would put the cases in their basement and if somebody wanted fifty cases of liquor, my dad was the one to call, and he'd tell the guy to bring his boat and he'd get the stuff from one of the places where the booze was stored . . . from one of those basements of his neighbors . . . then the guy would come and get it and take it to Detroit."

Whitey broke into crime under his father's tutelage during Prohibition. His earliest dealings go back to Mac's Bar on Jefferson Avenue in Detroit where he passed "hot diamonds" to the famed Purple Gang. The diamonds came from Toronto and he took them across the border to be sold to the gang and delivered the money, "and I, of course, got my cut, too."

Those, too, were the days when he was a bouncer in the local "cathouses" in Windsor. From his size and strength even now, one wouldn't doubt why he was hired.

Pitt Street was where all the action was in Windsor. Most of the traffic was from Michigan, "and with five or six guys in the car you knew what they were looking for . . ."

In those days, Whitey said, the madam who ran the brothels, gave business cards to winos who initialed them and passed them over to those looking for a good time.

"They would get paid a buck for every one that came through . . ."

Most prostitutes, brought in from Quebec during the Depression, operated out of twelve or fourteen houses on Pitt Street.

"They were beautiful . . . young . . . some only fifteen . . . came from big families . . . and didn't have much money . . . but after they got going they could make up to a $1,000 a week.

Windsor whorehouses paid off the authorities and prostitution flourished. Whitey was paid $1,000 once to take a "fall" for a madam. He spent two months in jail but got a $150 suit as a bonus.

Whitey has about the best education money can buy. He attended Loyola College in Montreal. All this education, Whitey said, has aided him in the "paper" profession, as forgery is known.

According to Maclean's, Benoit had a band of cheque-passers spread across Ontario and Quebec and forged cheques in a gully near his place in Tillsonburg, Ontario were he also ran "a cathouse and blind pig."

Police couldn't find the forging equipment. They even ripped up the floor in his hotel room.

His system was nearly foolproof but an informer gave it away. Whitey did four years for that one.

"No one questioned Benoit's authority," the Maclean's article says, "he never passed a cheque himself but he was the boss, the brains."

The article said, "they (the authorities) knew he had been in the racket for fifteen years and he had served only one six-month stretch for a bad cheque passed in Kitchener."

This luxurious home in LaSalle was built to Vital Benoit's specifications during Prohibition. It was just down the road from his roadhouse, the Chateau LaSalle (where Whitey was born) and the Hoffer Brewery, which he also owned.

The system was so tight that it even worked if a clerk got suspicious. A cheque passer attempted to cash a phoney paycheque in a shoe store and the clerk called the company listed on the cheque. Benoit had someone manning a telephone booth to answer the call and verify employment. Whitey laughs about how he fooled the police for years by signing cheques with his left hand. The police always took writing samples made with his right hand. He said he can still copy anyone's signature after studying it for five minutes.

Whitey is just taking it easy now. Why bother with anything else now, he shrugs. He's not living badly.

"The street isn't the same anymore . . . it used to be quite a place . . . but now I don't even lock my door anymore . . . it wouldn't matter anyway because they know better than to break in on me."

Occasionally newcomers to Pitt Street challenge Whitey. A recent challenger found himself sailing through the front door of a pub.

Standing there looking down the street, there is no doubt he is still the undisputed king here.

A Congressional Directory always provided some enlightenment.

Chapter Ten

The Amiable Giant of Prohibition — James Scott Cooper

James Cooper was one of the few giants from the Prohibition Era to die rich. Having raised himself from humble beginnings and working as an office boy and "news butcher" Cooper became one of the wealthiest and most powerful liquor barons in Canada.

The bright, amused eyes and the crooked bow tie epitomized the congenial and unpredictable nature of James Cooper. His photographs in the newspapers seemed to reflect a peculiar blend of playful enthusiasm and reckless daring. Cooper was a man of adventure, an enterprising hustling speculator, an experimenter, a thinker and a tireless worker, who would sit amid a stack of newspapers and financial reports in his chauffeur-driven car on his way to the office, absorbed in reading about the latest inventions and money developments. It was a good life — people catering to his every whim, opening doors, doing their utmost because of who he was. His name commanded attention and respect. He was the ostentatious millionaire who built the luxurious and enviable Cooper Court, a rambling, grand mansion that earned him a position among the elite of the financial set in the town named after liquor baron Hiram Walker.

But Cooper wasn't part of that snooty, self-righteous class of Walkerville. More than anyone else who had accumulated a fortune during Prohibition, James Cooper remembered his past. His quick ascent to wealth had not blurred the vivid memory of what it had been like to struggle and what it had been like to be poor. Cooper benevolently dispensed his riches, channelling great amounts of money into orphanages, schools, recreational schemes and farming ventures. He was considered a likeable philanthropist.

Like so many in Walkerville, Cooper's fortune was earned in booze. But in one sense, James Cooper was never considered to be a bootlegger. He never rowed boats laden with crates of whiskey, and he never stole silently from Windsor carrying illicit shipments of liquor to Detroit's blind pigs. Cooper was far more conservative and clever. Instead he sought and found the inevitable loophole in the laws, whereby he could sell and deliver liquor to Ontario residents on a completely legal basis.

Although Ontario had voted for Prohibition in October 1919, residents were still permitted to purchase liquor for "home use." Since saloons, bars and traditional liquor outlets were boarded up, booze for private consumption had to be imported. Ontario's distilleries and breweries were not allowed to sell stock to Ontario residents on a direct basis. As a result, Quebec's distilleries became the main suppliers of Demon Rum — until James Cooper's arrival on the scene.

Cooper had discovered there was nothing in the law to prevent Ontario distilleries from filling any orders not originating *within* the province, he could set up shop across the river in Detroit and take orders over the telephone from customers in Windsor. He worked both on a commission basis

Jim Cooper, the amiable philanthropist, who worked his way up from news vendor to millionaire selling booze in huge quantities. He was one of the very few bootleggers to die rich — which he did, mysteriously, on a German ocean liner in 1931.

for Hiram Walker and Sons and as a director for Dominion Distillery products and virtually gave Hiram Walker the green light in making deliveries of its products.

A close associate of Cooper's told the *Border Cities Star* (February 16 1931), "He simply walked into his Detroit office in the morning, picked up the Ontario orders and cheques on his desk, and came back across the river to leave them at the distillery. The firm would then make deliveries in Ontario or elsewhere, on the strength of those orders. This was quite legal." And it was an arrangement that lasted for two years. It was Cooper's brand of importation, since the distillery in Windsor merely acted as a warehouse, while the liquor was really being sold from Detroit.

When Ontario laws changed to prohibit importation, Cooper immediately took up the lucrative "export" business. Appointed by the Walker distillery as its agent, in a very real sense Cooper became "the businessman bootlegger." Arrangements were made on paper and conducted behind a desk, but liquor was still the commodity — and it was being funnelled into blind pigs and bootlegging joints in Detroit like all the illicit intoxicants flowing from Windsor ports. Cooper's exports appeared legal and above board, but there was no denying it — in some people's estimation, Cooper was a bootlegger. He was no different than the other exporters at the Mexico Export Company and the Bermuda Export Company, who directed massive cargoes of Demon Rum from the more than ninety docks that crowded the shoreline of the Detroit River. But because of Cooper's manner and his bearing, he appeared less corrupt than the others who openly bribed provincial officers in isolated railway sidings at night. Cooper managed to escape those shady dealings and the accompanying reputation. He cleverly created for himself an esteem in the community as a charming financier with an altruistic nature.

The son of William Cooper, a locomotive engineer who was killed in a train accident on the Grand Trunk line, James Cooper was born in London, Ontario in 1874. He attended school there, and his teachers, who considered Cooper to be a bright scholar, predicted a successful career for him. Following high school, he went into routine office work, first with H. Leonard and Sons in London, and then for the Grand Trunk. After two or three years, a dispirited Cooper asked to be transferred to a brakeman's job. Shortly afterwards, he quit the Grand Trunk to work for the Pere Marquette Railway out of Detroit. From there he landed a job as a "news butcher," selling candies, cigarettes, fruits and newspapers on the trains running between London and Rochester, New York. On one of these runs Cooper met his first wife. A few years later she died, leaving him a "tidy" estate.

From there, Cooper drifted from job to job, and eventually was appointed manager of a large brass foundry in New York, where he remained for several years. Returning in 1910 to the Windsor-Detroit area, he operated several saloons, speculated in real estate and soon came to be recognized as a flashy promoter. In 1918, one of his schemes not only attracted wide attention but helped revolutionize farming in Essex County. Cooper bought a 105-acre farm near Belle River and set about to tile the acreage so that spring planting could commence ten to fifteen days earlier than normal. Draining with clay tiles was something that had never been tried in the rural areas outside Windsor. Cross ditches were the only means of drainage. Tiling seemed like an expensive and risky proposition, but it proved to be the long awaited innovation needed in Essex County's farming community.

Cooper's success with the experiment spread, and soon neighboring farmers wanted to tile their own farms, but none could afford to. Learning of this, the adventurous Cooper declared he would sell tiles at cost to farmers. When they agreed, Cooper hired a crew to commence construction of a tiling factory on his own farm. In no time at all, the new business was manufacturing more than 10,000 tiles and 20,000 bricks daily.

The Belle River experiment led to other experiments. Cooper's ideas on increasing yields per acre led to a reversal in the trend of importing large shipments of fresh vegetables from the United States. Cooper proved that Canadian farmers could be self-sufficient. He constructed gigantic greenhouses, introduced new crops to Essex County and even demonstrated that southwestern Ontario could curb the large importation of eggs by setting up extensive hatcheries to meet its own market demands. In time, Cooper had fashioned a small reputation for himself, but this was nothing compared to what the Twenties would bring, for with Prohibition he would become a giant of his time. It was from his Detroit order office that Cooper made his fortune. But this didn't mean he abandoned farming or his experiments and investments in agriculture. In fact, farming was Cooper's "first love." He told a newspaper reporter at the height of his liquor wealth that all he had ever wanted to be was a farmer, that urban living had never appealed to him and had never brought him much satisfaction.

Cooper's investments in agriculture were vast and unusual for his time, and they had a major effect upon southwestern Ontario. Cooper

The first Cooper Court, built during Prohibition for a mere $40,000, but not quite to his liking. He decided to move downtown, to Walkerville.

virtually revolutionized the egg and poultry industry in Essex County, developed orchard and grape production, introduced tobacco farming, boosted the dairy and cattle industry, initiated the widespread practice of deep ploughing and mechanized farming, created muskrat farms, increased sugar beet yields and established enormous sheep ranches. Cooper's influence knew no bounds and was matched only by his incredible generosity and devotion. Farm boys, for example, were handpicked by Cooper to be sent, all expenses paid, to the Ontario Agricultural College at Guelph to learn about the most advanced and innovative methods in farming. Mechanized farm equipment was scattered and moved from farm to farm to enable farmers to increase efficiency, and to meet the heavy marketing demands of farmers in the district, Cooper also built the Belle River Seed and Grain Company.

The must ambitious venture for Cooper, however, was at St. Anne's Island near Wallaceburg. Here in 1925 and 1926, he leased the entire 2,600-acre island and developed the land. He built dikes and canals and homes for his crews. In 1928 his efforts began to pay off. From 300 acres of tobacco alone, Cooper's return was more than $65,000.

At the center of this whirlwind of rural activity stood Cooper. His influence, power and money seemed to be symbolized in the first Cooper Court he built — the massive, two-storey structure at Belle River. Constructed in 1920 at a cost of $40,000, today the building is a hotel and restaurant. Four years later when the huge profits and demands of Prohibition began to roll in, Cooper commenced work on a new Cooper Court at Walkerville. This second mansion, into which James Cooper moved in 1925, far outshone the first, and in fact, virtually overwhelmed all of Walkerville, surpassing even the grand Willistead built by Chandler Walker, a son of Hiram Walker I.

The magnificent forty-room Cooper Court at Walkerville occupied an entire city block and cost James Cooper more than $200,000. The colossal organ which piped music to every room in the mansion and played music rolls like a player piano but with complete fidelity of natural tone, cost Cooper more than $50,000. In one wing of the building there was a conservatory and a terrazzo-tiled swimming pool. The large pool was an all-glass enclosure with a domed roof. Dozens of potted plants adorned the ledges of the pool or hung from the glass roof. Dressing rooms were provided at either side. The top floor of the home was taken up almost entirely by a large ballroom, but off to one end there was the billiard room. This was also used as a schoolroom for the Cooper children when the family first

The second Cooper Court, which outshone other mansions in the area by far. Taking up an entire city block, it had an indoor swimming pool, and a massive pipe organ, which delivered music to each of the forty rooms. All that remains of the last Cooper home are the gate house and a meagre faded sign.

moved there. James Cooper had arranged for a nun to call every day and direct the education of his son and two daughters. The children also studied French and music. At the other end of the ballroom, Cooper had ordered a cedar lined room to store winter clothing and furs, and next to this, had an exercise room designed, equipped with rubbing tables and an electric reducing cabinet

But life in Walkerville wasn't so glorious for Cooper. Throughout the Twenties when prosperity and good times reigned, besides being tormented relentlessly by inquiries into huge liquor profits and widespread smuggling, Cooper was also plagued by high blood pressure and hardening of the arteries which eventually required a move to Switzerland.

James Cooper, whose influence and money extended to distilleries and major shipping and export companies, became the obvious target of the Federal Government's scrutiny into wrongdoing and unpaid duties. Cooper fought the issues head on, vehemently claiming at a 1926 parliamentary committee in Ottawa, investigating Customs duty on liquor, that Hiram Walker and Sons, for which he acted as an agent, had not defrauded the Canadian Government. At the dramatic Stevens Customs Committee hearings, Cooper dramatically unfolded the background operation of liquor exports. He said

Dominion Distillery Products, of which he had been a director, purchased liquor from Hiram Walker and Sons and sold it to their customers. Cooper also acted as a "go-between" for both companies, and as a result would tack on his own profits. Those profits amounted to one dollar per case for Dominion Distillery Products and one dollar for Cooper.

Under questioning, Cooper calmly admitted that he sold liquor to "a whiskey jobber" by the name of Scherer in Detroit. He said he didn't know the whereabouts of the rumrunner, but confessed if he needed to make a deal with Scherer, he could be contacted through the Statler Hotel in Detroit. Cooper emphasized that duty on those shipments to Scherer, and others like him, had already been paid to the Canadian Government, emphasizing, too, that liquor he bought from Hiram Walker and Sons, had never been "short circuited" to Windsor locations, thereby failing to clear Customs.

But Cooper wasn't off the hook. A Royal Commission investigation in 1927 revealed more of the intrigue in the liquor trade. An angry Cooper disrupted proceedings in Windsor when he claimed he had been coerced into paying into "a rat fund" organized by A. F. Healey, a former member of Parliament (1923-1925), now president of Mutual Finance Company and Guaranty Trust.

Cooper told former Ontario Liberal Leader N.

W. Rowell, the commission's counsel, that, "We have a politician here named Healey. He was elected to Parliament. A week after he was elected he called me to his office and told me to see William Eagan, a lawyer here. I went out and saw Eagan in front of Tim Healey's office, and he told me I had to pay two dollars a case on all liquor I exported and twenty-five cents a keg on beer. I kicked, but I paid him $272 right there.

"Eagan said to me, 'That's not enough,' so I went back to Tim Healey. I kicked, but he told me I'd have to see the 'Big Man.' I asked him who that was and he said it was John O'Gorman of Toronto."

Told to go to the Prince Edward Hotel (Windsor) to meet O'Gorman, who was also connected with the Super Cement Company in Detroit, Cooper went to see him, but told O'Gorman he wouldn't pay "another cent."

Copper confided to Rowell that all he ever paid to Healey's associates was $272, but then his troubles commenced. He said Healey's legal influence and position caused him undue complications with exports and eventually resulted in Cooper having to pay out more than $1,000 per carload for exported whiskey.

Healey denied Cooper's accusations to the *Border Cities Star* that same day (May 6 1927), pointing out that Cooper had in fact come to his office and boasted "of owning nearly every prominent official along the border and hinting that if I would cooperate with him there would be millions for me." Healey told the *Star* that he ordered Cooper to leave "and stay out."

When Healey appeared before the Royal Commission's hearings in Hamilton a week later, he told Rowell under questioning that he knew nothing about "the rat fund," and that Cooper instead should be under scrutiny because of his illicit liquor business.

Healey who had been elected in a by-election in 1923 said, "He (Cooper) came into my office and told me, 'I have something to show you. I have my books with me,' and he (Cooper) took of his hat and reached into the lining of his hat and said, 'These are my books.' He took out two slips of paper about the size of an ordinary letterhead, and then proceeded to unfold the greatest tales it has ever been my experience to hear, and named prominent people on both sides of politics."

Healey also acknowledged that Cooper had boasted of earning more than $6 million a year from liquor sales and exports and urged him to cooperate so that he could share in these profits. Cooper wanted Healey to use his influence in government to bring about relaxed liquor export

Helen Cooper, wife of James Cooper.

laws. But Healey refused, and again denied ever knowing about a "rat fund."

Cooper's lawyers didn't press the matter, and Healey's charges were left unchallenged. The focus of the commission also switched to other export companies who were defrauding the Canadian Government, and soon Cooper's revelations were ignored.

Toward the end of the Twenties, Cooper decided to leave Walkerville and take up residence in the high altitudes of Switzerland. His illness had left him nearly an invalid. Two weeks before his death in 1931, Cooper returned to Southwestern Ontario on a business trip, but had to disembark the train at London, Ontario, because he had been overcome by sickness. The *Border Cities Star* (February 10 1931) reported that "finding that he (Cooper) was unable to complete his trip to the Border Cities, he sent word to Belle River for Mr. M. V. Pougnet (his secretary and business manager) to go to London, where Mr. Cooper and his secretary conferred for three days. Mr. Cooper left London a week ago yesterday, remarking that he intended to take the first fast liner across the Atlantic."

Cooper hastened to New York and bought passage aboard the *S. S. Deutschland*. It was on this journey across the Atlantic that the

Walkerville millionaire fell overboard and drowned. His body was never recovered. News of the mishap reached Windsor February 10 1931 when Helen Cooper, Cooper's wife, sent a cablegram from Vevey, Switzerland that "Daddy fell overboard yesterday. Body not recovered."

Pougnet told the *Star* that when he had seen Cooper a week earlier in London, Ontario he was "despondent" over his health and that "he could not understand why he was as ill as he was, and why he should have to suffer as he did, after trying to do so much good."

But despite his illness, some concluded that Cooper actually fled the Border Cities because federal authorities and Michigan bootlegging gangs were fast on his heels. Some suggest he actually cut short his Southwestern Ontario visit because he learned that he might be the target of vindictive gang leaders from Detroit who felt they had been cheated during the bootlegging days of the Twenties.

When Cooper died he left an estate of $488,892 to his wife Helen and their three children. That amount did not include the Walkerville mansion, which years before had been transferred into his wife's name. Cooper also left behind the Belle River Cooper Court and more than 500 acres of farmland at Belle River, St. Joachim and Tilbury, in addition to the large stake he had in St. Anne's Island near Wallaceburg.

Cooper's financial empire had been vast and diverse. It had been built on ingenuity, clever insights into the existing laws and loopholes of government regulations — and it had been built on booze. The liquor industry had raised Cooper from obscurity to the pinnacle of Walkerville's high society. But unlike many from that era who had made big money from whiskey, Cooper resisted the temptation to invest in the stock market, and as a result was one of the few to emerge unscathed from the October 1929 crash. His business manager said Cooper "had never lost a dime."

Pougnet told the newspapers at the time of Cooper's death that the Walkerville millionaire's only fault was his big hearted generosity. He conceded that although Cooper was wealthy, "he gave it away as fast as he got it," and noted that the public's memory of Cooper's philanthropy was "only an inkling of the magnitude of Mr. Cooper's gifts." Pougnet said Cooper preferred to keep his gifts private, but they extended far and wide. In Belle River, Cooper built the town's first high school, the first ball park and even paid for all the children in Belle River to have haircuts and their teeth fixed. In London, Ontario, the town of his birth, Cooper poured his money into two orphanages, and every year, transported the children to Port Stanley for an annual picnic for which he picked up the tab.

Cooper, like Harry Low and other giants during Prohibition, was a legend in his own time. In the lengthy *Border Cities Star* obituary, there are countless stories about how Cooper had never turned his back on southwestern Ontario or its people and those who had helped him in his youth. One recounts how he had been stopped by an elderly wayfarer for a handout, and Cooper, recognizing this was the same man who had given him a silver dollar when he was down and out, checked the man into the Prince Edward Hotel and lavished food and new clothing on him.

But there was the vindictive side of Cooper, too, who opened his door one time to a tramp who he instantly remembered as the one who had been responsible for having Cooper tossed off a Grand Trunk passenger train when he was a boy. The man lied to the conductor, saying that Cooper tried to steal a free ride aboard the train. Cooper had not forgotten, and ordered the man removed from the premises and even threatened to set his dog on him.

The only vestige of that time and the extravagant forty-room mansion in Walkerville is a coach house which still sits inside an iron gate bearing the faded sign, "Cooper Court." The sprawling grand home had to be dismantled and the land sold, as it became too expensive to keep up. Other than this, the memory of James Cooper is virtually erased, except for the few oldtimers who still remember hobnobbing with the amiable giant of Walkerville.

Waiter at the old Norton-Palmer Hotel, which was a notorious haven for bookie activity, the day that beer went back on sale.

Section Four

LIQUOR FLOWED AND THE DICE ROLLED

The Rendezvous. The Rendezvous' windows face east and west and were manned by spotters watching for police. Gambling and drinking were relegated upstairs, while one could indulge in heaping platters of chicken and seafood on the main floor.

Chapter Eleven

The Roadhouses

The shoreline of the Detroit River was like a diamond-studded bracelet with each glittering jewel a roadhouse. Michiganders nightly traversed the mile-wide river to moor their yachts till the first glimpses of dawn and then putt safely home back to the American docks. They were on the Canadian side to feast upon the hearty seafood and chicken dinners, soak up the lush, elaborate speakeasies and toss away easy-come, easy-go money in long, bustling, upstairs rooms crammed with gambling tables and flappers.

This was the Twenties in the Border Cities. It was the age when men wore floppy tweed caps, slicked their hair back like Valentino, wore spats, smoked Omar cigarettes or Player's Navy Cut and carried revolvers. It was the age of kiss-curl ladies, chiffons, printed art crepes and hats with vagabond crowns. It was the age when parents washed their children with Lifebuoy soap and their clothes with Rinso "the cold water washer" . . . then sped to the roadhouses for a night out to take in a little Bye Bye Blackbird, the Charleston, jazz bands . . . and, of course, to roll the dice and drink.

On those nights the music filtered out from the wide verandas and gingerbread barrooms of these fabulous roadhouses, and everyone within was lost in the mad whirl of music and dancing . . . safe in the knowledge that although it was illegal to guzzle and gamble, trusty beady-eyed "spotters" stationed in second-storey windows or makeshift towers were ready to sound the alarm, warning of a police raid. And if the law successfully got wind of the illicit gambling and liquor, it was only a matter of minutes before the booze was rolled away behind false walls or into hideaway cupboards along with the gambling paraphernalia. All that remained for the police to view were the huge steaming platters of perch, frog legs and chicken . . . hastily carried out to bored customers accustomed to such interruptions.

There are remnants of those days. Alice Vuicic,

owner of the **Rendezvous Tavern** at Tecumseh, Ontario, can push open a storeroom wall panel on the second floor of the restaurant to display where gambling equipment had been stashed when the warning was sounded. That entire second floor during the Twenties consisted of two large rooms for customers specifically wanting to drink and gamble.

Mrs. Vuicic wasn't the owner then, but discovered the false walls several years ago when her husband, George, left Kirkland Lake to buy the hotel. The Rendezvous had been one of several roadhouses in Essex County built close to the water to provide easy access for illegal shipments of liquor. It was also the typical Canadian establishment with a relatively relaxed speakeasy atmosphere for Michigan residents who motorboated across the river or lake.

Few of these roadhouses exist today. Those that do are now catering to the country and western or disco crowds. Among the survivors from the Twenties are the **Chateau LaSalle** in LaSalle and the **Westwood** in Ojibway at the western extremity of the riverfront. (There is also the **Sunnyside,** a mile from the Chateau LaSalle, but it was completely rebuilt after a fire destroyed it in 1972.) Also on the west side, but in Windsor, is the **Chappell House.** In later years it was called the **Lido Tavern,** but all that remains of it are the charred ruins of once a grand roadhouse. It was here that the fanatical Reverend J. O. L. Spracklin* shot and killed Babe Trumble.

To the east, there is the **Bellvue, Abars Island View** and, of course, the **Rendezvous.**

Michael Vuicic, general manager of the Renedezvous, said the food may have been good in the Twenties — large helpings of perch, pickerel, frogs legs, chicken — but the meals were really "a front" for the gambling and drinking.

*A profile of Spracklin and the Chappell House slaying appears in Chapter 13.

The Buzzer Bar. The bar at the Rendezvous was called "the buzzer bar" because it was rigged with an alarm system warning of impending raids by the police. When the Vuicics replaced the old bar, they had to tear out all of the wires from the antiquated buzzer system.

"You could eat all the perch you wanted downstairs for fifty cents . . . and upstairs there was the gambling and the booze."

When the old bar was removed and replaced several years ago, the simple, but reliable, old buzzer system was torn out. "This place was wired in with four other roadhouses — the **Edgewater Thomas Inn, Abars Island View,** the **Golden House** and **Tecumseh Tavern.**

"They would buzz that the police were on the way and all the stuff would be stashed."

Vuicic said bottles were flung from the second-storey windows into a moat fronting the building. It was also from this second floor that spotters were situated to watch the movements of the police. Old photographs of the Rendezvous reveal just how deliberate the builders of the roadhouse were in the placement of the windows which face the east and west routes of the road. If a raiding party was spotted, the buzzer would be hit to warn the other hotels that a raid was about to occur.

The Rendezvous was built in 1926 by Wilf and Harold Drouillard, who leased it to Danny Bell

Sr., who in turn leased it to the Vuicics in 1943. The roadhouse was finally bought by the Vuicics in 1946.

At the time of that purchase, the roadhouse was dilapidated. It had been neglected for several years by Danny Bell, who was also operating two other places — the Bellvue and the **Royal Tavern.** These were far more popular than the Rendezvous after Prohibition. Bell only kept the Rendezvous in order to secure a larger beer quota from the Ontario Government. Vuicic said Bell's routine was to send his men over in a pickup truck to load up the beer and haul it downtown.

"I know this because when my father bought it, Bell's men arrived to pick up a load of beer. My father told them they couldn't have it because he now ran the hotel."

The two large second floor rooms of the Rendezvous were altered after Prohibition because the new laws in Ontario stipulated that an establishment had to have at least six rooms to have a licence to serve beer. Bell built the six bedrooms but they were never used, according to Mrs. Vuicic.

The Edgewater Thomas Inn was run by the lovable Bertha Thomas, who paid off police officers and gave away money generously to orphans and the poor. Bertha built the Edgewater from a small time restaurant into a fashionable hotel.

"In those days, you'd do just about anything to stay in business," she said.

The only surviving hotel that was wired in with the Rendezvous is Abars Island View, a towering three-storey building, the name of which derived from the Hebert family, the original owners. A fisherman, Henri Hebert, in 1893 registered the trade name, "Abars," because he found the French pronunciation of his name was more familiar in its anglicized spelling. The hotel remained in the family for three generations, and the name became a symbol of fine cuisine. Built to serve the stagecoach lines, the hitching rail at the front entrance remained long after automobiles made their appearance. At the turn of the century, the roadhouse became a leading nightspot on the waterfront and lured high society visitors from Detroit. Formal dress was the order and local patrons were sometimes discouraged from dining there.

At the entrance sat the flamboyant Mrs. Hebert, dressed in jewels and furs, to greet her guests — the Fishers, the Dodges, the Fords, Jack Dempsey, Al Capone . . . or team members of the Detroit Tigers and New York Yankees who often crossed the river to come to Abars because regulations forbade them to be seen in Detroit speakeasies. They directed their launches into the slips and docks provided behind the roadhouse which sat right at the mouth of the Detroit River.

The Golden Hotel in Tecumseh, which shared the buzzer system with Abars and Rendezvous, burned in 1976. It was ninety years old, originally known as the **Bedell Hotel.** One of the four original inns in the community, the Golden had a livery stable for its customers and large open facilities for eating and drinking.

Alphonse Pitre and his wife purchased the hotel from the Town of Tecumseh during Prohibition and operated it for fourteen years. His inn, along with the Tecumseh Tavern, was a good "stopping off" spot for travellers. The Tecumseh Tavern, built in 1903, was destroyed by fire in February 1977.

Bertha Thomas in early years with an unidentified companion.

But of all the inns and roadhouses the Edgewater Thomas Inn was the most unique and remained the most fashionable eating and drinking spot in the Windsor area. The inn, owned by the eccentric wealthy Bertha Thomas, burned in 1970. It had been called Martini's at that time. All that remains is the stone residence that once stood adjacent to the original roadhouse.

Maclean's in an August 1953 article described the old Edgewater and Bertha: "Of all the inns around Windsor, Bertha Thomas' place was the most popular. Bertha was buxom, beautiful, full of personality, a Canadian counterpart of Manhattan's Texas Guinan. Her meals were good, her drinks were good, her band was lively."

Bertha was legendary. People recall her with fondness and admiration. She was considered "a pioneer" in the restaurant and roadhouse business in the Detroit-Windsor area. As the former Bertha Haf of Detroit, she came to Windsor as a widow to purchase a small three room riverside eating place. She cooked meals and served customers herself until she could afford both additional space and waiters. In the Twenties, the Edgewater Thomas Inn with its

gingerbread entrances, mahogany panelled walls, its fabulous "shore dinners," the hideaway gambling and plush interior, became a favorite of Detroiters. As business increased and her popularity as a hostess grew, Bertha added more and more space. By her death in 1955, Bertha operated one of the most widely-known and patronized dining and partying establishments in the area.

But it was during the Twenties that Bertha made her reputation. Thomas' Inn was equipped with secret passageways and hidden wine cellars. During Prohibition it only took the "tip of a stick" and the shelf of liquor slid down a chute. Moments later bottles of soda and soft drinks appeared in their place. Musicians had duties, too, when Thomas' Inn was the target of a raid. Their chore was to rush to customers' tables and dump liquor from the glasses on to the well-padded carpets. On one occasion when a band member missed the rug and some of the booze splashed generously upon the dance floor, it was mopped up by the raiding party — with charges laid against Bertha. But the clever roadhouse owner wasn't to be outdone. She proved that the dance floor had been recently varnished and that the varnish used had contained, curiously enough, alcohol.

Bertha Thomas in later years.

"Spotter" for Bertha Thomas.

Bertha's parking attendants also had extra duties. Louis Baillargeon, for example, was officially employed to park the cars of customers, but in fact was used as a "spotter." Hired as a young boy by Bertha who felt Louis lacked the proper homelife and advantages of other children, she paid for his schooling and kept him at work. Before directing him to park cars, she sequestered Louis in a strategic window location of the hotel where he was duty bound to do his homework and keep his eye on the movements of the police.

Bertha was among the few roadhouse owners who didn't have to worry about the police. Often it meant she had to place ten-dollar bills on the floor in a trail leading from the entrance of the hotel to the back door exit. The police simply followed the path strewn with money — and left the inn without charging her under the liquor laws.

Bertha's wealth was attained during the Twenties, and throughout the years following Prohibition she dispensed it generously to the community. She often helped struggling friends by paying their mortgages. In later years, she gave fabulous Halloween parties for the children in Riverside, Ontario (now incorporated into Windsor).

"But if she didn't like you, you were in trouble," remembers a former Riverside Police officer, who added, "if she fancied you, then you were in good stead."

He said although many believed Thomas' Inn to be a fashionable nightspot, it was really "a high class blind pig," and when it burned many of the hidden rooms people often talked about were uncovered.

"She had all kinds of places to hide the booze . . . and there were buzzers all over the place . . . outside under the window sills or in the little shack they had for the parking boys . . . there were buzzers inside near the bar and in various other rooms . . . and there were false walls that would open up . . . she had it all figured out."

Bertha, he recalls, too, was "a real show girl," especially the time a Detroiter had fallen into the river near one of the docks behind the roadhouse.

"Well, Bertha jumped in after her, and of course, the police then had the task of saving both."

There was also the tragic moment when Bertha was robbed and beaten in the late Forties. Three fellows had broke into the roadhouse after the police had made its routine check on the place.

"Excuse the expression, but they really beat the piss out of her — I remember one fellow got twelve years for that and the other, eight."

No matter how many times Thomas' Inn was raided by the police during the Twenties, it was

The Chappell House. The hotel had a large ballroom and was a popular gambling and cockfighting spot. Here Reverend Spracklin shot the owner, "Babe" Trumble.

always back in business in less than ten minutes. "A fine was nothing to her," another policeman said. "It was just part of the operating expenses for Bertha."

Westward along the riverfront two other roadhouses which operated during Prohibition were the Bellvue (still open) and the **Westside** (now JP's Disco). The speakeasies and gambling atmosphere and the good food were the attractions, and the places stayed open all night long. Cars with Michigan and Ohio plates were a common sight, and pickups with shipments of illegal booze arrived boldly and regularly.

Sometimes roadhouse owners themselves delved enthusiastically into the gambling. One hotel owner, who had been losing all night, challenged another hotel owner to put his establishment against his. With a throw of a dice it was decided . . . and the challenger lost. The next day he made arrangements to transfer the ownership of his roadhouse to the winner.

Besides the roadhouses, there were regular hotels in Windsor, including the **British American,** the **Ritz** (not the present one) and the **Windsor Hotel**. These were not in the same class as the roadhouses, which had an easier and classier atmosphere.

Further to the west of Windsor the Chappell House was the dominating roadhouse. Built within a few feet of Sandwich Street, it had a sign over the entrance which read: "At All Hours." There were accompanying signs on the railings advertising frog legs, chicken and fish dinners.

This roadhouse with its prominent veranda was actually the second Chappell House. It was built by two brothers — Henry and Harley Chappell. They opened their first in 1865 on the Canadian Steel Corporation property in Ojibway nearby. They sold this and bought **Mineral Springs Hotel** in Sandwich, then in 1897 opened up the second Chappell House on the present site.

The Chappells ran the roadhouse until it was taken over by the Trumble family. But even before the Trumbles bought it, the roadhouse had gained a wide reputation for its sumptuous meals. The Trumbles ran the hotel until 1949.

Although today this roadhouse, the site of the Spracklin-Trumble shooting, is in ruin, evidence of Prohibition still exists. In a back room a strong box bearing the name "B. Trumble" had been left. It is a reminder of its former owner whose name blazed across the newspapers when he was

Westwood Hotel, a typical roadhouse with secret sliding shelves concealing bootleg liquor, was a haunt for rumrunners.

slain by the Methodist minister in 1920. The shooting came to be regarded as Prohibition in microcosm — the fanatical forces of Temperance pitted against the rumrunners and whiskey exporters.

Also, in the basement of the burned-out roadhouse, a "secret room," with simulated cement blocks made of wood still exists. The wooden blocks have been inserted into a brick wall to conceal a small room used to store liquor.

In those heady days of Prohibition, the Chappell House shared the atmosphere of other roadhouses with its extravagant parties and gambling, but it also offered the sport of gamecocks in the deep recesses of the rambling old building.

Near the Chappell House the **Westwood** had its share of parties and customers. Victor Bourdeau, its owner, sometimes shows customers a wooden shelf that slides out to reveal a small cache where liquor was once hidden away. The roadhouse, once owned by the Reaume family that gave Windsor one of its most colorful mayors (Art Reaume), at one time was closer to the Detroit River, but was moved to its present site.

Further along the Seven Mile Road, as it is known in Windsor, there are two roadhouses

which gained international reputations — the Chateau LaSalle and the Sunnyside. Oldtimers recall that some of the frequent visitors to the latter included Jean Harlow and members of the Purple Gang. Those were the days when slot machines lined the walls and 21-tables and crap tables dominated the large rooms. Liquor flowed easily and without end.

The Chateau LaSalle gained its reputation under the ownership of Vital Benoit who was regarded in the LaSalle area as the giant among rumrunners. The owner of the Hoffer Brewery next door and the man who paid for the streetcar tracks to bring customers from Windsor, Benoit's efforts in no time transformed the hotel into a popular haunt.

Chateau LaSalle is one of those hot spots of the Twenties which have survived and become as *Maclean's* declared "merely respectable . . . refined." The "giddy" decade, as the magazine described it, was reflected in their roadhouse style — the Venetian glass globes, the gingerbread and the flappers. Evidence of that era has all but disappeared except for the false walls and shelves and hidden rooms. These stand as reminders of the hectic pace and tone of Prohibition.

(above) American border patrol, with their speedboats, in harbor.
(below) The curses of strong drink.

YOU CAN'T DRINK LIQUOR AND HAVE STRONG BABIES
CAN YOU IMAGINE A COCKTAIL PARTY IN HEAVEN?
SOW ALCOHOL IN THE BODY, REAP **D**isease
isgrace
efeat
eath

FOR **My** own brother's country's **Sake** I WILL BE A TOTAL ABSTAINER

HOW IS ALCOHOL RELATED TO **F**oul ilthy iendish WORKS OF THE FLESH?

INDULGENCE IN ALCOHOL LEADS TO
Folly
Meanness
Sin
Disgrace
Misery
Disease
Insanity.

Section Five

THE LAW, THE CUSTOMS, THE TICKET COLLECTORS

The rumrunners were pitted against as surly a lot as their own — they had to face the beady eyed customs people, the policemen, the ferryboat operators, and, of course, the fanatical circuit riders or evangelists of Prohibition. The following unfolds briefly profiles of Charles Johnson of the Old Ford City Police department who battled bootleggers, of George Large who worked for Canada Customs and issued the infamous B-13 export papers to rumrunners, of William King who sold tickets to ferryboat travellers to the United States and, finally an abbreviated look at another commodity smuggled during Prohibition, and also includes the story of the Fighting Parson, Reverend J. O. L. Spracklin.

The Coast Guard, with the Detroit skyline behind.

Chapter Twelve

Officials on the Fringe

Rumrunners weren't the only individuals in the thick of Prohibition. So were the policemen. They broke down doors, axed crates of booze, dumped liquor into the water, arrested bootleggers, shut down blind pigs, and battled with fists and guns whiskey dealers throughout Prohibition. Sometimes they triumphed, other times they failed miserably.

Charles Johnson, now 81, is a retired policeman from the old Ford City Police Department and the Windsor Police department. He retired as a staff sergeant in 1963 after forty-four years in police work. When he started with the Ford City Police in 1919 he was a motorcycle driver. Later he was promoted to inspector. The force was amalgamated with Windsor in 1935 and he was appointed sergeant.

Johnson worked on just about every detail, from bomb squad and bootlegging to detective and homicide.

Johnson remembers Prohibition vividly. He says the "export docks," or the places from which liquor and beer were shipped out of the country, were strung out along the riverfront "like some huge bootlegging dream." The docks, he said, stretched from Lake St. Clair, the St. Clair River, the Detroit River and all the way to Amherstburg, Ontario. They even had an export dock on Pelee Island "where the Americans used to load up with whiskey and take it back across to the States side." Lake Erie's export docks, Johnson recalls, were devoted to serving Cleveland, Toledo and Akron, while the Detroit River "freight" was intended for Detroit and nearby parts in Michigan. The docks along the St. Clair River and Lake St. Clair shipped to Mount Clemens and Port Huron. Of course, these export docks were not supposed to be used as clearing houses for shipments to the United States. Booze was banned in the United States and the export papers only permitted the exporters to send it to countries where Prohibition wasn't in force. But the rumrunners merely marked other destination points on their B-13 papers and the booze was cleared through the Customs — then went to the United States instead.

"It was all a sham — I mean everyone knew what was going on, but you couldn't do anything to prevent it."

At the start of Prohibition, however, Johnson recalls bootleggers hauling booze from Montreal.

You used to be able to get it from Quebec, I recall, and with a twelve dollar money order. A person would get a case of whiskey, and they would ship it down here. The express charge would be $2.99. And then he could take it any place around the waterfront. If he had connections he could get $120 in American money. And the discount was twenty-two per cent on top of that.

So the biggest majority of the poor people used to buy one case of whiskey, and when they sold that case of whiskey they had enough money to buy twelve to fifteen more. That's how they made their money so fast, and you could sell every case you wanted. There was no limit. The Americans over there were paying $120 a case for it. That was in Detroit. But now in Cleveland, Ohio they tell me it was worth far more than that. Now I'm not sure, I couldn't prove that.

Johnson also recalls the Americans coming over to the Canadian side.

The Americans started coming over when it went dry over there (Volstead Act, January 1920), and they started buying everything they could get their hands on. One hundred cases was nothing at a time for these guys. I've seen 300 to 400 cases of beer going to Detroit in a big boat, one of those forty-five foot boats. They could take over 200 to 300 cases of whiskey, too.

Johnson recalls one bizarre case that led him into catching a rumrunner who was smuggling narotics as well as beer.

Yeah, there was a rumrunner from the other side (United States) who had come over and stole a top off an old boat — cut it right off. He just selected the size and shape he wanted, and sliced it right off. Of course we had an idea who it was, and we went across the river (Detroit River) in a boat to scout around. We found the top right on the property. Of course, I couldn't do anything about it because we didn't have any jurisdiction in the United States, so we called the Harbor Master. He wanted us to go down to City Hall in Detroit to press charges of theft under international law. Well, the man who owned the boat refused to prosecute or to press charges. He figured it would involve so many court days — maybe years — before it was settled, so he said for us to forget it. But we told him to press charges of theft on the Canadian side with the idea that when he returned we'd nail him. So, we waited for him — a long time, too, maybe two or three years.

Finally I got a telephone call from some woman one night. She said if we wanted to catch this boy he was down at one of the docks. So I took a couple of men with me and down we went.

He jumped in the river. I sent the sergeant down there, and they pulled him out of the river. I then grabbed him, handcuffed him and took him up and locked him up.

But when I was searching his boat I found he had a load of beer, but I also noticed some boxes about a foot-and-a-half long and about twelve inches high, cardboard boxes. I opened one, and saw that it was a box of cocaine. Another box contained morphine and opium. There were six or seven tubes half full, glass tubes of opium. So we had this joker locked up.

At that time we were unable to prosecute — it had to be a federal charge. The Mounted Police (Royal Canadian Mounted Police) had a detachment in Windsor. So I sent one of my men to get them. I turned the dope over to them, so they could prosecute. That rumrunner got three years in Kingston prison.

He was over here again two years later and the FBI from Detroit came over one day and looked me up and showed me a picture, and said "Do you know this man?" I said, "Yeah. Seen him the other day." He's wanted in about fifteen states for bootlegging." I said, "Well, I seen him the other day."

I had seen him at least two or three times before the FBI asked about him. He used to come down from Riverside and drive through old Ford City as if he was going to Detroit in his coupe. I used to see him about lunch time generally. So I told the FBI I'd keep a lookout for him, and sure enough the very next day, there he was. I whipped around in my car and stopped him.

I asked him, "Do you know they are looking for you on the other side?"

He replied, "I know that. That's why I'm over here.

So I said, "You won't be for too long. I'm going to take you in. You're wanted over there — the FBI has been searching all over for you."

The man tried to coax and beg me not to take him in, but I showed him the warrants out for his arrest. Then I took him and threw him in the can and called the FBI. They came over right away to get him. But they couldn't take him back to the United States — they had no jurisdiction. All the FBI could do was to get him charged under the Immigration laws. At that time if you made a declaration at the border crossing that you weren't wanted on any charges, they'd let you through Customs.

So the guy was charged under the Immigration laws . . . with the hope that he'd be deported, and once deported the FBI would nab him. But it didn't happen that way.

The judge let him out on $500 bail, and of course he went back to the States . . . but not under the watchful eye of the FBI . . . they missed him somehow. In any case they didn't catch him right away. I think there must have been indictments right through Detroit to California and Florida for him for bootlegging. And so anyway they finally chased him down somewhere and he got two years in the pen over there. They threw all the charges at him and put him away.

Later on I knew his buddy that used to work with him, and when the bootlegging was over (after Prohibition), he kind of straightened out. He got a job teaching school in Detroit. Anyway, this fellow told me one day what happened to this guy we had chased during the bootlegging days. He committed suicide. They found him in his bathroom one morning with half his head blown off. So that was the end of him."

Johnson recalls that besides the bootlegging, there was an extensive gambling racket in the Border Cities.

In those days when Prohibition started there was the odd poker game, crap games and whatnot . . . but in time they opened up huge halls. They had gambling, roulette wheels, crap games, poker games, fan-tan horse racing — that was all included in those gambling joints. And that ran all the way through Prohibition. It was big time here.

East Windsor had a lot of gambling. It was done mostly in the roadhouses, the out-of-the-way places, you know. They'd haul in the slot machines. They had anywhere from a nickel to a dollar machine going. But of course most of this stuff, I'm sure, was run from people from the States. They had all the money behind it.

WEEKLY · FILM · NEWS

ol. 1   No. 3!

DEVOTED TO THE INTERESTS OF THE J H KUNSKY THEATRICAL ENTERPRISES.

CONTROLLING
The
WASHINGTON
LIBERTY
GARDEN
ALHAMBRA
COLUMBIA
EMPRESS
ROYALE
CASINO
THEATRES

WEEK

September
5th
1915

J. Warren Kerrigan

DETROIT MICH
2206.12.DIME BANK BLDG.

"He'd collect money out of the slot machines. But that man finally got out of it. He started in the theatre business in Detroit..."

Years ago when I was a boy going to school, I remember there was a man who owned all the theatres in Detroit. He used to come over here and run one of those funeral cabs with a team of horses and he'd collect his money out of the slot machines. Of course he had to pay out so much a percentage on whatever they took in. Then he'd go home with a bag full of nickels, dimes, quarters, silver dollars . . . it was a good going operation for him . . .

But that man finally got out of it. He started in the theatre business in Detroit, and then he started in the radio business. He had a big home here situated on Riverside Drive in old Ford City, a million dollar home. And he got all that money from gambling and bootlegging. His name was John H. Kunsky, and he later changed it to John King. He was a Jewish fellow, a nice fellow, as I remember.

Johnson said besides gambling, prostitution was also a booming business in the Border Cities. Americans would come to Canada because the atmosphere was far more relaxed. The roadhouses were isolated from the towns and cities and far enough away from the police stations.

They used to get the girls from Quebec. They'd be fourteen to eighteen years of age. Beautiful looking girls, too, and they were in it for the

dough. The pimps would bring them down from Montreal and the rural areas of Quebec. Montreal was a clearance spot. They'd bring them right here to old Ford City. Walkerville was pretty clean. You'd never find them there. Sandwich wasn't too bad. Windsor was the worst. Pitt Street was literally infested with prostitutes.

The girls hung out at the Prince Edward and Norton Palmer right in downtown Windsor, trying to pick up trade, and there were streetwalkers right on Ouellette Avenue (the main street of Windsor), in fact, any place where they thought they could make a pickup that's where they went. And that was the main dough for these girls from Montreal. We used to snare them and throw them in the can. If we could prove our case, they'd get thirty days . . . and then they were right back on the street. But at that time you had to prove they had committed the act, you see, and that was difficult sometimes.

Chinese smuggling was also another lucrative business related to Prohibition, Johnson said.

Chinese smuggling was big business at one time. They used to have three or four different gangs out here in the City of Windsor. And they would take so much a head to take a Chinaman to the States. I've seen them load up five or six at one crack and take them across.

They used to say they put them in bags. Now, I've never actually seen this, but it's true from what I've been told. It was the talk all over Windsor. They used to put these people in big bags, weighted bags. If the United States patrol boats got too close to them, these rumrunners — they'd also be taking whiskey across — would drop them overboard. Whether that's true or not, I'm not sure.

The Chinamen that got through were scared. Contact used to be made here to take them across, and they'd be delivered to a certain spot over in the States. The rumrunners were never paid until they were actually delivered.

After the Chinese smuggling started, there was smuggling of other nationalities, and they'd take them in boatloads. Ten or fifteen or twenty at a crack. They'd never let them take anything with them, only what they were wearing. There were piles of suitcases left behind and those big wicker baskets. They wouldn't let them take a thing. Half the time the smugglers would just grab the stuff they were carrying and just throw it into the river and order the people (the aliens) to get into the boats.

Johnson said the rumrunners were a clever, brash lot. They became so attuned to running whiskey across the border that they had figured out all the angles. That meant bribes, clever ways of concealing the booze,

Daring rumrunners would slide under the ferry's fender, concealing themselves from the police and hitching a free ride.

designing faster and more efficient engines for speedboats, rigging up signals and lights, sending out decoy boats and "just plain outwitting the customs and police."

Johnson said, "There used to be a rumrunner who hauled liquor in a big Chandler or Studebaker. He had the back seat taken out.

He went over there one day and pulled right up to the Customs fellow and said, I'd like to speak to you fellows. You know, I'm a bootlegger." And the customs guy said, "Oh yeah?" And he knew it. Well the bootlegger asked him if a deal could be struck. He said, "I can come over loaded any day, and I'll give you so much a case." Well, this one officer was pretty honest, and he figured he was being pretty clever, so he agreed with the bootlegger that the next time he was making a haul of whiskey, he would give him the go-ahead sign and let him through Customs. So anyway, the two struck a deal and at the appointed time, the bootlegger drove over and this fellow, a Customs officer, was ready for him. He had two or three other Customs men with him, and they searched through the car from one end to the other, tore out the front seat and everything. Someone got underneath it, and they looked in the back and under the hood, in the trunk, everywhere. They

didn't find a thing. Not a drop of liquor anywhere. Nothing.

So the Customs fellow says to the bootlegger, "I thought you said you were going to bring over a load." And the bootlegger, smiling and all, said, "No. The day I was talking to you was the day I had the load."

But there were other ways, too, to get the booze across the border.

When the law was really hot, the patrol boats were really up and down, and it was practically impossible for smugglers to sneak ashore. The rumrunners used to go down and get underneath the ferries. The ferries were running at that time. They tied the end of the boat underneath the ferry which had a big guardrail, and that big guardrail extended well over the hood. They would tie their boat there and be towed across the river.

I met Al Capone. He was down here at one of the export docks. That's where you'd find these guys. They were here making deals. Capone seemed like a very nice fellow, very gentlemanlike. He was over here dickering with the exporters about liquor. He came down to see Harris and Caplan who ran an export dock. I suppose he wanted to know who was the best here to haul his liquor. Capone would take a thousand cases a day out of the docks here.

George Large, now 80, worked for Canada Customs in Windsor for forty-one years. He saw Prohibition from a unique vantage point — he issued B-13 papers to the rumrunners who supposedly were taking booze to faraway places but in fact hauled it across to Detroit. In the course of his work, he met the wealthy Jim Cooper, and after Prohibition, Large was involved in the seizure of Harry Low's vessel, the Vedas. Large was a Customs collector for four years and retired in 1965.

Large remembers the formation of the export docks soon after Prohibition came into effect in both the United States and in the Province of Ontario.

There was a leeway in the law. You could buy all the booze you wanted right here in Ontario, but you couldn't sell it here or serve it in the bars, but you could export it to any country that didn't have Prohibition. So that's what the exporters were doing, or at least, that's what they said they were doing.

Anyway, you could export liquor and beer from Ontario. You made your export papers out, what we called "B-13" papers, and you could export the stuff to St. Pierre Miquelon. From Windsor to St. Pierre.

The whiskey was loaded on these rowboats and big boats, good sized boats with outboard motors, and they were loaded in the daytime. You couldn't turn the papers in after five o'clock at night, so the rumrunners would load them in the daytime. And in the night they'd run across to the United States.

Of course when the boat would tie up, they would just start their motor up nice and easy — they were on the American side — just go to wherever they were going.

Then the federal officers couldn't see them coming across. They wondered how they were getting over there. That's how they were getting over there. They pulled that stunt on the Walkerville ferry, the Windsor ferry, and the Windsor car boats. And they hauled any amount of stuff over there that way. Especially when they put the heat on. They would have quite a number of patrol boats on that side of the river.

The rumrunners also used to get a good fast speedboat and fill it with empty boxes that looked like whiskey boxes.

They'd have the other boats all loaded with whiskey. This real fast boat would take off to the American side, and of course the feds and the patrol boat followed after him. While they were after him, the other boats would be sure to cross the river.

The rumrunners pulled that trick a good many times until the patrols got onto them, and then the patrols used to let the fast boat go and just sit there and wait and see if the rest would come. At night the rumrunners used to load those luggers down so low they only had a foot of free board, and they were so close to the water that it was hard to see them, unless they happened to get into a light and see something moving. They looked just like a big raft, that's what they looked like.

The rumrunners had plenty of ideas on how to avoid detection. Some of them tried to drive loads of whiskey across Lake St. Clair on the ice.

They would carry heavy planks and when they came to a piece of open water they made a bridge. Some of them got through but a lot of them were stopped by patrols.

We seized about 300 cases of whiskey in St. Joachim after a good sized boat ran up the Ruscome River to get away from police.

In those days a case of whiskey was worth about eighty-five dollars in American money and the exchange sometimes ran as high as twenty-two percent.

Large said the infamous American gangs — the Purple Gang, the Little Jewish Navy and even Capone's "hoods" were in the Border Cities continually during Prohibition.

Some of these boats were carrying eighty to 100 cases, maybe even 200 to 300, depending upon the size of the boats. This liquor was brought into Ontario and down to the export docks.

I remember working at Reaume's Dock near Brighton Beach (just outside of Windsor). The rumrunners would load up the boats. There might be 100 cases of beer for one boat, and they'd (rumrunners) hand us four B-13 papers for that one boat. We would take it and check it over. These forms were all signed and everything, made uptown, all typed neatly with the destination St. Pierre Miquelon, stamped on it. At five o'clock the boats would all be loaded up and that would be it.

When night came these fellows (rumrunners) would be back to pick up their shipments. They had signals when to leave and when not to leave. When it was the right time, they'd head across the river to Detroit.

These B-13 papers were really a farce. We all knew what was going on, and we knew the stuff was all going to Detroit, but it wasn't our jurisdiction. Once the stuff left the docks and left Canadian waters there wasn't a thing we could do. If it got diverted, that wasn't our fault.

After Prohibition I was working as a clerk in the old Post Office building right downtown. And as you went up the stairs, there was a little room on the left. It was kind of a storage room.

We used to take those export papers and put them in there before they were to be filed away.

Well, when I went up there two years after Prohibition ended, those export papers were still there. I think they were up there for two more years before they were thrown out. The Customs officials here never worked on them at all. They were never sent on to Ottawa where they were supposed to go. They were supposed to be sent on every day. We were asked to put them in there — in that room — until they had a chance to go through them. They never went to Ottawa at all. There were so damn many of them and they (the Customs) didn't have the staff to handle these papers, so they just ran them by the boards. Oh, there must have been thousands and thousands of these B-13 papers. There was a room full of them.

As I say, Cooper was fanatical about some things. He'd get something into his head, and nothing would stop him from going ahead with it. Like that time he was heading to Montreal on a train. He told me about this.

He was riding to Montreal when he saw a lot of ducks in a field, so he thought that's a good idea — I'll just put a lot of ducks down at St. Anne's Island.*

"You see, Jim Cooper invested heavily in St. Anne's Island and started the tobacco business there. He brought in Kentuckians — skilled tobacco growers, and he built houses and hired people to work the land.

"Anyway, he just got it into his head that he'd like to see some ducks down there, so he bought ducks by the score and transported them down there. But it was a crazy venture.

Cooper tended to be eccentric and terribly impatient. Large recalls how Cooper's chauffeur would drive the millionaire to a show in Detroit.

The chauffeur would have to sit there in his car all during the show waiting for Jim, and if he wasn't right at the door the moment Jim appeared, then Jim would hop into a cab and head home. Sometimes the poor chauffeur had to sit there all night. He was afraid to leave in case Jim hadn't come out yet.

Large remembers the broad-smiling, amiable Cooper who, whenever he was crossing the border would give him a bottle of Canadian Club.

To Large, Cooper wasn't a bootlegger in the strict sense of that definition. He said he had found a clever way of legally selling liquor.

"I really don't think he was dishonest."

*St. Anne's Island is part of Walpole near Wallaceburg.

Large remembers others who smuggled booze across the border:

There was one fellow who used to go over to Walkerville. He went to work there every morning. One day he came back with a big load of stuff in his car, and he told me while I was examining his car that he was just taking home a bunch of stuff from his office since he wasn't going to be working in Walkerville again. Then he told me that he used to take ten bottles of whiskey across to Detroit every day. He told me he put it in the false bottom of his car."

George Large during Prohibition got to know the wealthy Jim Cooper, who built one of the most fashionable homes — Cooper Court — in old Walkerville. He met Cooper while working at the New York Central Railway yards as a Customs officer.

I remember him telling me that he used to pay the Provincial Police off. I don't know this as a fact, I'm only quoting him. He used to pay the OPP's off in big bills. You see they used to unload these cars at Walkerville, where the station is now, in those yards up there. And they'd unload them at night.

They had to protect them, so to get the protection they used to pay the OPP's off, paid them off in big bills. So they used to kick about getting rid of a $100 bill in 1925.

So, Jim says one night, 'I'll fool them, or give them what they want.' He wrapped up three thousand dollars in one-dollar bills in newspaper. His man gave it to a police officer, in the boxcar, or something, I don't know how it happened, but anyway, when the policeman went to open it, the paper holding it busted and the bills blew all over the yard. They had a hell of a time there picking up the money.

Jim was a great guy to laugh about things like that.

George Large was also an invited guest to Cooper's Court and remembers how it was one of the largest mansions in Walkerville.

It was a great big home, and it had a gigantic swimming pool with a dome. Oh, I was at Cooper's home several times. It was very luxurious for those times — even for today's times.

He had a big Persian rug, and it would have gone all across the size of a normal living room and dining room of any big-sized home — and it was at least that wide as well. It cost him, I think, about $10,000 at that time.

I also remember the organ he had installed. It cost him about $50,000. It was installed right in the house. But you know, Jim couldn't play it at all, but he was fanatical about hearing music — good music. So, he got an organist from the

The *Vedas,* seized by the police and at anchor in Windsor. It had been nabbed by Customs as it floated off Colchester Light and towed to Windsor.

Anglican Church, the Ascension, to play for him. This organist was an accountant on Walker Road, and Jim hired him to come and play hymns for him every morning at eight for a half hour.

This organist told me how he had to go to Cooper's Court five mornings a week — just before he went to work — and play these hymns for Cooper. He told me old Jim would come bouncing down the stairs in his shorts...singing all the way down. Oh Cooper just loved that music.

The seizure of The Vedas, *Harry Low's rumrunning vessel was vividly recalled by Large. The oceangoing ship was seized by authorities after Prohibition.*

It was impounded by the Mounties. I think it was picked up way down east some place. Anyway they brought it down and docked it right downtown at the former Canada Steamship offices (site of Holiday Inn in Windsor). It sat there, I'd guess, for about a year. Finally we were told to take a crew on and destroy the beer that was still stored within it. We were told to throw it into the river.

So I took about six officers down there and brought all this beer up on the decks and we literally poured all this booze — bottle by bottle — into the river, then threw the bottles

overboard. I don't know how many hundreds of cases there were. I think we were there about ten afternoons destroying this beer. Just threw it in the water — bottles and contents.

Some of the boys however started drinking this beer down in the hold, but God, it had been down there for about two years, and they really got sick.

The first time that Large realized that even the small-time rumrunner had a lucrative business operating was the night he returned to Reaume Export Dock at Brighton beach.

One afternoon I came home and I realized I had forgotten to bring the B-13 papers with me, so after supper I said to my wife that I've got to go down and get those papers. We were very conscientious about them. We thought that any time we exported by the ferry or railroad or any place, these papers were being sent up to higher authorities and that they were being checked out. So we were very careful.

Anyway I went into the office and found a great crap game going on down at the dock. There were about ten or twelve guys down there on the floor, and believe it or not, there were $1,000 bills being slapped down. I had never seen a $1,000 bill. But there they were — these fellows — just rolling the dice.

As ticket collector on the Windsor Ferry at the foot of Ouellette Avenue, William King saw many bizarre methods of taking liquor across to Detroit. He worked on the ferry from 1924 to 1932 right in the midst of Prohibition.

There were lots of people going across with liquor. Lots of them. Oh, they had a lot of different ways of taking it across. Some of them had cars, and they built tanks underneath each side of the drive shaft, and they would fill them up. A lot of them would fill up a spare tire, put a little air into it, so it wouldn't rattle. And a lot of them took out the back seat and filled in there. And they'd carry it across on their person as well. Oh, yes. There was one fellow there who used to make about three trips a day. He carried two quarts — that's all he carried. He carried them on his back. He walked very straight, you never seen under his coat at all. He made about three trips a day.

The Customs people got wise to all this activity and decided they'd check all the lunchboxes being carried across. Oh, you should have seen it that morning — there were plenty of lunchboxes left on the boat...lots of them.

King remembers the Customs seizing cars if they believed the drivers were attempting to smuggle liquor to the United States.

One time, however, they stopped a mail truck...the American mail truck. There was a big colored guy driving. A young Customs officer asked him what he had in the truck. He pulled him over to the side and asked him to open the truck up.

"No, I won't open it! I'm not allowed to open it until I get back to the post office!"

At that time all the mailmen used to carry .45s, but the fellow beside this colored guy carried a shotgun.

This Customs officer said, "Well, I'll open it." The colored fellow pulled out his .45 and said, "Go ahead. Take hold of the lock and you're dead! I'll shoot you if you take hold of that lock."

They had quite a row over it. Finally the Customs officer called up the Postmaster at midnight and asked him to come down. The Postmaster demanded to know what was the matter, and the colored guy told him what was going on. So, the Postmaster walked over to the Customs official and turned his badge over to check the numbers on it, then said, "this is the last day you'll be working with Customs." And it was. The Customs fellow was fired. And the reason is, you can't stop a mail truck. They just go from post office to post office. There might be the odd bottle on them, who knows, but you can't stop the trucks.

In those days however everyone was bootlegging, and the stuff came on the ferries just as regular as the commuters. I remember the landlady where I lived was even a bootlegger. She kept her liquor in a coffee pot.

A sidelight to King's story is that contraband literature as well as contraband liquor was being smuggled on the Windsor Ferry.

American readers were introduced to James Joyce's *Ulysses*, a book banned in the United States, when the first forty copies of the Irish novelist's work were smuggled to Detroit on the Windsor Ferry in the midst of Prohibition.

A Curtis Publishing salesman, Barnett Braverman, a friend of Ernest Hemingway's, was working in Windsor but living in Detroit at the time. He took copies of *Ulysses* one at a time across the river where he mailed them to friends in the United States.

Chapter Thirteen

The Fighting Parson

Reverend J. O. L. Spracklin more than any other person during Prohibition symbolized the dramatic fight between temperance-minded people and the rumrunners. His campaign was waged like a war against the whiskey dealers.

Today at Sandwich United Church the oldtimers prefer to forget one of their former pastors. But his name is not easily buried in the church's records. His identity surfaces occasionally in anniversary editions of *The Windsor Star*, in regional historical sketches and in high school essays.

He is remembered for his dynamism, fanaticisim, charisma, and for carrying out his mission with relentless iron will. He was not one to be pushed aside, but he set himself apart. He was Reverend J. O. L. Spracklin, pastor of the Sandwich Methodist from 1919 to 1921.

His brief charge at the church, however, gave him a place in the history of Prohibition. More than any other figure during that era, Reverend Spracklin epitomized the dramatic confrontation between the forces of temperance and the ranks of rumrunners.

On November 8 1920 the zealous pastor burst into the Chappell House to face its saloon owner, Beverley "Babe" Trumble, in a gun duel which Spracklin won. The young minister, charged with manslaughter, was acquitted. He fled the area for good, but the episode and his high-spirited rampage along the riverfront came to an abrupt end — but not in the minds of those alive at that time.

In less than five months from July to November 1920, Reverend Spracklin polarized the extremes of Prohibition. With guns strapped to his belt, he wailed from the pulpit at Sandwich Methodist about the low-life of the community. When not in the sanctuary, he roamed the streets till the early hours of the morning, busting down doors with pistols blazing and a squad of men trailing behind who were tougher than the surly rumrunners. And when not being chauffered in his large touring car provided by Ontario's Attorney-General William E. Raney, he was patrolling the Detroit River with the provincial government speed boat, *Panther II*, zooming into remote docks and canals to spy upon and catch whiskey dealers red-handed.

Everyone came under the scrutiny of Spracklin's persistent war against Demon Rum. No one escaped him, not even the members of his own congregation. It is said while he preached on Sunday mornings, his thugs rummaged through parishoners' cars for booze... just on the off chance.

Spracklin trusted no one . . . that seemed to be justification in his receiving the job as a free-lance liquor licence inspector. He was personally selected by Raney, and was given a free rein in the Border Cities. The attorney general wanted someone who believed in the temperance cause, not simply an employee, but a fierce believer. In gun-slinging Spracklin he found that man.

Spracklin took on the task of cleaning up the border with unrestrained enthusiasm, and very soon was called "The Fighting Parson" by newspapers. He became a kind of teetotalling Wyatt Earp, who stopped at nothing to win — even if that meant carrying a stack of blank search warrants which he filled out himself.

The crux of this drama is his rivalry with Babe Trumble, the saloon keeper at the Chappell House, who blatantly disregarded the new

Reverend J. O. L. Spracklin

temperance laws in Ontario by serving liquor. The roadhouse was only an eighth of a mile from the church and its all-night entertainment went on unobstructed, much to the chagrin of the crusading Methodists.

Ontario had just passed its Prohibition laws in October 1919, outlawing bars and clubs like the Chappell House, but the roadhouse openly flouted the new regulations. This may have raised Spracklin's ire, but a long-time feud between the two may also have touched off the vicious confrontation at Sandwich.

Spracklin and Trumble had known each other from childhood. Their mothers were close friends in Woodstock where both families originated. But Babe and "Leslie," as he was known, were never close. A challenge existed between the two, not the violent or resentful brand that ever led to a fistfight, but a subtle personality duel that undercut their lives.

Trumble was flashy and had little difficulty in acquiring friends, while Spracklin, not a loner, but an individualist, kept to himself. Whether deep-rooted jealousy on Spracklin's part separated them, isn't known, but rivalry brewed like a poison between the two.

One story recounts how Spracklin was waltzing with a pretty girl at a school dance, when Trumble suddenly appeared at the doorway. That's all it took, apparently, for the wide-eyed girl to abandon Spracklin for the flashy Trumble.

Another, tells of a field day race when Spracklin trailed behind Trumble to finish a close second, but not the winner.

The most blatant conflict between them is best exemplified in their roles at Sandwich, a town now amalgamated with Windsor. There Trumble, in 1920 a well-to-do businessman and owner of a fashionable roadhouse, was gaining recognition and wealth, while Spracklin, a newly-appointed pastor of a church, languished with low pay and little authority outside the sphere of his congregation. But the situation for Spracklin was to be altered. The power that he sought in the community finally surfaced in June 1920.

Monday night, June 21, Spracklin towered above a cowering Sandwich Council, demanding a thorough investigation into the wide-spread sale of liquor at nearby roadhouses. The young minister harangued council members saying, "this historic town has become the dumping ground for the lowest element; an element which we might well be rid of and which comes to us from all parts of the United States to obtain what they are looking for — strong drink.

"They come to the Border Cities for it and secure it largely in the town of Sandwich. There is a flagrant disregard for the law and so far the police have made no effective efforts to cope with the situation. The streets have become unsafe for our mothers, wives and daughters on account of the open debauch which is going on here.

"At any time of night, you can hear men passing your street door using the most obscene language; drunken, rolling, spewing, fighting men in all stages of intoxication as a result of the illicit sale of liquor which is being carried on."

The target of his attack, however, was the Chappell House and the ineffectual Police Chief, Alois Masters of the Sandwich Police. Spracklin claimed he counted nearly thirty drunken men and women leaving the roadhouse, "by the front entrance that night, with the chief of police sitting on the front steps . . . twirling his thumbs." One girl came out, Spracklin said, who was "so drunk that she rolled all over the porch," and a man left the building "so loaded with liquor that he had to be helped to the end of the verandah, where he tried to sober up.

"Girls came out in such an intoxicated state that they had to be helped to the automobiles by their escorts, or they would have fallen down the steps."

And Spracklin said, one girl in a drunken stupor sat for a moment on Chief Alois Masters' lap before he told her to leave.

Spracklin's demands were clear and emphatic. He wanted not just an investigation, but a reorganization of the police department and a special campaign to clean up these lawless activities.

Council gave him that assurance. But it wasn't quick enough for the minister who raised the subject once more the following Sunday with his congregation. He challenged Trumble and the police chief to carry out their threats of lawsuits. Then on July 5 Spracklin returned to council and to another packed room of spectators. This time he was denied the opportunity of speaking. In fact, Mayor E. H. Donnelly threatened to have the pastor removed by the police if he didn't leave willingly. Spracklin was instead asked to put his charges in writing.

Meanwhile Trumble vehemently denied that his roadhouse was the scene of such vileness. He told the *Border Cities Star* in an interview, "liquor has never been sold in my house with my consent, and I am prepared to deny that Mr. Spracklin saw the drunks coming out of my hotel as he said. I have discharged several waiters for having whiskey in their possession."

On July 19, Spracklin was back at council to submit his charges at a stormy meeting, and according to the next day's account in the newspaper, "at the conclusion of the scene (in

The Spracklin Gang. They carried guns, clubs and blank search warrants. Two were dismissed for being mere thugs.

the council chamber) with the mob surging about him, shaking their fists in his face, calling him names, threatening him with personal violence, the Methodist minister stood defiantly and announced . . . 'I am not afraid of you, I can use my fists if necessary.'" He then elbowed his way through jeering spectators and shouted to them he was departing and wasn't afraid to walk home by himself. Behind him, he left a two-page typewritten report, charging the police chief and the law enforcement committee of council with neglect of duty.

Less than a week later, buoyed up by rumors Attorney-General Raney was considering the appointment of Spracklin as head of a special force of liquor licence inspectors, the outspoken pastor warned he would lay charges against Chief Masters under the Ontario Temperance Act. The act specifically stated, Spracklin said, that any constable failing to enforce the liquor laws could be dismissed from the force and fined ten dollars.

Sandwich Council, taking up Spracklin's challenge of an investigation, carried one out only to announce that the minister's charges were unfounded and false. But this coincided with word from Toronto that Reverend Spracklin had indeed been appointed a liquor licence inspector. The brash pastor didn't hesitate to undertake his new role that same evening (July 30 1920) when he was invited to join two other

inspectors in a raid on three roadhouses. Charges were laid at all three spots. Two days later, Spracklin exposed three more drinking holes, one in which he battled his way out of a fistfight with the bootleggers in a free-for-all brawl.

By August 5, of that year, Raney gave Spracklin the support he needed by the appointment of twenty-four more inspectors for the Essex Region. From these, Spracklin hand picked his squad of men, some like the Hallam brothers, who were considered mere thugs.

A former Windsor police officer, who was part of a bootlegging squad then, remembers Spracklin's men as "punks." He said, "I can remember (Spracklin and his squad) went down to LaSalle because they knew there were some shipments being made.

"Well they got them, and they brought the boats back. I was asked to meet them and give a hand. Well I could see them coming along the river . . . and those two brothers — the Hallam boys — were in the back drinking and falling all over the place. They couldn't stand up. They were just like a bunch of drunken sailors . . . and now Spracklin, he wasn't even looking at them . . . oh, I don't think he ever took a drink."

But if some of his squad were dishonest, Spracklin's own intentions were sincere.

In the beginning he basked in this newfound attention, and became the most feared inspector in the six months that he was permitted to reign.

But fear didn't stop the rumrunners from retaliating. On October 4 of that year, the parsonage was riddled with bullets, shattering its windows and nearly hitting a former inspector with the Sandwich Police Force, G. A. Jewell, who had been sitting at a table in Spracklin's home reading a newspaper.

On Halloween night, Spracklin's house again was barraged by bullets in another spree, one bullet whizzed past Spracklin's wife and embedded itself in a staircase wall. That night the pastor's squad took rooms in a Walkerville hotel and placed furniture against the doors.

Speaking before a Detroit congregation later, Spracklin said, "Every time my young wife goes upstairs, she has to pass the marks where bullets came through my parsonage."

Threats on his life also came through the mail and over the telephone. Sometimes they were sent to his mother and father, who lived in Windsor. Spracklin told a *Toronto Star* reporter that despite the intense pressure upon him to quit, he refused, even if it meant carrying a pistol with him wherever he went. Later, he contended he could no longer meet a stranger in his downstairs study of his home, unless he wore a gun.

The rumrunners feared Spracklin's reckless parading along the border, but they stopped at nothing to waylay him. In one instance, they even tossed him into a canal near LaSalle.

Besides assaults, some tried to remove Spracklin by legal means.

By October, Inspector M. N. Mousseau was terribly disgruntled by the free-for-all clean up campaign that Spracklin had commenced. As head of the department in the district, appointed long before the pastor was selected by the attorney-general, Mousseau claimed this divided authority was destroying the control of the war on Demon Rum.

The inspector warned the board of licence commissioners on October 21 1920 that unless Spracklin ceased his free-lance activities, he would quit.

Mousseau mainly objected to tactics used by Spracklin's men, especially the Hallam brothers, who were nothing but half-cocked brutes in his estimation. He said since he was chief inspector for the region, it should follow that he should control Spracklin and his squad. But under the arrangement made by Raney, Mousseau had no such power. And Spracklin wasn't about to relinquish his command.

The following day, Spracklin dismissed the Hallam brothers, but without explanation. He said merely it was the result of "certain information which he had obtained." A clue to

the cause might be an earlier news report describing how Spracklin and the two brothers had jumped aboard a yacht owned by a lawyer, O. E. Fleming, and waved their pistols about and carelessly and recklessly searched the boat. Held captive was not a band of rumrunners, but a group of frightened ladies.

This was typical of the kind of searches made, but Spracklin would pay for this one in particular the following spring. Also characteristic of Spracklin's raids, or specifically those conducted by the Hallam boys, was a total disregard for valuables. Stories tell of how they broke open chests of drawers and ruthlessly damaged countless cabinets in their haphazard manner. There are also tales of the squad roaring down the Detroit River in their patrol boat slicing rumrunners' boats, in two, leaving the occupants to swim to shore.

But although Spracklin dismissed the Hallams, under no circumstances would he be placed under Mousseau's command. To the *Border Cities Star*, he said, "I intend to maintain that status even should Mr. Mousseau find it necessary to withdraw from the service."

But Spracklin's enemies mounted an effective campaign to remove him. On November 3, he appeared before the temperance committee of the Ontario Legislature in Toronto to hear Mousseau's vehement opposition to Spracklin's use of firearms. Mousseau declared that it was better in his opinion to let a load of liquor get away than to shoot. Sometimes he thought that lack of judgment overbalanced enthusiasm with Spracklin. Mousseau added that he himself had only been assaulted once and he had never carried a gun.

The chief inspector's warning, "There are troubled times ahead for him," received support from Dr. Forbes Godfrey, MPP who said to Spracklin, "That gun will get you in trouble sometime."

But Spracklin retaliated by challenging the chief inspector to match up the number of convictions against his own. A taunting Spracklin boasted greater accomplishment in the short span of time than that of Mousseau.

The committee, impressed by Spracklin, whose spectacular methods had caught the attention of all Ontario, was swept up in support of The Fighting Parson.

Spracklin however came under attack for carrying with him a handful of blank search warrants. One committee member complained, "Why not have martial law and be done with it?" But in a sharp retort, the pastor replied, "Well, you'll have that unless conditions are soon cleared up."

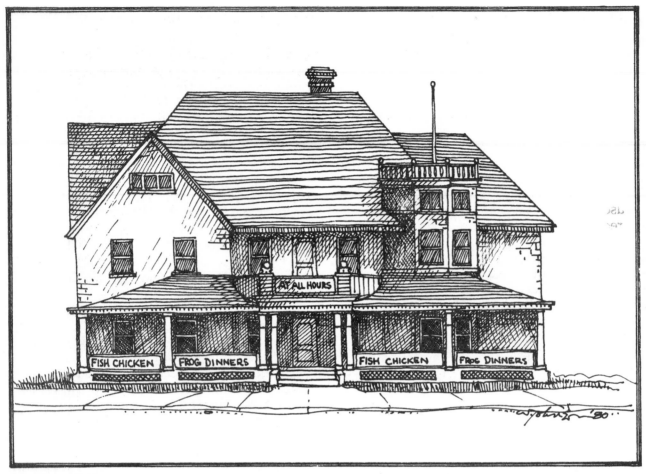

The Chappell House

He argued booze had been going across the Detroit River at a phenomenal rate, but since his appointment, roadhouse selling had been reduced by more than eighty percent. That he had searched drinking establishments after midnight was true, but that shouldn't seem unusual when, these places didn't actually shut down until 4 A.M.

Spracklin insisted, "I don't want this miserable job for the enforcement of the Act with all the risks I am taking and the disruption of my house, unless I can go back tonight or tomorrow feeling that I have the absolute confidence of this committee and the Government."

He was able to return to Sandwich with the endorsement he sought. The chairman of the board, J. D. Flavelle, declared, "No other place is as bad as Essex, therefore extreme measures must be taken where there are extreme conditions . . . Mr. Spracklin went in as a matter of public service. I think the ends justify the means." The board thus voted to keep both inspectors in a divided command. But Mousseau's warning must have been ringing in the committee's ears just a few days later when news that Spracklin had shot Trumble reached them.

The "troubled times" that the chief inspector had predicted came sooner than expected. Only three days after the hearing in Toronto, November 6 1920, a startled public read the headlines in newspapers all over Ontario that Babe Trumble had been shot and killed by the Sandwich minister.

Now all the justification for becoming a minister and for assuming responsibility as a liquor licence inspector flashed before Spracklin. He also had to reconcile the on-going rivalry that existed between he and Trumble and what the newspapers made of it.

That eventful morning of November 6 1920 Spracklin had been roaming the streets of Sandwich in his touring car with his squad when he passed the Chappell House. It was about 3:30 A.M. He noticed an unconscious man, Ernest Deslippe, on the front lawn of the roadhouse. When Spracklin stopped to investigate, Trumble secured the lock at the front door barring his entrance to the saloon.

Spracklin, desperately wanting to question Trumble, broke a window of the hotel and climbed in. He raced through the main dining room, into the main hall and through to the bar in search of Trumble, but couldn't find him. He retraced his steps, this time meandering through the pantry and kitchen of the roadhouse, then into Trumble's private dining room where he met him face to face.

It was then that Spracklin shot Trumble, claiming the hotel owner had flashed a gun. "It was his life or mine," a tired Spracklin told police later that night.

Spracklin fled, but only to the bullrushes and weeds across the road from the Chappell House, where he watched large expensive cars with Michigan license plates rolling up to the roadhouse. Coming to lend support, he discovered later, were American mobsters who had heard of the shooting.

Spracklin finally gave himself up, not to the Sandwich Police, but instead to the Windsor Police whom he believed would give him a fair hearing. Hours later the *Border Cities Star* with second-coming type style wrote: "'Babe' Trumble Shot and Killed; Spracklin Held Pending Probe."

No immediate charges were made against Spracklin. But the inquest itself into Trumble's death began the night of the shooting and didn't finish until Monday night.

During these proceedings Spracklin testified that "Babe Trumble pressed his gun against the pit of my stomach. 'Damn you, Spracklin,' he said, 'I'm going to shoot you.' I knew then it was his life or mine."

But Lulu Trumble, Babe's wife, contradicted the testimony, claiming, "My husband had no gun. He had only a cigarette in his hand when he went out and met Mr. Spracklin."

The minister and his men, she said, appeared at the doorway of the roadhouse's living quarters, demanding to speak to her husband. But Trumble, walking toward Spracklin, insisted he produce "badges" for his squad.

Mrs. Trumble said, "I heard the report of a gun right after and that is the last I remember, except that Beverley cried, 'You dog, you have shot me.'"

Trumble then stumbled to the bedroom and died in the arms of an assistant, Edgar Smith.

The jury's verdict was justifiable homicide and Spracklin was exonerated and freed.

That same day Babe Trumble's body was placed beside his mother's in the mausoleum at Windsor Grove Cemetery. The funeral had been held at the house of Hamilton Trumble, the father of the slain roadhouse owner.

One of the mourners ironically was Mrs. Joseph Spracklin, mother of the Fighting Parson. The *Detroit News* November 9 1920 wrote, "There is one mother on the border who has wept for Mrs. Beverley Trumble and her two children,

Babe Trumble shot and killed.

Robert and Leslie, now fatherless, following the shooting of Mr. Trumble Saturday morning . . . That woman is Mrs. Joseph Spracklin . . . Mrs. Spracklin for the last four months has dreaded the ring of the telephone, the knock on the door, for with each she anticipated the news that her boy, Leslie Spracklin, had been killed. Letters threatening to kill Spracklin were sent to the home at 148 Cameron Avenue each week. They went into the fire as soon as they were opened. But the threats remained in the mother's mind.

"'The last few months have been terrible, and I knew Saturday morning when by five o'clock Leslie neither had telephoned nor come home that something had happened,' the mother said."

Mrs. Spracklin had been friends with Ellen King, Trumble's mother, from Woodstock. The two had played together and Mrs. Spracklin used to do Ellen's arithmetic in the "fourth form."

"If only it did not have to be Bev that was shot," Mrs. Spracklin told the *Detroit News* in an interview, adding, "We all knew them so well, but it just seemed to have been fate."

Following the inquest's decision, sympathetic support overwhelmed Spracklin. The *Border Cities Star* November 13 1920 wrote, "Probably no public official in the history of the community has suffered more criticism and risked his health and life so often in the pursuit of duty."

The Christian Guardian insisted the real issue at Sandwich "for many months has been an open flouting of the law on the part of those represented by the unfortunate man who was buried so suddenly. And that open and barefaced and altogether unscrupulous breaking of the law is a very serious matter."

It was emphasized that Spracklin has been "fearless, and intensely alert . . . and has made himself a terror to evildoers, and it is no secret that his life has been in danger more than once.

"His ceaseless activity has not been agreeable to lawbreakers and their friends and his enemies . . . but we are glad that so far he has escaped alike their malice and bullets."

Meanwhile W. H. Furlong, a Windsor lawyer and friend of the Trumbles — he had been a pallbearer at Trumble's funeral — was prepared to press for a charge of manslaughter against Spracklin.

By the end of November, Spracklin's motley band was dismissed by Attorney-General Raney and replaced by Superintendent W. J. Lannin, the former chief of police at Stratford, Ontario. *Panther II* and the great touring car, a Paige, were transferred to the new inspector November 27 1920. Spracklin returned to Sandwich Methodist, humbled by the frenetic experience as a liquor licence inspector and the fanatic campaign which ended so tragically.

But his name wasn't to disappear so quickly from the news. Ahead of him were months of worry and a lengthy trial. Mrs. Trumble's lawyer and other friends petitioned the attorney-general to charge Spracklin with manslaughter and put him on trial. More than 2,000 signatures supported this demand in a petition sent to the Ontario government. Spracklin himself urged the attorney-general to consent, realizing his innocence had to be proven once and for all.

Raney finally announced Spracklin would be charged with manslaughter. It came not long after the shooting, in fact less than two weeks later. Arraignment was done at the end of November. By December a date of February 21 1921 was set for trial. Sir William Mulock was named as the presiding judge, while Munro Grier, a Toronto lawyer of Furlong's choice, was appointed prosecuting attorney. R. L. Brackin, Liberal member of the legislature for West Kent, was hired to defend Spracklin.

The trial actually started February 22 and more than 600 people had to be turned away. Spectators lined up at the entrance of the Sandwich Court House at 6:30 A.M. And rumors spread that Hamilton Trumble had gone into the sheriff's office the day before hurling threats at Spracklin. The proceedings got under way at

Police spirit Reverend Spracklin away after the inquest into Trumble's death.

8:30 A.M. with Mrs. Trumble testifying her husband had had no gun in his hand, when Spracklin shot him.

A spectator at that trial, in an interview, reported that whole bins of guns were collected by the police from spectators pressing to get a seat. Hallways and stairwells of the court house were jammed, and when it came time for lunch, few moved from their spots, so that they could stay close to the courtroom.

Mrs. Trumble, pregnant with a third child, mounted the stand but kept one of her children in her arms until Sir William ordered her to hand him over to her father-in-law. Brackin delved deeply into her assertion that not only did Trumble *not* have a gun, but had never owned one. He questioned her about how Trumble brought in a cash register to be repaired a year before and how he had pushed a pistol up against the repairman's head, demanding that he fix the machine.

Mrs. Trumble hotly denied this, telling Brackin he only owned rifles, never a handgun.

But Mrs. Trumble wasn't the only one who was skillfully cross-examined that day. So was Spracklin, who confessed that he wore a .45 calibre automatic Colt at all times. He also revealed that it had been drawn when he went into Trumble's roadhouse. Grier also established that the weapon wasn't registered with the police and wasn't the kind permitted by the law.

At this point in the trial, the persistent question was whether Trumble had a gun in his hand that night. The police had found no evidence of one, and Lulu Trumble steadfastly clung to testimony that Babe Trumble never owned one. Brackin poked holes in these claims, but she continued to deny her husband ever had a handgun.

One thing was established — the rivalry between the two. Almost a month before the shooting, Spracklin had searched Trumble's car outside the Chappell House, with Trumble branding the pastor-inspector a "cur," warning him, "You'll get yours!"

But the first break in the chain of testimony came February 23 from Jack Bannon, a notorious rumrunner, later sentenced to Kingston Penitentiary for kidnapping John Labatt. He revealed to a stunned court room that he saw Mrs. Trumble snatch a gun from her husband's hand after he was shot.

The startling revelation was made when the dramatic Brackin jumped to his feet to cross-examine the witness. Bannon had just been asked by Grier whether Trumble had a gun. Bannon said he didn't. An undaunted Brackin asked if Lulu Trumble had a gun in her hand, and Bannon nonchalantly admitted she did.

The sensational statement caused a flurry of clapping in the court room. Sir William angrily demanded those who had made that sudden outburst should stand up and be removed by the police. No one got to their feet.

Two other dramatic turns in the case occurred that day; Ernest Deslippe, the fellow who had been beaten up outside the hotel, died in hospital of pneumonia; and Ed Smith, the man in whose arms Trumble died, changed his story about seeing Trumble with a gun. Smith had told the physician, summoned to the Chappell House after the shooting, that Babe Trumble had drawn a gun on Spracklin.

Brackin's masterful cross-examination poked holes in all that Smith said. He snarled at the witness: "What did you carry with you when you went to Detroit on the morning of the shooting?" Brackin was struggling to force Smith to admit he had fled to Detroit with the gun and had either dropped it into the Detroit River while on the ferry or had sold it at a secondhand shop in the United States. But Smith held firm to the story that Trumble didn't have a gun at all.

The following day, February 24, the two attorneys addressed the jury. Brackin far outshone his opponent Grier, who seemed

Jack Bannon, a key witness at the Spracklin trial, photographed later at Kingston, where he served time for snatching John Labatt.

ineffectual and confused. Brackin wove together the intricate tale of the pastor-inspector and the roadhouse owner and the mounting rivalry between the two. He criticized the provincial government for appointing Spracklin, saying, "I don't think it was fair; I don't think it was right for the Government of Ontario to say to this minister of the gospel, 'You complain that conditions in your town are vile, that they have reached the unbearable point; you therefore assume the responsibility of remedying them, of cleaning up the situation you complain of.' Had I been a member of the Government with the necessary authority I would have sent a regiment of soldiers to cope with the situation here."

Brackin also accused Mrs. Trumble of lying: "Yesterday (she) kissed the sacred book and swore to tell the truth . . . she stood there and she lied, and lied and lied." Finally turning to the jury, Brackin said, "If you need a chain of lighthouses to guide you on your way, you have only to think of the threats against Spracklin's life."

Spracklin found Not Guilty.

Grier stood firm on the evidence given by Mrs. Trumble and Smith. He challenged Brackin's assertion that Mrs. Trumble wasn't as grief-stricken as she might have been, and dismissed the evidence given by Bannon, since it contradicted his testimony at the November inquest.

The jury deliberated for only fifty-nine minutes and returned with a verdict of not guilty. Spracklin was set free. Over the next few days there was an endless string of editorials in newspapers, congratulating him for his war against rumrunners. The *Border Cities Star* came to his support: "If there existed any stain upon the good name of Leslie Spracklin it has been wiped out."

But this respite was short-lived. His border rampaging came back to haunt him. Only a month after his trial at Sandwich, Spracklin was back in court, this time being fined $500 damages for trespassing on the yacht of Oscar Fleming, a Windsor lawyer. This was the vessel he ransacked with the Hallam Brothers in the beginning of his border war on booze.

Spracklin appealed to the Second Appellate Court in April the following month, but it held up the previous decision. Chief Justice R. N. Meredith and four other judges declared the pastor-inspector was blatantly unfit for his responsibilities and that he lacked proper experience, tact, patience and knowledge. In the case of Fleming, the court said his behavior was "stupid and inexcusable."

In the *Canadian Annual Review,* the judgment made was quoted: "If the law is to be respected and properly enforced, the enforcement of it must never be committed to such persons as the defendant, it must be left to trained, experienced and impartial officers of the law." And the *Toronto Telegram* on April 8 called Spracklin's command of the border "Raneyism running amuck . . . It was Raneyism that shot Beverley Trumble. It was Raneyism which went buccaneering on the Windsor river."

But rumors that Spracklin would be shot frightened the family, and even the congregation. On a couple of occasions, the pastor-inspector returned to Windsor from excursions out of the city to calm the reports that someone had attempted to kill him. But the threats were real. On April 6 1921 in London, Ontario when he was asked to attend a church service, someone passed a note to the pastor of that church, "Don't let the murderer come here tonight. We will get him."

His name had not been forgotten. It was very much a household name. Spracklin however did turn up at a hockey game to play with London

Motors in London. Spectators, hearing of the event, crowded the arena to watch the burly, tough-minded pastor. The *London Advertiser* reported at one point in the game, he broke through the defense and came down upon the goalie on a breakaway, but didn't score. Nevertheless it earned him a standing ovation.

But lack of applause in Sandwich drove him away. Despite support of the Border Cities Ministerial Association, he underwent one more trial — this one behind the closed doors of Sandwich Methodist. Spracklin was accused by some women in his congregation of having made sexual propositions. A kangaroo court of sorts was held in the church hall, and Elton Plant, a correspondent for the *Detroit News*, attending that meeting, recalled how those accusations against the pastor-inspector forced him from Windsor. Spracklin fled quietly. In fact, the United Church of Canada's archives in Toronto list him in its church, but without a charter, from 1922 to 1925. Spracklin actually left Sandwich to take over a charge in Cheboygan, Michigan in 1922.

The Cain-like Fighting Parson at that time began his wanderings, from church to church in Michigan. First Midland till 1929, a short leave of absence, then at Homer, Davisburg, Bay City, Clio and finally Oscoda.

Spracklin died at Greenbush, Michigan May 28 1960. He was 73 years old at the time. His death drew no publicity. He had finally been forgotten. There had been the occasional attempt by the movie industry to portray The Fighting Parson's life on the screen, but the Spracklins refused to grant permission.

The *Woodstock Sentinel-Review* on November 8 1920 may have summed up the tragedy at Sandwich the best way in light of the ferocious temperance campaign against rumrunners and whiskey dealers:

"There has been too much emotionalism, perhaps on both sides in this temperance campaign, and where there is too much emotion there is likely to be too little clear thinking. The tragedy at Sandwich may set people thinking, as the outrages associated with the Fenian rising set Gladstone thinking. And so some good may come of it."

Members of The Purple Gang and associates at time of arrest.
(left to right) Sam Drapkin, Joe Bomerito, Jimmy Licavoli, Nick Desmond, George Rose, Abe Axler.

Section Six

The Purple Rule of Terror — The Purple Gang of Detroit

A *Detroit News* reporter wrote that the true story of the famed and notorious Purple Gang reads "like a Hollywood script." He wasn't far off — a movie was made of the terrible underworld gang, and it starred a younger Robert Blake of the former *Baretta* series on television.

The gang, which terrorized the liquor trade and gambling and prostitution rackets throughout Michigan and Ontario, was labelled by crime writers as one of the most vicious in United States history. For a while, it was said, the Purple Gang gave Al Capone trouble.

The notorious gang got its start in the Twenties at the height of Prohibition. Where and exactly how it got its name, no one really knows. Not even the leaders of the gang itself. But some versions have it that the name comes from the purple colors of Northwestern University. Another says the nucleus of the gang while skipping classes at the old Bishop School on Detroit's Winder Avenue, spent hours in a rented cottage in Canada near Lake St. Clair. There they traipsed about in purple swimming trunks. When an older and rougher group took command, it assumed the name by which the younger boys liked to be known.

The widely accepted version, however, actually dates back to the now almost forgotten remarks of a Hastings Street clothing merchant. He was said to respond to the stories he had heard of petty crimes being committed by a young gang of hoodlums: "They're a bad lot; off-color from other fine boys of their own age. They're purple."

The boys to whom he referred were a youthful band who were committing depredations on the near East Side of Detroit. One *Detroit Free Press* writer said, "The boys snatched ice cream, gum, candy, cookies and fruit from hucksters and stores. They ganged up on children their own age. Sometimes they strong-armed grownups."

Merchants began to fear this gang and seldom reported to the police what they were doing. They feared reprisals. And as Prohibition neared, these hoodlums saw big, easy money ahead. Its early leaders included Harry Millman, Eddie Fletcher, Abe Axler and Irving Millberg. All but Millberg died as they had lived — by guns of the underworld. Millberg died of natural causes while serving a life term in Marquette Prison for murder. Another mob member to die naturally was "The Professor," or Charlie Auerbach, who furnished the arsenal for the gang. And there were others who were imprisoned, including Harry Fleisher, his brothers, Sammy and Louis, Ray Bernstein, Morris Rader and Joseph Stein.

The Purple Gang's story isn't simply an American one. It was this gang which arranged for some of the biggest shipments of illegal liquor to the United States. Their dealings also extended to Canadians in many other ways: the sale of hot diamonds, dope and even prostitution.

Probably the story which best exemplifies the style and vicious nature of the gang is the Collingwood Massacre. The story is told here in two versions: one by a *Detroit News* reporter who flashes back to the 1931 gang-slaying of three men; and the other by Judge Donald E. Van Zile who presided over the case and wrote his account of the trial for the *News* a few years later.

Before this event, in those early years the Purple Gang's name meant little. But as the deeds of the gang became more and more brazen and their activities in shaking down blind pigs and gambling houses more widespread, the name came to mean something. Especially with the Collingwood Massacre. But prior to this, there were other large events which linked the name of the Purples to violence. The label came to mean terror. "It meant slugging and clubbing . . . sometimes murder," wrote John McManus in a 1945 article for the *News*.

The Milaflores massacre of 1926 is blamed on the Purples, but the police or courts were never able to prove it. It was in the Milaflores Apartment Building that three gunmen for a St. Louis gang were mowed down by machine-gun fire in an apartment rented by Axler and Fletcher.

The Purples had been considered small-time punks until that day in 1926 when Frankie Wright, Joseph Bloom and Reuben Cohen were shot down as they waited to be admitted to the Axler-Fletcher apartment where they had been invited to "a peace conference." The massacre, it was said, was the result of a gambling-house shakedown in which Meyer "Fish" Bloomfield, stickman for the late Doc Brady's Grand River Athletic Club, was kidnapped and ransomed for $50,000.

Wright, Cohen and Bloom were supposed to have double crossed the Purple Gang in the Bloomfield deal, so they were shot down. The police never officially solved the case.

Two years later the gang made its next appearance when it was accused of extorting money from cleaners and dyers in Detroit in the warfare waged for two years between two groups of wholesale cleaners and dyers. Two cleaners — Sam Polakoff and Sam Sigman — were murdered. The trial lasted for weeks, but ended with an acquittal for all.

But besides the story of the Purple's mass murders, there is also the story of the Licavoli Squad and their involvement in the liquor trade and gambling operations in Detroit. Although there weren't any major confrontations with the Purples, the two did battle over control of the rackets. The Licavoli brothers on occasion lived across the river in Windsor.

Chapter Fourteen

The Purple Gang: A Detroit Gang that Terrorized the Liquor Traffic
By Joseph Wolff

Detroit was quiet. The hoodlums, the gorillas and the musclemen of the illicit beer and liquor trade were in hiding. The alcohol cutting business and the bookmaking establishments were at a standstill from Grosse Pointe to Wyandotte and known gangster hangouts were as deserted as the old Michigan lumber camps. But the peace and quiet was ominous and strained.

It was forty years ago, September 16 1931, and the gangland killing two days before, already dubbed the "Collingwood Manor Massacre," had joined the ranks of such sensational Prohibition murders as Chicago's St. Valentine's Day Massacre of February 14 1929.

Harry Toy, then the Wayne County prosecutor, had issued orders for an underworld roundup and the dragnet had its impact on the community. Heading the top of his list were four members of Detroit's infamous Purple Gang, and law officers throughout the country were ordered to bring them in "dead or alive."

The city, almost accustomed to daily violence among the city's bootleggers and gamblers, reeled in shock at the brazenness with which three former members of the Little Third Avenue Navy (Little Jewish Navy) had been executed.

Dead were three transplanted Chicago gangsters who had moved into Detroit a few years before and, with an assortment of hired gunmen, had tried to get a piece of the Detroit action — something that even Chicago ganglord Al Capone had refused to do. The trio, however, had undoubtedly underestimated the power and ruthlessness of Detroit's own underworld.

Herman (Hymie) Paul, Joseph (Nigger Joe) Lebovitz and Joseph (Izzie) Sutker were brought to Detroit from Chicago in 1926 by leaders of the Oakland Sugar House Gang, an outfit that was among the main suppliers of alcohol for several bootlegging organizations in the area. The Sugar House needed "rod men" — hired killers to protect its lucrative alcohol trade while it was waging war with powerful downriver gangs.

The trio did their job well, but soon their own greed moved them into the rackets and they became associated with the Third Avenue Navy, a gang so called because it landed its river cargoes of Canadian Whiskey in the railroad yards between Third and Fourth.

Trouble had been brewing for months in the beer and liquor business because of the Depression, stricter law enforcement and the racketeers feuding among themselves. The trio's activities added to the unrest.

Association and friendship meant nothing to them and in the early Thirties they had imported their own gunmen into Detroit. They disregarded the underworld code.

They hijacked from friend and foe alike. They double crossed the men with whom they were in alliance and were found so untrustworthy that no one dared work with them. They refused to stay within their own boundaries in the alcohol and whiskey trade and encroached on domains of other gangs.

Federal authorities had "turned the heat on" the downriver alcohol cookers for beating up one of their agents and the downriver mob enlisted the aid of the trio to supply them with alcohol at a reasonable price. The trio, however, took advantage of the situation, demanding higher prices. Not only that, but they began cutting into the gang's business. taking away some of the mob's regular customers.

The movie version — Allied Artists romanticized the Purple Gang in its 1959 film starring Robert Blake. Note the cases, not sacks, of "CANADIAN WHISKEY".

Sutker, Lebovitz and Paul were blamed for nearly every action that added to the unrest among rival Detroit gangs.

At the time of their deaths, huge orders for illicit booze for the coming American Legion convention had been placed with various bootleggers by the blind pigs and cabarets around the city.

Suddenly a series of hijackings began and the trio was blamed. Once during these tense days another gang, in an effort to get even and regain some of their stock, sent some hijackers to raid the trio's warehouse. One of the hijackers was shot to death during the attempt.

The trio's imported gunmen had begun a series of extortions, extracting protection money from blind pigs and bookmakers, selecting among others friends of such gangs as the Purples. This effort was shortlived, however, when the Purple Gang sought out and found the extortionists, forced them to repay several of their clients and ordered them out of town under penalty of death.

In the spring of 1931, the trio set up its own bookmaking operation and Sutker, heading this phase, took in a local hoodlum, Solomon (Solly) Levine, as a partner to help in its operation. For a few months before the assassins struck, the East Side Mafia had been giving their handbook a big play and in late August had put over a big parlay worth several hundred dollars.

Fearing vengeance if they did not pay the debt, the trio bought fifty gallons of alcohol from the Purples on credit, diluted it, and undersold the "market price" to make a quick profit.

The east side gang came back again with another "boat race," a fixed horse race, taking the handbook for even more money. Again a deal was made with the Purple Gang to get fifty gallons on credit. Again they diluted the stock and undersold the market price.

And so the stage was set. They had pushed their luck. Their activities spelled death; it was just a matter of time and which gang would move to stop them first.

On September 14, Solly Levine ran into Ray Bernstein on the sidewalk outside of a restaurant on Woodward at Temple. Bernstein, the accepted leader of the Purple Gang, made the initial peace overtures, telling Levine the Purples wanted to do some business.

Describing the casual meeting later, Levine quoted Bernstein:

"We've got everything straightened out and we're going to let you boys handle the horse bets and alcohol when you straighten out that bill." Levine knew that the trio owed the Purples for the alcohol.

He told Bernstein the boys needed more time to pay off the bill, that the Legion convention was near and they would have an opportunity to sell the liquor. The pair parted after Bernstein told him he would make contact when the Purples were ready for the meeting.

Levine was a natural to act as intermediary between the rival factions, whether to arrange a peace meeting as he was led to believe or to unknowingly set his partners up for murder.

Levine and Sutker had been operating the betting parlor for four months. He had known the trio since shortly after they arrived in Detroit five years before and had had dealings with them. On the other hand, he had a longtime acquaintance with many top men in the Purples and had grown up in the same neighborhood as its toughest operators.

The possibility of a "peace meeting" with the Purple Gang gave the three partners a sense of security. They felt they were now an accepted part of the Detroit underworld and could negotiate with other gangs on equal terms rather than as hirelings.

On the night of September 15, Izzie Sutker was carefree. A couple of his henchmen had driven to Port Huron to pick up his 18-year-old girl friend, Virginia White. They returned early in the evening and dropped her off at a cabaret where she spent the evening with Sutker over a few drinks and listening to a three-piece combo.

Hymie Paul went home early, had a couple of drinks by himself and went to bed.

Lebovitz also seemed confident that all was well. He went out on the town until the early morning hours. He had such a good time that he had a tremendous hangover on the morning of September 16 and didn't bother to shave.

That morning Levine was in the handbook at 706 Selden with a few cronies when the phone rang about midmorning. He grabbed a pink horsebet ticket and wrote down an address — 1740 Collingwood, Apartment 211, three P.M. It was the message the trio had been waiting for.

After the phone call, Levine called Sutker, Lebovitz and Paul and told them of the arrangements. The three strolled into the Selden handbook shortly after noon and chatted until they left at 2:45 P.M.

With Levine driving Sutker's car, the four pulled away from the betting house. They were laughing as they passed a corner drugstore and waved to a couple of detectives who had stopped to buy some cigars. They were also unarmed; it wouldn't look good to carry weapons to a peace meeting.

Levine, the only person to talk about the meeting in statements and testimony, detailed the events of the fateful afternoon. The ride to Collingwood took about fifteen minutes and Levine pulled the car in front of the apartment house at about three P.M. The men walked up the short entryway and pushed the buzzer for Apartment 211. Ray Bernstein answered and greeted them in the second floor hallway before ushering them into the apartment.

There, according to Levine, were Purples Harry Keywell, Harry Fleisher and Irving Milberg. Levine was surprised to see Fleisher there because he heard Harry was wanted by federal authorities.

The men shook hands and the visitors were asked to sit on a long sofa. After a chat, Bernstein asked "Where is Scotty with the books?" and left on the pretext of calling their bookkeeper. The others continued to chat about details of financial transactions and about the trio's debt. Crowded together on the sofa, they failed to see any significance in that the Purples stood or sat some distance apart, directly across from them.

Bernstein had walked down to the alley behind the apartment and started the engine of the getaway car. He tooted the horn, then headed back to the apartment.

Suddenly the Purples drew guns and the room was filled with a hail of bullets. One whizzed past Levine's nose and struck Sutker in the head.

Levine sat frozen to his seat; the three men he had brought to the apartment made desperate but futile efforts to flee as slugs from smoking guns slammed into their bodies.

It was over in seconds. Levine was shocked that he had not been hit. He saw Keywell, Milberg and Fleisher huddle for a moment, then one of them turned to him and said "Come on!"

As the men retreated through the kitchen, each dropped his gun into a can of green paint they had left on the floor near the stove.

The registration markings on the weapons had been filed down and the green paint would eliminate any fingerprints.

They ran down the back stairs to the waiting car. With Bernstein driving, the car sped away, nearly hitting a little boy playing nearby.

Levine said he was driven a short distance and was released and told to return to the handbook. About a half hour after he arrived there, he was seized by detectives, who were making mass arrests of known underworld figures.

Bernstein and Keywell were arrested two days after the murders in a flat at 2649 Calvert. Heavily armed police surrounded the house but both surrendered without a fight.

Milberg was arrested September 19 in an apartment at 3311 Chicago. Police confiscated five pistols and a rifle. He, too, surrendered without a fight.

Fleisher, also named in the murder warrant, vanished and was not heard from until months later.

Levine testified at the preliminary hearing against the three men who were bound over for trial on first degree murder charges.

On October 28 1931, a little more than a month after the massacre, the murder trial opened with the selection of a jury. Hundreds jammed the hallways of Recorder's Court, hoping for a seat at the trial. All who got in were searched for weapons. Plainclothes officers were scattered throughout the crowd inside and outside the courtroom.

The jury was selected after 108 prospective jurors were questioned. Before the first witness took the stand on November 1, Fire Marshal G. S. Goldwater warned Judge Donald Van Zile that the courtroom and hallway crowds were creating a fire hazard.

As the testimony began, Assistant Prosecutor Frank G. Schemanske, now a Recorder's Court judge, announced that he had begun an investigation into rumors that the defendants' cronies were "squeezing" money for a defense fund from local handbook establishments who were compelled to contribute two dollars a day for "betting service."

The jurors were locked up overnight and weekends during the trial. They were given absentee ballots for the November election and the five guards protecting them had orders to admit no one but the judge himself.

Sol Levine remained the key witness, although the caretaker of the Collingwood apartment building and the little boy who was almost run over also testified and identified the Purples.

Forty witnesses testified for the prosecution. At one point in the trial, while police armed with machine guns watched the streets and alleys, the jurors visited the murder scene.

In summarizing the case before the jury on November 9, Prosecuting Attorney Toy said:

"I hold no brief for the victims and their occupation. This is no defense, however. These men checked their books with bullets and marked off their accounts with blood. They lured the victims to the apartment with promises of

Irving Milberg, Ray Bernstein, Harry Keywell at the "Collingwood Massacre" trial.

partnership and killed them when they were unarmed and helpless."

Harry Baxter, a well known criminal attorney and one of several hired by the defendants, tried to attack Levine's testimony by saying that because of the slayings Levine "fell heir to the bookmaking and alky business."

The jury returned to the courtroom on November 10 and after one hour and thirty-seven minutes found the three defendants guilty of murder.

The verdict brought bedlam to the courtroom. Friends and relatives of the defendants began to scream hysterically and court officers climbed onto chairs and tables in an effort to restore order.

And so, according to Chief of Detectives James E. McCarty, the conviction "broke the back of the once powerful Purple Gang, writing finis to more than five years of arrogance and terrorism."

To prevent a recurrence of a wild court scene, Van Zile ordered Milberg and Bernstein brought to his court for sentencing two hours before they were scheduled on November 17.

"The crime which you have committed was one of the most sensational that has been committed in Detroit for many years. It was, as has been said, a massacre.

"It was the passing of a sentence by you men, which even the State of Michigan could not impose; that is to say the sentence of death."

Van Zile then complimented the police for bringing the men "to the end of the trail" and, addressing the defendants again, he said with a note of sternness:

"And in traveling this trail, you have established reputations as members of the famous Purple Gang, which has undoubtedly placed you at the peak of racketeer gangs of the city of Detroit and has unfortunately brought an unsavory reputation to this fair city.

"This has all been to me a great tragedy, not only in its results to you, but also by reason of the fact it has demonstrated that such a thing would be done in what we call our enlightened age of civilization.

"I do hereby sentence each of you for murder in the first degree to imprisonment in the branch of Michigan State Prison at Marquette for life."

Neither prisoner spoke. They were dressed in new suits, shiny shoes and were clean-shaven. They were led away and Keywell was brought into the courtroom. Van Zile intended to send him to Jackson State Prison rather than the maximum security institution in the Upper Peninsula.

"I had intended to separate you three and sentence you to Jackson but I understand you

Ray Bernstein in a wheelchair. He is being released from prison 32 years later after suffering a stroke. Note expression on his face in the two pictures.

wish to serve your time at Marquette. Is that correct?" Van Zile asked.

"Yes sir," Keywell replied. He chose to remain a Purple gangster, even in prison.

A special Pullman car was quietly added to the northern Michigan-bound train at the depot on Wednesday, November 18 1931. Shortly before it was to leave at 9:30 A.M. a convoy of black cars pulled close to the depot siding. Shotguns and machine guns bristled out the windows of the convoy, in the middle of which was a Detroit Police wagon.

The three killers were placed aboard the Pullman and shackled to their seats with heavy chain. Seven Detroit police, all heavily armed, rode with them.

The faces of the gunmen were hard. One of them, Keywell had not yet reached voting age. The three remained cool. They joked occasionally, chatted with their guards; they read about themselves in the newspapers the guards had purchased at the depot, and they munched corned beef sandwiches and played pinochle long into the night.

Bernstein, still the leader of the Purples, flashed a roll of bills and tipped a Pullman waiter five dollars after breakfast.

As the train neared the end of its fifteen hour trip, Keywell, in hushed tones, questioned his leader.

"I suppose it will be tough at first?"

Bernstein replied: "Yeah. Like everything else, you have to get settled and organized. It will be new and strange at first, but we'll get organized. We always did."

"Sure we will," Keywell said.

But when the gray steel doors of the big brownstone penitentiary closed behind them on November 20, they lost all outside identity, Bernstein, 26, became No. 5449; Keywell, 20, No. 5450, and Milberg, 28, was given No. 5451.

Although their lives in Marquette prison were subdued, their names continued to come before the public as efforts to free them continued for many years.

In March 1932, their attorney sought a new trial, displaying an affidavit allegedly made by Levine which stated the trio were not the killers and that he had been forced to testify against them.

Levine had vanished from Detroit after the trial. Some said police had paid his way to France; other rumors placed him in St. Louis, Mobile, Alabama, Oklahoma City or elsewhere.

This appeal went as high as the Michigan Supreme Court which upheld the convictions.

Another was made in 1933, when Bernstein's attorney said he could prove Bernstein was making phone calls to Chicago, Cincinnati and New York bookmakers at the time of the murder. Milberg's appeal stated that his maid would swear he was home at the time of the murders. Both appeal bids failed.

Milberg died in prison in 1938 after serving seven years.

Appeals for Bernstein and Keywell continued. Recorder's Judge O. Z. Ide, who denied one such appeal in 1949, was asked a few years later by the State Parole Board for comments as it considered parole for the pair.

"This shocking, despicable and brutally organized Collingwood massacre is still fresh in the minds of the citizens of Detroit. It was a case that aroused the entire community." he replied.

Another alleged Levine affidavit produced for the parole board in 1961 quoted him as saying; "I wasn't there. I never went there. I never saw those guys that day."

That effort failed, as did one in 1963 to which the board replied tersely:

"The parole board feels that more years of imprisonment are needed before both men attain commutation status."

But that same year Bernstein suffered a crippling stroke in Marquette and was transferred to Jackson State Prison. He was paralyzed in the left side and his speech was impaired when,

wrapped in a blanket and in a wheelchair, he was brought before the parole board on October 31 1963.

He had served thirty-two years, seven more than the average lifer. He had no misconduct during his term and taught elementary classes to inmates after he himself had been educated. He also helped and gave financial assistance to other inmates.

Although he steadfastly denied he was involved in the Collingwood Massacre, Bernstein told the parole board: "I needed correction and I got it. I learned that crime certainly does not pay."

He was released on mercy parole January 16 1964, and was immediately admitted to the University of Michigan Medical Center. He died two years later on July 9 1966.

Harry Keywell had a spotless prison record for thirty-four years before his life sentence was commuted. He walked out, free, on October 21 1965.

He was released from parole in 1969 and has since married, obtained a job and attempted to live a quiet, normal life.

The same month that Keywell won his freedom, the last member of the Purple Gang in prison, Harry Fleisher, was also released.

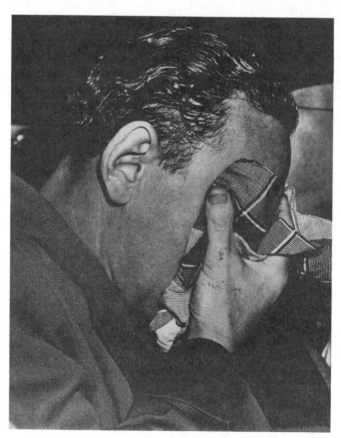

Harry Fleisher, under arrest in 1950, breaks down.

Harry Fleisher (left) with reporter and police.

He was never tried for his alleged role in the massacre and his stay in prison was for a different crime.

In June 1932, Fleisher, the object of a nationwide manhunt for months, walked nonchalantly into city hall and surrendered.

Although Levine's affidavits were produced on several occasions and defense attorneys stated they could produce him for testimony at a retrial of the three convicts, law enforcement agencies could never find him.

Police searched for three months before the Wayne County prosecutor was forced to dismiss the murder case against him, explaining to the court that he could not go to trial with any hope of success without Levine.

Although Fleisher's name was linked with various crimes, he remained free for many years.

In 1945 he was convicted in Calhoun County Circuit Court of conspiracy to murder State Senator Warren Hooper, who died in a volley of machine gun bullets and whose killer never had been found.

Fleisher also served three years, nine months of a federal sentence in Milan, Leavenworth and Alcatraz in the early Fifties.

His release in 1965 ended a thirteen year, two month sentence for the armed robbery of an Oakland County gambling house in 1945. Released from parole in 1969, he, too, is living a quiet life.

—*The Detroit News Magazine* — Appointment with Death — September 26 1971.

Chapter Fifteen

Detroit's Most Famous Mass
Murder
By Judge Donald E. Van Zile
as told to Harry E. Taylor

The bullet riddled bodies of three men were found in an apartment at 1740 Collingwood Avenue, the afternoon of September 16 1931, after a blast of gunfire that was only partly camouflaged by the exhaust roar of a racing motor awaiting outside. Within the hour the city knew of this new struggle for control of bootleg alcohol traffic and that the three members of the "Little Navy," Hymie Paul, Joseph (Izzy) Sutker and "Nigger Joe" Lebovitz, had fought a losing battle with the powerful Purple Gang.

Within the day the police had arrested the first sixteen gangsters in a fine meshed net that scooped in big fish and little fish of the two bootlegging outfits.

By September 19, Irving Milberg, Ray Bernstein and Harry Keywell, members of the Purple Gang, were charged with the murder and Solly Levine was held as a witness while police attempted to break through evasions and discrepancies in his swiftly changing stories.

Wives, sweethearts and the beautiful camp followers of the big-time gangs had been put through long grillings as police checked each of the suspects.

The murderers had covered their tracks well both before and after the killing. The site of the murder had been chosen a month before when a stranger, never completely identified, rented the Collingwood Avenue apartment. The murder guns were found in a can of green paint waiting in the apartment kitchen to obliterate all sign of fingerprints. The killers had moved so swiftly that witnesses near the scene told conflicting stories that carried little weight with the jurors.

But with all those precautions, the murderers had left alive an eyewitness, one man who gave as complete a description of the crime from beginning to end as if he had moving pictures with sound recordings. That man was Solly Levine, 30-year-old bookie and bootleg partner

who was spared because he was their school days "pal". He finally decided to talk.

The big job was for the police to keep Solly alive so he could talk when the time came to hear his story in court.

To the job of keeping Solly alive was added the task of protecting the accused from the quick justice of the slain man's friends and guarding the jurors against gangster intimidation and the possibility of a mass attack to break up the trial.

Extraordinary precautions were taken for the safety of all concerned in the trial.

With hundreds crowding the corridors of the Municipal Court Building, only 250 persons were allowed each day in the courtroom, an order that at one time brought an unsuccessful demand for a mistrial because the hearings were not "public" when any spectators were excluded.

Uniformed policemen and detectives stood at the door of the courtroom, putting each spectator under searching scrutiny, patting the hips of every man as a suspected gangster sympathizer. The handbag of every woman was opened to make sure no weapon was concealed.

Plainclothes officers mingled with spectators in the courtroom and overflow crowds in the corridors — lest a gun suddenly blaze at one of the principals in the unfolding drama.

Each juror called was questioned by Prosecutor Harry S. Toy as to his fear of reprisal should he find the accused men guilty — then confined within the court building under constant machine gun guard.

The one trip into the outside world allowed the principals in the trial was a visit to the Collingwood address by accusers, accused and jurors. The defendants were transported in a patrol wagon with machine and riot guns protruding from the rear door. The jurors were in a special bus with five police cruisers forming a front and rear guard, a detail of motorcycle officers on each side and armed officers within. Exact time of the excursion had been kept a secret.

Throughout the days of the trial Solly Levine had a personal bodyguard of twelve picked officers — picked for their fast-shooting ability — and was a voluntary prisoner within police headquarters.

Solly lived to tell his story. Slumping down in the witness chair, pale, nervous, obviously frightened, Solly told his story as eight of his twelve-man bodyguard flanked the witness stand, hands close to their pistol holsters. Levine said:

"I was a partner with Hymie Paul, Joe Lebovitz and Izzy Sutker. We owed Bernstein several hundred dollars for alky and I guess, too, they thought that we had been responsible for trying to cut in on their business and that we had hijacked some of the dope they were transporting. But we didn't have any idea they were trying to get us.

"Anyway, we were over in the bookie at 700 Selden Avenue — that is Hymie and Joe and Izzy and I — when a call came from Ray Bernstein that he wanted to see us because he had some suggestions he wanted us to get together on. He gave me the address of where he said his new office was at 1740 Collingwood Avenue, and I wrote it down on one of the pink slips we used for making bets — this is the slip here, I found it in my pocket afterwards.

"I wanted to know if I couldn't leave Izzy to watch the book for me but he said no, we were to all come. We wanted to go and get cleaned up and shave but he said come now. We all got in Sutker's car and drove over to Collingwood Avenue.

"We went upstairs to Apartment 211 and Ray met us at the door and shook hands with all of us and said he was glad to see us. Milberg and Keywell were there too and so was Harry Fleisher and we were surprised to see him and all shook hands with him because we'd heard the federal government was looking for him and he hadn't been around."

(Fleisher was the only one of the accused men the police could not capture and was not on trial with the other three.)

"They had a couch in the room and I sat at one end with Nigger Joe (Lebovitz) beside me and then Paul at the other end. Izzy was sitting on the arm. Bernstein, Milberg and Keywell sat across from us and Fleisher over at the side. Fleisher said 'Where's that fellow with the books?' and Bernstein got up to go downstairs and telephone.

"That was the signal! All of a sudden Fleisher pulled his gun and fired at Nigger Joe and the bullet went right by my nose. He asked me if I was hit; he seemed worried about that. At the same time Milberg and Keywell fired at the other two.

"All three ran into the kitchen to drop the guns in the paint pail and then said 'come on' and we all ran downstairs where Bernstein was waiting with the car motor racing and backfiring. We started to go.

"Then we missed Fleisher and in a minute or two heard several more shots. Fleisher came down stairs and said, Nigger Joe was still living a little bit.

At least one of the murderers was a better shot, it was evidenced by the coroner's testimony. Sutker had two holes right in the middle of his forehead not more than an inch apart. Police credited Milberg with that marksmanship.

Solly continued:

"We drove like the devil for a few blocks almost hitting a truck (whose driver later testified against the defendants) and just missing a woman and little child. Then we split up and Bernstein shook hands with me again and said:

"I am your pal, Solly."

"He gave me three or four hundred dollars and said to go back to the book and he'd pick me up later.

"I found out later that they were going to make me tell where some dope was and then bump me off. Bernstein, my 'pal,' had kept one of the murder guns and I'd be found in the ditch with that gun and a dead man would be blamed for the murder."

That ended Solly's testimony and both the jury and I believed he was telling the truth. Defense Attorneys A. Rodney Baxter and Edward H. Kennedy sought in cross-examination to depict Levine as the instigator of the murders; attempted to show that Levine was the one who actually owed the debt to Bernstein and named him to cover his own crime.

But the jury deliberated only one hour and thirty-seven minutes to find all three defendants guilty of first-degree murder on the first ballot, a courageous decision in view of the gangster's threats of reprisals.

I sentenced all three defendants to life imprisonment and with the exception of Milberg, who died in the penetentiary, they are still confined. The conviction went far to break up the notorious Purple Gang, James E. McCarty, then chief of detectives said later.

McCarty continued:

"The effect of Bernstein's conviction should be a great influence. He reached the top of the underworld and all it got him was a life sentence."

Turning state's witness brought Solly Levine a life sentence of fleeing the vengeance of friends of Bernstein and the others, although the police and prosecutor did what they could for him.

He first tried to run away to France. The prosecutor's office escorted him to a boat in New York but when he got to France the government wouldn't have him and sent him back.

Then he tried to go to Ireland and couldn't get a passport. The next thing I heard of him he was reported in Mississippi, Ohio and Canada all at the same time. Some friends of Bernstein sent me what purported to be a recantation from Solly — an affidavit denying the truth of his previous testimony — almost two years after the trial. That was when the convicted men were still trying to get a new trial.

I don't know just how they got the affidavit as I could never trace just where it came from. It would be hard to tell whether or not Solly escaped successfully.

Taken from The Detroit News, August 15, 1940.

Pete Licavoli.

Yonnie Licavoli.

Chapter Sixteen

The Rivals — The Licavoli Squad

The Licavoli Squad was the rival to the Purples in Detroit. Equally vicious, but somewhat more reckless and persistent, this gangland-style organization led by Thomas, or "Yonnie," Licavoli and his brother, Pete, became the most notorious criminals in the northern states.

The two brothers, who hailed from St. Louis, arrived in Detroit to cash in on the huge profits being amassed in the rumrunning racket. In no time, the gang dominated the smuggling operations on the upper Detroit River and virtually seized control over the bigger east side business in the city.

Yonnie was perhaps the most unfortunate of the two cold-blooded brothers. He was sentenced to serve thirty-seven years for murdering a man with whom his girlfriend had an affair. He was 68 years old when finally released from Ohio State Penitentiary, and upon being freed, he told reporters, "I have never killed anybody and never conspired to kill anyone."

But the former rumrunner and gang leader confessed, "I admit I was a bootlegger and broke the law. But I don't feel I should have been convicted of murder . . . no man should spend that much time in prison for anything . . . you might as well take him out and shoot him . . ."

Pete was the successful one. He skillfully dodged the law until the Fifties when he was finally caught for tax evasion, something that serves as a nagging moral reminder to successful crime bosses. It is said that Pete was arrested more than a dozen times, but only hit with two convictions. One was a $200 fine in 1929 for carrying a concealed weapon; the other for attempting to bribe a border patrol official to ignore the rumrunning operations Licavoli had organized between Canada and the United States.

The two brothers, with another gang member and friend, Frank Cammarata, came to Detroit after a fulfilling apprenticeship with the "Hammerhead Gang," a band of wild juveniles who terrorized St. Louis and earned its name from conking robbery victims over the head. From this, the boys acquired new roles as triggermen for one of the most feared gangs of bank robbers in that city. Working out of St. Louis, they knocked over banks in the surrounding countryside for miles around with almost monotonous regularity.

At a police convention at Memphis, Tennessee in 1926, more than 300 revolvers, submachine guns, shotguns and rifles used by the Licavoli gang went on display. These weapons had been confiscated by police over the course of pursuing the gang, but unfortunately, for the law anyway, the gang members were never caught.

Detroit for the Licavolis appeared more inviting. Liquor was far more lucrative than bank robbing. Payoffs were easily arranged and risks were few. But most outside gangs lured to Detroit in time stayed clear of the city because the famed Purples had tight control of the action. They had managed to secure rule over the downriver booze business, and instead of handling the task of hauling the cargoes across the river, they had set into motion a network of rumrunners from other gangs to handle the passage of booze across the border. One of those conspiring gangs was the Little Jewish Navy. Others included Canadian links to the Purples in Sandwich, Windsor and Belle River.

The Purples had also muscled their way into the blind pig industry in Detroit and were regularly exacting protection money from the owners. They had also created the Art Novelty Company to handle the booze traffic across the United States. The shipments coming to Detroit from Canada were repackaged under false labels, then taken by train or truck to spots in St. Louis, Toledo, New York and Chicago. Throughout Prohibition, Al Capone was the Purple's main customer. Thousands of cases of expensive Canadian whiskey, Old Log Cabin, were shipped to him. It was one of these shipments that, hijacked by the Bugs Moran gang in Chicago, led to the St. Valentine's Day Massacre in 1929.

144

Thus the Licavolis had a bigger-than-life task if they were preparing to secure a piece of the rumrunning action in Detroit. They had to face the Purples head-on, and eventually they did. Not only in the liquor traffic, but in the dry cleaning racket which had been originally organized by the Purples in Detroit. The two gangs rivaled for dominance in Detroit during Prohibition with the result of several open wars and slayings.

Jerry Buckley

Several other murders have been linked to the Licavoli brothers and their gang, but due to lack of evidence, the courts failed to prosecute. The most infamous of these was the slaying of Milford Jones, an acknowledged gunman from St. Louis at the popular Stork Club in Detroit in 1932. Pete Licavoli and another hoodlum, Joe Massie, rushed into the club and riddled Jones with bullets. Neither Licavoli nor Massie were ever brought to trial, because witnesses either fled the state or disappeared.

Another time, both Pete and Yonnie were wanted for the murder of Jerry Buckley, a muckraking radio commentator in Detroit, but miraculously avoided convictions.

Buckley, an admired broadcaster in the Twenties, was also widely praised for his good deeds on behalf of the needy in the city. One *Border Cities Star* reporter observed that "he wouldn't have an enemy in the world." But one September night in 1930, not long after Cammarata and Yonnie were released from

Kingston Penitentiary in Canada, Buckley was shot to death. He had been sitting in the lobby of the LaSalle Hotel in Detroit. Cammarata, recently released from prison, was believed to have driven the gunmen's getaway car, but no one could prove it.

Later a story circulated that a gangland defense fund of $25,000 raised on Cammarata's and Licavoli's behalf for the earlier Canadian conviction had been misappropriated by their Detroit counsel at the time — the same Jerry Buckley.

Buckley, it was rumored, had loaned $20,000 to someone to buy a house in Riverside, Ontario (now incorporated into Windsor). Buckley, according to Essex County Registry Office records held a mortgage on the home. The Licavoli gang had been swift to retaliate because Buckley had allegedly cheated them.

Buckley's involvement with the Licavolis wasn't known to the general public, but he did appear in the Essex County Court House in the fall of 1927 to act as the Detroit counsel for Yonnie Licavoli and Frank Cammarata. The case centered on the seizure of a loaded .38 calibre handgun in a side pocket of a car owned by Cammarata. The car had been parked in a lot outside the Prince Edward Hotel, in Windsor.

But upon a search of Rooms 501 and 502 of the hotel, the police uncovered another loaded .38 under the pillow in Licavoli's room.

According to a newspaper report, "this was an embarrassing turn of events for a couple of torpedoes from St. Louis who had adopted Detroit as their playground, and although under the suspicion of several police departments had beaten all the raps. Now they were in collision with the Criminal Code of Canada, with no prospect of a fix in sight."

Buckley's involvement wasn't mentioned until three years later when he was shot. During those years, Licavoli and Cammarata patiently waited out their time behind bars in Kingston.

But the trial was among the most dramatic from the rumrunning days. James H. Clark, appointed Canadian counsel for the two hoodlums, argued vehemently that the police had planted the gun in the defendant's car. Futhermore he insisted the possession of a handgun wasn't anything sinister, since the two were recognized rumrunners, and in that line of employment such hardware was standard equipment.

Justice Wright, unable to restrain himself, interrupted Clark to ask, "What necessity is there in this country of Canada for having guns of that nature? There has been a suggestion that these men had them for the purpose of rumrunning.

Lobby of the hotel shortly after Jerry Buckley was shot.

That is carried out on the Detroit River, not in the rooms of a hotel.

"Has the day come in this country when it is necessary for any person to have in his or her possession weapons of that nature?"

The Crown Attorney, C. W. Bell, on the other hand asserted that the two were not actually rumrunners at all, but hired gunmen from Detroit. Their purpose in Windsor was merely an extension of their mission in the United States.

The smooth talking Licavoli struggled to persuade the court to believe he wasn't a gunman at all, but an ordinary, hardworking rumrunner. He insisted he had nothing to do with the Detroit mobsters and related that he and Frank Cammarata had been smuggling liquor across the border that night. When they had finished, they dropped into the Madrid Club for "some fun." They remained there till three A.M., and at this point decided to check into the Prince Edward. But no sooner did they bed down when the police busted down their doors and arrested them.

The two were convicted for "possession of offensive weapons for a purpose dangerous to the public." They were sent to Kingston for three years.

Although Yonnie was lucky to escape conviction of the Buckley murder, he was finally caught and sentenced to life imprisonment for the killing of his rival in a love triangle.

While in prison, he wrote love ballads and copyrighted more than thirty-five songs. Detective Sergeant James Yokom of the Windsor Police at the time sarcastically remarked. "The only bars that Licavoli should have anything to do with are those long steel ones that run up and down his cell." Most of Licavoli's titles reflected the moody, wistful dreams of the inmate.

Yonnie's brother was more fortunate. He was put behind bars for only two years for tax evasion. But Pete was no small time criminal. In later years, following Prohibition, he was closely associated with the syndicate in the United States, and was regarded its leader in Detroit. In fact his next door neighbor in Tucson, where he lived for a time, was Joe Bonanno, the Syndicate Godfather.

At the time when Bonanno was attempting to hold on to the leadership of the mob, a bomb was placed in the garages of both their homes. The one at Bonanno's residence exploded.

In the Thirties however, the leader of the Mafia's connection in Detroit was none other than Joe Massie (sometimes spelled Massei). In the late Fifties, he was labelled as the numbers rackets boss in Michigan. Although he left the state in 1940, he maintained an interest in a Hamtramck auto dealership.

Massie's name is also familiar to Windsor Police because he owned a house on Windsor's Askin Boulevard while avoiding a bribery rap in Detroit.

Angus Munro, a columnist with the *Border Cities Star* said, "Gentry of this (the Licavolis) stripe always went about their chores armed. It was more practical. The era in which they flourished was one which held life lightly. Rival gangsters declared open season on each other the year round. For as little as $500 one could have one's competitor in business 'rubbed out'."

Pete Licavoli in 1952. Head of the syndicate in Michigan and friend of "godfather" Joe Bonnano.

Chapter Seventeen

The Good News

The good news.